AN UNSETTLED

I0535753

PAST

C.L. BREES

Copyright © 2016 by C.L. Brees

All rights reserved.

No part of this book may be reproduced in any form or by any electronic or mechanical means including information storage and retrieval systems, without permission in writing from the author. The only exception is by a reviewer who may quote short excerpts in a review.

This book is a work of fiction. Names, characters, places, and incidents either are products of the author's imagination or used fictitiously. Any resemblance to actual persons, living or dead, events or locales, is entirely coincidental.

C.L. Brees

Printed in the United States of America

First Printing: July 2016

Rostveit-Brees Media

Cover Design by Bookcoverzone.com

ISBN-13: 978-0-692-70823-1

AN UNSETTLED PAST

Dedicated to my beautiful friend Amanda—thank you for twenty-five years of laughter, support, and everything in between. If it weren't for you, this book would have never existed.

AN UNSETTLED PAST

1

ALEX'S PATIENCE GREW THINNER AS HE and John lingered in the parking lot of the local 7-Eleven. Their friends rarely took this much time grabbing and paying for the onslaught of junk food they needed to fuel their minds. However, as graduation inched closer, the stressful moments became more plentiful at Ridgewood High, and even a health-food junkie like Alex craved a sugar rush.

Alex tapped John on the shoulder before he shrugged. "Girls, am I right?"

John couldn't hold back his smirk, and with a friendly head nod, he reached out his arm to crank the radio louder. The upbeat music was what both guys required to pump them up for the long day ahead.

As the song reached its climatic crescendo, out of nowhere a hail of bullets erupted, and the next thing Alex saw was the front doors of the store blow outward and the glass shattered onto the ground. Without pause or consideration for his friends trapped inside, Alex sank beneath the steering wheel and pulled John down.

Alex hollered over the automatic gunfire and pounding bass. "Are you hit?"

John patted his chest. "No. You?"

"I'm okay."

The amount of time between the initial shot and when it stopped escaped his mind. The only thing Alex did was crouch as low as his body would allow. Through his cracked window, the air permeated with the distinct smell of burned gunpowder, yet amongst the lawlessness, suddenly everything became quiet. The two boys exchanged glances, yet not a word crossed their lips, and Alex inhaled and let out in rapid intervals. Alex asked for God to deliver a sign that everything was clear.

Not even moments later, the sign appeared in sensational fashion with squealing tires leaving tread marks embedded into the asphalt as a blurry van sped from the parking lot. And suddenly a bombardment of obscenities spewed from his friend Heather's mouth, some so vulgar even the most hardened sailor would cringe.

Alex clutched the handle, yet the voice inside told him to resist opening it. Instead, he raised his head over the steering wheel and saw Heather propped against the glassless door frame. Her face was an intense shade of crimson red, and her arms thrashed about. Relieved to discover her unharmed, his eyes shifted restlessly, and he spotted John affixed to his backpack as if it were his savior.

"Stay here," Alex advised.

John bobbed his head.

Alex thrust the door open and bolted past the fragments of glass and towards the entrance. "What the hell happened?"

Heather scoffed and proceeded with her out-of-control hand gestures. "Uh, isn't it evident?"

Alex peered around Heather's scrawny shoulders and long blonde hair. "Where's Amy? Have you called the police?"

Heather responded. "She's okay. She called while they were knocking the store over. Too bad for her she got busted and then got an attitude with one dude."

"Is she okay?"

"Eh, he gave her a wicked bruise. She'll live."

"Wait. This guy beat her?"

"Yup. Smacked her right across the face with the gun."

Alex tried to go in, and Heather pushed against his chest, backing him out. "Hey, hey, hey. Don't you watch *Law & Order?*"

"Sometimes. Why?"

She folded her arms across her chest. "Rule number one: never, ever, enter a crime scene."

"Whatever. I gotta get to Amy."

Alex charged once more and again Heather's perfectly manicured hand pushed against his chest. "You're dating a cop, and you, of all people, should be aware you'll contaminate the scene."

Mindful he'd never coax her into letting him inside, Alex proposed a compromise. "So, since you won't let me in, can you do me a favor?"

"We'll see."

"Can you bring her to the door?"

Heather pondered his request, and after a few seconds, a smile adorned her face. "Okay, hang here."

Alex lingered as Heather vanished into the store. A minute later the two ladies came into view, and he caught sight of his best friend, stumbling along in a daze while Heather assisted her.

Ecstatic to see her alive, Alex stretched out his hand and gripped hers. "Amy, thank God you're safe. And little miss, it's dated, not dating. Pay attention to your tenses."

Heather could sense his eyes piercing into her; however, given the present situation they discovered themselves in, she let it slide. Amy walked closer to Alex, and the sunlight caught the side of her face, unmasking a massive bruise on her cheek. He pressed his hand against her face.

"Looks worse than it is," she said.

"What happened?"

"These guys barged in here and—." Her explanation cut off by a stream of deafening sirens resonating from cop cars, ambulances, the fire department.

Alex dropped his head and traipsed to his car. He tapped on the passenger window, and John relaxed his grasp on the black backpack and peered up.

"You can get out now; they're gone."

John opened the door and stepped out onto the pavement. "You sure it's safe?"

Alex didn't have time to acknowledge John's question. Squad car after car rushed into the lot and Alex searched for one car in particular: twenty-three. And as the last vehicle pulled into the lot, he saw it, and Alex covered his face while his friends whispered behind his back.

"Well, things got more interesting," Heather whispered to Amy.

Alex caught her wise-ass remark and jerked his head around. "Not funny, I need one of you to intercept."

John saluted like a private in the service. "It'd be my honor, sir."

"Whoa. Way too young for that."

John grinned and stepped into the parking lot while Alex turned around to face Amy and Heather. "So, some guys burst in here and what? Robbed the store?"

Heather cocked her hip to the side. "Shot a couple people, robbed the place, and little miss attitude here decided to meddle, and you see what having a big mouth gets you."

"Wait. People are bleeding in there?"

"Yeah, but no reason to rush, though."

Alex wrinkled his nose. "And why not?"

"Because…"

His voice climbed an octave, "Because why?"

"They're dead," Amy chimed in, "everybody is dead."

His knees went out, and he collapsed to the ground. "How many?"

"Two, perhaps three. It's not like I stayed around and did a body count. Protecting Amy was higher on the list."

Alex covered his face and inhaled. Heather usually worked his nerves, however, at least this morning it wasn't Amy for a change. From across the parking lot, a police officer shouted over the megaphone. "Ridgewood Hills Police. Don't move."

Alex glanced over his shoulder at the considerable presence of officers, several with their guns drawn on them. He raised his arms above his head and spun his body around to face them.

"Turn around, lock your fingers on top of your head, and get on your knees," an officer roared.

Alex checked his surroundings and watched as two officers approached John and chucked him face down against the pavement. With one rapid movement, they handcuffed him, and Alex chuckled to himself at the over-dramatic display of manpower. Nonetheless, he followed their instruction as to not become another innocent victim in the parking lot.

Alex nodded to Amy and Heather to follow. With everyone with their backs to the officers, a swarm rushed in. They put handcuffs on their wrists and jerked each of them from the ground.

Slicing through the disorder, Alex caught a recognizable voice. "Hey, hey. Wait. I know them."

Alex closed his eyes. He didn't wish to see him, nor hear his voice. However, given the predicament, Alex was in no position to have a choice in the matter. He held his eyes closed, and his nostrils flared as a familiar cologne grew closer. As his fury reached a climax, a slight touch of a strong hand rested on his shoulder, and he clenched his fists.

Why's he touching me?

His eyes came alive, and indignation burned. Inches from his face crouched his ex with his standard hard stare. "Alex, are you okay?"

Their eyes locked. "You know, Mike, I don't need you to rescue me."

Mike's eyes scoured the space and found their way back to Alex's. "Uh, in case you didn't notice, it seems you do. I know these guys, and a few of them are hoping for any excuse to shoot someone."

Alex remained unaffected. "No one is killing anyone else today. So, do us both a favor and step away."

"Why are you acting this way?"

Alex fixated his eyes on Mike's face and gritted his teeth. "Walk away now. Don't give your colleagues an actual reason to lock me up."

Mike rose to his feet and lingered over him. "One day you'll realize I've been nothing but honest and devoted to you."

Alex aimed his face away while another officer approached Mike and pulled him aside. When voices raised, Alex scooted closer to eavesdrop of their conversation.

"What the hell, Temple?"

"I know them, and I doubt they had anything to do with this."

"I understand, I do. However, restraining them is for our safety, so instead of circumventing policy, give me a hand getting them into the cruisers."

Mike held back his emotions. What he wanted to tell his colleague was to mind his own business. Instead, he shuffled towards Alex.

Alex glanced up in time to see him coming. "Don't even think about touching me ever again."

Getting the message loud and clear, Mike rerouted and approached Heather and Amy. Alex remained on the curb with his hands cuffed behind his back as he watched Mike escort the ladies away. To aggravate Alex even further, Mike asked his two close friends, "Does he treat you the way he treats me?"

Alex brushed off the snide comment while an officer helped him to his feet. Not wishing to agitate any of the cops, Alex continued his respectful attitude and directed his attention on the officer helping him. "Thanks. You mind if I ride along with the one there in blue?"

The officer remained mute. And it wasn't until moments later Alex discovered he got his way when the officer shoved him into the back of his cruiser beside Amy. Alex glanced over at his best friend, who gazed out the window and struggled to hold back tears. "I'm glad you're okay."

"Me too. Why are we being arrested?"

"I doubt they are. Sure, the cops may ask us questions, but it's nothing to stress about."

Amy laid her head on Alex's shoulder as the officer opened his door and cranked the engine over. "Hey, kids, everything is okay. None of us here think you had anything to do with this."

"So why are you taking us to jail?" Amy asked.

"Jail? I'm taking you away someplace safe. I'm sure the detectives will need to ask you some questions, though."

"What a relief. For a second, I imagined you would lock us away."

"Nah. Officer Temple is an excellent judge of character. If he says you're not connected, chances are it's true."

"Ah, right, Officer Temple…," Alex responded with a hint of bitterness.

Amy nudged Alex with her head.

"What? Don't start with me about him."

The officer interrupted. "Between us, I'm not sure what our sleepy little 'burb is becoming."

"What d'you mean?" Alex asked.

"Can you recall the last time we had a triple homicide in Ridgewood Hills?"

Alex shook his head. "No, I can't. When?"

The officer cocked his head back. "Never, that's when."

His reply left them both speechless. However, he was correct. The tranquil atmosphere had shifted around town, and incidents such as this lit a fire under Alex's ass to move as far away from this cookie-cutter suburb as soon as he could.

"I'm aware it's not my place to ask, yet I saw on the news last week about a spike in the crime rate in Denver. Could it be spillover?" Alex asked.

"Could be. Say, what'd these guys look like?"

"Filthy."

"How so?"

"Shaggy. Dirty fingernails. They reeked of cigarettes and vodka. I'm sure neither of them could choose a stick of deodorant out of a line-up."

The officer grinned at her terrible joke. "Anything else special about them?"

She angled her eyes upward. "Yeah. They both had what I think is an Eastern European accent. I'm positive they aren't from around here."

"What makes you presume they aren't from here?" Alex asked.

"You ever heard an Eastern European accent in town?"

Alex mulled over her question. "Nope."

"Exactly."

The car pulled out of the parking lot and swung left towards the police station downtown. Alex leaned his head against the leather seat and shut his eyes.

Guess it's just my luck.

2

ALEX AND AMY LOITERED IN THE BARREN HALLWAY of the Ridgewood Hills Police station where they sat in their dreadful plastic chairs and anticipated their opportunity to chat with the detectives. An hour ago, two men zipped John and Heather away, and with so much time passed, concern gnawed at Alex.

Maybe they threw them in a cell? Perhaps they will do the same to us?

A few moments later Alex made out the unmistakable thud of Heather's clunky shoes as her heavy footsteps rapped against the marble floor. He leaned forward in the chair and caught sight of John and Heather hustling down the corridor.

Alex scoffed. "Took them long enough."

"Why?"

"Who knows. I'm sure we'll have our chance to discover why soon enough."

Heather plopped into the chair next to Amy, leaned in, and mumbled. "Be prepared."

"For what?"

"The questions are excessive as if they're trying to rule us out as suspects."

"Are they crazy? Do we remind you of killers?"

John chimed in. "I had the same thought. These cops must be so bored since they're making more of this than it calls for."

"How fucking brilliant. I'm missing class to be treated not unlike some common gutter-trash criminal because two guys picked today, of all days, to plunder a store and massacre a few people," Amy grumbled.

"We're in the same boat. It'll go quicker if we answer the detective's questions."

"You're right. You always are. And the fact you're always so swift to have an answer irks me," Amy said as she studied two men in suits walking towards them.

It wasn't long before Alex and Amy found themselves in the exact room their friend's moments ago departed. Inside was a table with four chairs and a video camera set-up. They both took a seat and folded their arms across their chests.

The younger detective wasted no time. "So, you're aware why you're here, so let's cut to it, shall we?"

They both uncrossed their arms.

"What can you tell us about this morning?"

Amy clenched her lips tight. "Well, since I was in the store when it happened, I'll go first."

The two detectives pressed their pens to the paper.

"The two guys ran into the store. I assumed they were regular customers just in a hurry. My friend Heather distracted me, and I amused myself for a few moments. That's when it happened; all hell broke loose."

"Can you elaborate?"

"They pulled out a gun and yelled. All I could do was crouch out of the line of sight."

"What happened next?"

"On the sly, I called 9-1-1 and stashed my phone in a rack of potato chips. By the way, when will I get it back?"

"Don't worry, we'll fetch it…soon. Continue."

"Okay, so I discarded the phone, and a minute later the smaller of the two raced down the aisle and snatched me to my feet by my hair. He asked me about the phone, but I lied to him. The next thing I know a gun is pointed at my head—," Amy paused.

Alex leaned forward in his chair as she broke down. "What's wrong?"

"I could have been murdered. I still feel the metal against my head—." Amy buried her face in her palms, and her tears flowed heavier now.

Alex reached for her hands. "Amy, tell them what you saw. These maniacs are on the loose. We're gonna get through this…the two of us."

"Okay, I'm sorry; he pointed the gun at my skull and instructed me to choose who they were going to kill. I told him I wouldn't do it. So he tossed me to the floor and the next thing I know bullets are flying past me, glass shattered everywhere, and people shouted for help."

"Way too much for someone of your age to go through," the older detective said.

The younger detective spoke up. "Are you sure we can't persuade you to get checked out at the emergency room? That's a pretty bad head wound you got there."

"Thanks," Amy replied as she reached for a tissue to dry her face, "I'll be fine. Can I go home now?"

"Soon. I promise. Now, Mr. Jones, what do you recall about the incident?" the older detective asked.

"I can't add much. I was outside in the car with John."

"And you didn't hear or notice anything unusual leading up to the robbery?"

"Did I see anything? Did I—," Alex began, "I saw the front doors of the store as they blasted them away."

11

"So, did you get a glimpse at either of the suspect's?"

"You're joking, right? I was too busy ducking and pleading for the blitz of bullets not to strike us."

The older detective snubbed a hostile Alex and remained fixated on Amy. "Miss Williams, the officer who brought you in, told us you noticed these guys had an accent."

"Yeah. And a few times they spoke in another language."

The detective leaned in closer. "If you had to guess—."

Amy had the answer to the query and cut him off. "Which language? I'd have to say it was either Czech or Russian. I know a little German, and it wasn't that."

"Precious information. If we locate these guys it'll be obvious to know we got the right ones," the detective perked up, "Now, Miss Williams, would you be able to meet and describe these men to a sketch artist?"

Alex interjected. "Detective, as you can see, my friend is in no condition. Can we pick this up again tomorrow after she has had time to relax?"

"Miss Williams, it would be a tremendous favor if you could stick around a while longer," the detective as he tapped his pen onto his notepad.

"Detective, I can't. I want to help, I do. As Alex said, I'm in no condition right now. If you arrest them, I'll come down and do a line-up or anything you need."

Hesitant, the detective rose to his feet "No problem, I get it. You're free to go. Oh, and Miss Williams, if we require further information, we'll be in contact."

"You know where to find me."

Alex shook the detective's hand and escorted Amy to the exit. As they were about to step out, the detective had one final thing to add. "Oh, and Mr. Jones, your mom is downstairs waiting. Officer Temple was kind enough to drive your car over here."

"Did he now? Well, detectives, thank you for your time. If there is anything else that we can assist you with, please let us know."

"We will. Oh, and Alex, we do miss having you around here. I hope things work out for you."

"Aww, Alex they miss you."

Alex scrunched his face. "I beg you to stop."

Alex and Amy walked into the corridor and caught sight of his mother, Carol, scrambling along the corridor in her blue hospital scrubs.

She looks pissed.

They wandered along, unhurried, and bumped into Mrs. Jones. She threw her arms out and wrapped them tight around Alex.

"My God, what happened this morning?"

"You mean the police didn't tell you?"

"Tell me what? Someone enlighten me on why you're at the police station, and why I had to delay performing a surgery?"

"We witnessed an armed robbery and triple homicide this morning at the 7-Eleven by the house," Alex said.

"Funny. Now tell me the actual story."

John cocked his head. "Um, Mrs. Jones, that's the story."

"Dear God," Carol responded.

"I've never experienced anything so horrific in my whole life," Heather said.

"Well, you guys have been through a hellish morning and hovering around this police station isn't making it any better. I'll call your parents and tell them you're at our house and safe."

"That'd be perfect," John said.

Amy dropped her head. "Yeah, better you dealing with them than me."

Everyone stayed inside while Carol stepped outside to call everyone's parents. About five minutes later, Carol returned through the double doors

13

and dangled Alex's car keys in her hand. "I saw Mike outside, and he gave these to me."

"Wait, you gave him a set of keys to your car?" John asked.

"Of course. We dated for a year."

Carol interrupted. "Now, go home and recuperate. I'll see each of you tonight for supper around seven. If you have time, stop by the store, and pick up supplies. We'll keep it low-key, so go with spaghetti."

"Deal. Thanks again for coming to our rescue, mom."

"Yeah, yeah. Next time, some heads up. Scared the crap out of me."

Alex tapped the roof of the car and everyone piled back in. No one spoke a single word, only a sufficient amount of grumbles. And Heather, helpless to keep silent for more than a few minutes, broke the silence.

"People, I have two points to express. First, we must find a different spot for snacks in the morning, and second, I want to go home for the rest of the day. I need some time to reflect."

3

THE BLACK BMW PULLED UP TO A LARGE, brick, two-story house on Birchwood Drive. Before the car even came to a complete stop, Heather already had the rear door flung open. Alex slammed on the brakes, just missing the curb, and Heather stepped out onto the fresh-paved asphalt.

Alex clenched his jaw—*typical.* She leaned into the driver's side of the vehicle, kissed Alex on the cheek, and retreated. Alex stared at her with an expression of utter horror as she stood in the gusty breeze letting her hair blow freely.

Heather ran her fingers through her brunette hair and spoke in a seductive voice. "Thanks again for dropping me off, Alex. See you guys later."

"I'm not gonna touch this situation. Nope," John said.

"Sure, yeah, we'll see you at dinner."

"Of course."

"And next time, wait until the car comes to a complete stop before opening the door."

"Calm down. I'd never jump out of a moving vehicle."

"I don't need unnecessary worry in my life."

"That's your problem, Alex—you fuss too damn much about, like, everyone."

"If I didn't worry, I'm sure some of you wouldn't be around still."

Alex flipped a U-turn right there instead of driving a few extra feet to the cul-de-sac as usual. Heather waited on the curb and waved until the car disappeared around the corner. She grinned and then strolled along the red-brick walkway to the front door.

Heather wasn't like the others. Some days her faculties ran like a well-oiled machine, she was likable, coherent…however, there were days like today, where she was wacky, euphoric, the same as someone suffering from bipolar disorder.

Alex recognized the best way to help people with undiagnosed mental illness was to treat them as he would anyone else. However, just because he cared, it still didn't stop him from watching his back and keeping a careful distance. Heather wasn't the first bi-polar friend in his life, and Alex was sure she wouldn't be the last.

She approached the front door, inserted the key, and gave it a good twist. The massive door creaked open, and she stepped into the darkness of a still foyer. She twirled her hair and plopped her backpack on the floor behind the door. She meandered down the long hallway towards the kitchen, with each stride her footsteps echoed off the beige walls.

Once in the kitchen, she took out a tall glass, and set it on the counter before rushing to the refrigerator and took out a half-full carton of orange juice. She lifted the glass to her mouth, took a sip, as the faint sound of the telephone rang in the distance. Annoyed, she aborted quenching her thirst and ran for the phone in the living room.

"Hello?"

"Good morning, Detective Scott from the Ridgewood Hills Police. May I speak with Wendy Burgess?"

"She isn't in. Anything I can help with?"

"Who am I speaking with?"

"Oh, sorry, this is her daughter, Heather Burgess."

"Right. Weren't you just here an hour ago?"

"Yup. So, what's this about? Is everything okay?"

"Well, it's regarding your sister, Kelli. Can you please have your mother call me back at the station when she returns?"

"Of course. I'll let my mom know."

The call ended, and Heather stood emotionless with the phone still clutched in her hand.

What's the hellion done now?

She shook her head, returned to her backpack, and pulled out a notebook and chemistry book. Heather flipped through the textbook as she pulled out a barstool. A few seconds passed, and she revisited the juice she left on the countertop. As the rim of the glass touched her lips, the garage door flung open and in rushed her panic-stricken mother.

"Mom, what's wrong?"

"Kelli, is she here? Have you seen her today?"

"Saw her this morning."

"Is she here?"

"She's not. What's going on?"

Wendy Burgess walked away, unconcerned why her older daughter was not in class. Instead, she was hellbent on finding Kelli.

"Kelli? Kelli are you here?" Mrs. Burgess hollered throughout the house.

Heather grunted and closed her notebook. "She's not here, I swear. Woman bring your ass down here and tell me what's going on."

Mrs. Burgess emerged from around the corner, breathless. "The police… they called me at work—." She paused to catch her breath.

"Yeah, they called here too."

"Your sister. They say she's at the police station."

"Funny. I didn't see her there."

Mrs. Burgess crinkled her forehead. "What d'you mean?"

"Did I stutter? I left the police station an hour ago, and I assure you Kelli was nowhere in sight. Besides, if they called you, why are you here and not there?"

"I believed she was playing a prank—I mean, we both know how she becomes when she's starved for attention."

Heather smiled and watched as her mother rushed back up the staircase to the second floor.

This woman is hard-headed.

Heather stood at the foot of the stairs. "She's not here."

Heavy footsteps thumped down the stairs for a second time, and Mrs. Burgess stopped on the second step from the bottom and gazed at Heather with reproving eyes. "Grab your shit."

"What for?"

"We're going downtown."

Heather stomped her foot. "I'm not going."

"And why not?"

"I've already spent the better part of the morning with the police. Now you want me to go back? Pass."

Mrs. Burgess pressed her right hand against her hip and cocked her hip outward. No wasn't an answer she got often. "Grab your shit and move your ass. I don't give two shits if you spent the night in jail, your sister is in some sort of trouble, and I'm not leaving you in the house alone."

Heather huffed, slammed her book closed, and marched ahead of her mother towards the garage door. She twisted around and placed her hand in front of her. "Fine, whatever. I can't wait to leave this prison."

"Prison? If you want me to treat you like an inmate, I can. You're grounded for three weeks."

"What? No."

Mrs. Burgess brushed by her. "Yes. I can't figure out what's gotten into you lately. Why do you always have to be a bitch?"

"Why? I learned from the best, mom."

"Have you completely lost it? Do you want us to send you back to the therapist?"

"Back to the quack who needs a lifetime of therapy herself? Sure, go ahead and waste your money."

The back and forth arguing continued a few minutes longer, with Heather losing the battle. The past few years, Heather struggled with emotional issues brought on by her rocky relationship with her parents. While Heather found her feelings natural, her parents didn't have the same nonchalant view.

The car backed down the driveway and Heather slouched in the passenger's seat with her arms folded across her chest, watching the cookie-cutter houses pass her by. She reminisced about Kelli, knowing how much of a prankster she was, Heather was sure she was acting out again given no one paid her any attention of late. Heather was too busy studying; their parents spent too much time riding her back every chance they got. Where did that leave Kelli?

Heather broke her intense concentration on the world passing by outside, picked up her chemistry book, and returned to chapter twelve.

***

AT ABOUT THE SAME TIME, ALEX AND the rest of the crew pulled up to a drive-thru window at a nearby fast-food restaurant. What better way to drown out the traumatic events of the day than stuffing their faces with greasy burgers and fries. With bags in hand, Alex handed them to

John in the backseat and pulled out of the parking lot and back onto the soggy main street.

"What's on the agenda?" Alex asked.

"Study a few hours, and I'm hopeful afterward I can do nothing. What about you, Amy?" John asked.

"No tests for me until next week. So, suppose I'll spend the afternoon watching my stories."

"Stories?" Alex asked.

"You know, soap operas."

John ignored her comment. "Alex, what's on your agenda?"

"Lit paper due tomorrow. I can't afford anything less than a 'B.'"

"Stop stressing. You're one of the smartest kids at Ridgewood High. You'll do amazing."

"Thanks for the enthusiastic support."

A red light interrupted their flow, and Alex noticed a white van, similar to the same one he saw flee the 7-Eleven hours earlier.

There's not a chance in hell those robbers would hang around town. Relax.

The light changed, and he refocused on the road. He tittered under his breath. "One more stop, guys."

"What'd we forget?"

"Groceries for dinner. If I leave you two in the car, promise you'll be alive when I return?"

Amy bit her lip. "I adore John; although from time to time he annoys the shit out of me."

"Yeah, Alex, we're not savages or anything."

Alex hung a left into the shopping center. "Perfect."

Alex slid the car into park, smiled, and stepped out as drizzle coated his jacket. Although Amy tried to deceive everyone with her brave facade, Alex foresaw a meltdown in her future, and he'd be there, as usual, to prop her up when it happened.

Along the way towards the store, an overwhelming sense washed over him. He swung his head around, noticing the same white van parked towards the back corner of the lot. Panic seeped in, and he stopped in his tracks.

Something isn't right.

The situation bothered him to the point he forced himself to return to the car. A few yards away, Amy lowered the window. "Everything okay?"

Alex messed with his collar. "I've gone crazy. Do me a favor and glance over at the white van parked to your left. Look familiar?"

Both Amy and John inconspicuously rotated their heads.

"No. Should it?" Amy asked.

"Wait, wait, wait…yeah, it does."

Amy's mouth gaped open. "It does?"

"It could be. Looks like the one from the 7-Eleven."

"Should we call the police?" Alex asked.

"If I murdered three people and robbed a convenience store, I'd be long gone. I'm sure we're safe."

"You're right. I should chill and stop being so jumpy."

Alex changed course and continued to the entrance of the store. As hard as he tried to forget about the van, it would not leave his mind.

Stop overreacting.

The grocery errand took ten minutes, and as Alex got closer to the car, he noticed the white van had disappeared. With the brown paper sack pressed against his jacket, he smiled and continued moving towards the car.

After the wild morning they had, their afternoon gradually improved. However, downtown at the police station, life was about to spiral out of control for the Burgess family.

***

MEANWHILE, ON THE OTHER SIDE OF TOWN, a silver Mercedes SUV sped down Sixth Street. Wendy Burgess was in a rush, and no traffic light or vehicle would stand in her way.

Heather grabbed ahold of the handle above her head. "You're driving like a lunatic. Please, slow down."

Mrs. Burgess ignored the pleas and pressed on.

"Mom," Heather screamed. "You're worthless to her if we crash."

"Stop complaining—we're here."

Wendy slammed the car into park and exited the vehicle faster than Heather had ever seen. With her mind otherwise occupied she forgot the keys in the ignition and Heather shook her head. She closed her textbook, set it on the floor, and grabbed the keys before removing her seatbelt.

Heather stepped out onto the curb and searched for her mother. When at last she located her, she whizzed by an officer forcing him to spill his coffee to the ground. Wendy vanished inside before Heather had crossed the road.

With panic in her voice, Mrs. Burgess rushed the main desk where a broad-shouldered officer typed away. She interrupted, "Who is in charge?"

"Whoa, ma'am, I'm going to need you to take a breath. I'm the desk sergeant this afternoon."

She took a deep breath and composed herself. "I'm Wendy Burgess. A Detective Scott phone me earlier about my daughter."

"Right. Have a seat, and I'll fetch Detective Scott."

Heather walked in and stood next to her mother. "Why won't anyone tell me what's going on?"

The sergeant grimaced. "Mrs. Burgess have a seat, please."

"I'll stand if you don't mind."

She remained at the desk, pacing back and forth, and drawing attention to herself. Heather stepped away and occupied one of the plastic chairs which lined the wall of the lobby.

The unknown kept her in suspense. And Wendy Burgess was not the type of woman you kept waiting too long. Five minutes passed, and the sergeant still had not come back. Feeling defeated, she lingered next to Heather.

"Mom, you gotta calm down. It's a police station, and you're not making any friends with your attitude."

Wendy crouched, emotionless, staring straight ahead at the empty desk. Two sets of heavy footsteps echoed through the deserted corridor, and every eye focused towards the noise.

Some lanky middle-aged gentlemen approached, and when he got closer, he extended his hand out. "Mrs. Burgess I presume?"

She jumped to her feet. "Yes, and this is my daughter Heather."

"I'm Detective Scott. Sorry I kept both of you waiting. I needed to confirm information before we spoke."

"What information? Don't tell me she's been arrested again?"

Detective Scott placed his strong hand against her shoulder. "I'm afraid it's far worse. If you follow me."

Heather stood and followed a few steps behind. Her footsteps clanked against the marble floor, and Detective Scott stopped and turned.

"Eh, might be best if you wait here, miss. Not sure this is the best thing for you to see."

Mrs. Burgess planted her hands on her hips and cocked her head. "Where I go, she goes. I won't leave her out here amongst the gutter-trash of Ridgewood Hills."

The detective leaned forward. "Your call. Shall we continue?"

"Where are we going?"

"Around the block. Not far."

The two ladies exchanged perplexed glances before they directed their heads back to Detective Scott.

"Around the block?"

He slumped his shoulder forward and hung his head. "I won't beat around the bush any longer."

"Spit it out already," Mrs. Burgess scoffed.

"There was a homicide this morning—."

"I know. I was there…remember?"

"Eh, not those murders. A single homicide in Centennial Park."

Mrs. Burgess gasped. "It can't be. No way, Kelli put you up to this, right?"

"I wish I could say she did, however, she didn't."

Her already fair skin grew paler with each passing second. "No. I have to see for myself."

The detective held the front door open and extended his arm. "Right this way."

***

THREE HOURS EARLIER, KELLI BURGESS WALKED along the tree-lined streets and perfect lawns of Evergreen Gardens and out into town. The walk to her friend Allison's took twenty minutes, which on an average day would be uneventful. Little did she know evil was brewing in Ridgewood Hills, and today would be unlike any ordinary day.

Kelli rounded the corner of Sixth and Elm, three blocks away from Allison's, when a white van crept along her side. A shiver climbed up her spine from the consciousness of eyes behind her. Creeped out, she increased her pace, and the van matched her speed. She stopped and squinted. Unable to make out a face, she stepped off the curb, removing one earbud in the process. The moment her foot touched the pavement, the van tore off at a high rate of speed.

Kelli scoffed, puffed out her chest, and inserted the earbud back in her ear. As she stepped into the crosswalk of Spruce Street tires squealed, and as she looked to her right, the van hit her full-force. And as her life flashed before her eyes, she smashed against the hood of the white van.

The rear door of the van opened, and a tall, masked man jumped out and grabbed Kelli and pulled her inside. Kelli was in and out of consciousness, and the moment she came to, she wailed. "Oww."

"Keep quiet, bitch."

As she looked into the man's blue eyes, her eyes burned with tears. With a stutter in her voice, she asked, "Where are you taking me?"

"Don't worry about it right now."

She screamed and banged against the side of the van. "Help. Help me. No, get off."

The man calmly reached into a black duffle bag and pulled out a roll of duct tape. He tore off a long piece with his teeth and pinned her down to cover her mouth.

"I hate when they scream."

Kelli remained frozen. *What do they want with me?*

The van came to a screeching stop, and she caught a glimpse out the front windshield, and they were waiting at the on-ramp to the expressway. Unrestrained, she attempted to be as discreet as possible as she reached for the door handle, and wiggling it a few times, it still wouldn't budge. She was locked in.

After accepting every option was exhausted, the realization sunk in that they had her trapped. As the van took a hard left, panic crept in.

Why are we heading back in the same direction?

The driver whipped around another corner at a high rate of speed, and the man in the back banged against the metal door. "Yo, not cool, bro."

Kelli mumbled, and the man peeled away the tape. "Are you going to kill me?"

He didn't respond. Instead, he bent over and, in an instant, whacked her across the face. The blow took her breath away, and she gasped as tears streamed down her face.

The man clenched his teeth. "Stop. Crying."

Unmoved by her emotions, he moved behind her and placed a red blindfold across her eyes. She squirmed, trying to break herself free from the man, except his grip was more potent than she assumed. After a minute of struggling, she gave up and surrendered to his demands.

The driver jumped from the vehicle and raced around to the side where the two men removed her with force from the van. She twisted her head from side-to-side, not able to tell where she was or if anyone was around to help. With nothing logical left to do, Kelli took a leap of faith and kicked and moaned at the top of her lungs.

If I'm going to die, I'm going out with a fight.

Her efforts didn't last long. The hard, cold muzzle of the gun pressed into her back, and the pungent stench of tobacco wafted from the man's mouth as he spoke. "No one is around to help you."

She understood these would be the last few minutes of her life, so she mustered up her energy and kicked the shorter man in his shin. Quite a ballsy move, however, the man dropped to the ground and released his tight grip. Now, with one arm free, she escaped the clutches of the other man and ran, tearing the blindfold from her face. Her freedom was short-lived once the men regained their bearings and snatched her up again.

"Huge mistake. Huge."

Nearby were the park restrooms and the two men pushed her into the men's room and dead bolted the door. Raising her hands above her head, they tied her to the metal stall divider to ensure she couldn't escape again. The adrenaline pumped through her veins and tears spilled harder along her swollen cheeks.

The man snatched the tape from her mouth, and she gulped for air. "I promise I won't tell anyone about this. It's not too late. You can just let me go."

They took turns brutalizing her. One jabbed her in the ribs with the gun while the other stood there spewing lewd comments and every few seconds the man would let out a raspy laugh. Even with her vision now obscured, there was no mistaking the amount of hate which exuded from their souls, and she thought, *kill me, and get it over.*

After they had their fun for a few moments, the taller man pulled a hunting knife from a holster on his side and walked up next to her. He pressed the glacier-cold steel against her drenched cheek.

"Any last words?"

"Tell my family I love them and I'm sorry for everything."

The man laughed. "Anything else?"

A calmness sank into her soul, and she bowed her head. "No."

And with a quick thrust, the man dug the knife deep into her abdomen and watched while her blood spilled onto the filthy, piss-soaked ceramic floor.

Kelli cried out in pain, and the man pulled out the roll of duct tape and wrapped it around her face several times to silence her screams.

His soulless eyes met with his coconspirators. "Finish her."

And with those two words, he withdrew the knife and stepped aside, allowing the other man to finish her off. He pulled back the slide of his Sig Sauer and with one shot, a hush fell over the room. They stood, watching as her limp body dangled from the stall and the shorter guy whacked his arm against the other. "Let's go before the cops show up."

***

27

BACK DOWNTOWN, WENDY AND HEATHER DESCENDED the marble stairs outside the police station to the sidewalk below. Detective Scott remained a few steps ahead although Heather trailed along in a daze. Before long, the three stood at the secured door which led to the satellite office of the Chief Medical Examiner of Jefferson County.

Mrs. Burgess rushed past the detective and pulled the door handle. "It won't open—why won't it open?"

Detective Scott stepped forward and pulled out a generic plastic card from his wallet. "You need an access card."

Detective Scott tapped it against a black box and the magnetic door released. He pulled the door and allowed them to enter first. The lobby wasn't anything to write home about. White walls with a couple photos hung above a set of comfortable chairs.

"Have a seat, and I'll check if they're ready for us."

"Mom, why are we here?"

"I don't know. It's possible the police made a mistake."

"I sure hope so."

Mrs. Burgess's cell phone rang, and she fumbled to recover it from her purse. "Hello?"

A harsh masculine voice greeted her. "Wendy Burgess?"

"Yes, who's this?"

"I'm the man who murdered your daughter."

"Why—why are you fucking calling me?"

"To pass on a message from Kelli."

"You murder my daughter, and you have the nerve to call me?"

Wendy Burgess was on her feet and hollering so loud the receptionist rushed to retrieve Detective Scott. After a minute, he ran into the waiting room to see what the commotion was. Mrs. Burgess wiped tears away and paced. The detective approached bit by bit, not wanting to interrupt her conversation.

28

"Well, you gonna tell me?"

"She said to tell you she loved you and she's sorry for everything."

Detective Scott looked at Heather, "Who's on the phone?"

"No idea. It must have to do with my sister."

Now in tears, Mrs. Burgess flopped into the chair. She covered her face with her hands and strained to wipe the wetness from her red cheeks. Detective Scott snatched the phone.

"This is Detective Scott with the Ridgewood Hills Police. Who's this?"

"If you're smart enough, you'll figure out." The call disconnected.

Wendy Burgess hunched over in the chair, the tears streamed down her face, and she cried out as it hit her—her baby would not be coming home. The receptionist raced around the desk carrying a box of tissues and crouched next to her. Mrs. Burgess peeked up at Heather and waved for her to go. Aware of what her mother wanted, she looked at the detective.

"I'll go and identify the body. It's obvious my mother is in no condition to do it."

The detective was uneasy and approached a devastated Mrs. Burgess. "I can give you a moment if you need it. We don't usually let minors identify bodies."

Heather interrupted. "Excuse me, I'm eighteen; I'm pretty sure I can handle this."

The detective looked once again at Mrs. Burgess, and with nothing more than a nod she approved. "Okay, follow me."

They passed through the double doors and into a long, sterile, cold corridor. About halfway down the bright overhead lights grew brighter the closer they got to the room where her sister rested. They arrived, and Heather froze as soon as she stood in the doorway. She stood there, staring at the stainless steel tabled covered in a white sheet with a distinct outline of a petite body underneath. None of the years she watched crime dramas on television prepared her for this.

29

She closed her eyes and clung to the door frame. She drew a deep, audible breath and the smell of formaldehyde filled her lungs. Detective Scott touched her shoulder gently, and as Heather exhaled, she gagged for air.

"You sure you're ready?"

Heather opened her vacant eyes wide and stared ahead. They sauntered side-by-side into the cold, sterile room with a lone stainless-steel table fixed to the floor. The technician waited for the go-ahead and peeled back the white sheet to reveal the cyanotic face of her sister.

Heather stood stone-faced for a moment, disturbed at the sight she was looking at. A single tear trickled down her cheek, and her nostrils flared several times before she spoke. "It's Kelli."

The detective motioned for the attendant to cover the body and guided Heather back into the hallway. Once outside, Heather fell against the wall and allowed gravity to bring her to the ground.

"What's happened to our once great town?"

"I have no idea. I do know we're going to figure it out."

He reached out his hand to help her up. Instead, she rested her head atop her knees and continued to cry. Aware they weren't leaving any time soon, he hunkered down on the floor next to her and wrapped his arms around her shoulders.

Heather gave her face a final wipe and looked over at the detective. "Thank you. I've always believed cops were assholes."

He glanced her direction, nodded, and grinned. The two stood to their feet and walked down the same corridor back to the waiting area. Before they arrived at the double doors, the detective stopped and leaned in to whisper. "If you need anything, here's my card. Call me day or night."

"Thanks. I will."

They walked through the doors, and Wendy Burgess stood, but then collapsed again into the chair. Heather ran to her side to comfort her and as the two women embraced Detective Scott approached.

A few minutes passed, and Wendy pulled away and glanced up at the detective. "What do we know so far?"

"The truth…not much. We've requested help from the Denver Forensics Lab, and we still need to await the ME's final report."

Wendy Burgess sucked back the mucus dripping from the tip of her nose. "Was she murdered? Did she suffer?"

Heather rolled her eyes. "The killers called you, mom. And I'm certain it was over quick given her wounds."

Detective Scott rested his hand on Heather's shoulder. "We're treating this as a homicide. The ME will make the final determination though."

"You'll keep us posted on any developments?"

"Yes, ma'am, I give you my word. I'll personally call if anything comes up."

"Thank you, detective."

"Of course. Now, about the call earlier—was there any caller I.D.?"

"No, it was 'unknown.' Will you still be able to trace the call?"

"I'll check into it. Could be a major break in the case."

"Good. You catch these bastards, and I want to be there when the judge gives them the death penalty."

Detective Scott grinned and ran his hands against her back. "Well, not much more we can do now. You two should go home and rest. I'll call if anything changes."

4

AFTER LEAVING THE MEDICAL EXAMINER'S OFFICE, THEY approached the car while Heather fumbled with the keys. She had to do something to distract her traumatized mind from the sight only minutes ago she witnessed. Heather shot a glance at her mother, who leaned against the passenger side door. Her bloodshot eyes, flaming-red cheeks, and disheveled hair put Heather on notification she was in for the most challenging day of her short life.

Heather clicked the key fob and the doors unlocked. Once inside the privacy of the car, they lingered in silence before Heather cranked the engine over. What could she say to her mother in a moment like this? There were the clichés everyone always used. However, none of them were appropriate given the situation.

Heather remembered back to the conversation she had with Kelli earlier in the morning. Little did she know at the time, but it would be her last. It was the usual bitching and moaning like every other morning. Had she had known it would be the last time they'd speak, Heather would have said things differently.

She sucked back tears and twisted the key in the ignition. She wanted to remain strong, keep it together for the family, yet in the end, the weight of her emotions tumbled, and she broke down.

Mrs. Burgess reached her hand across and squeezed Heather's hand.

"I can't believe I was such an ass to her this morning."

"You two have always been high-strung. I'm pretty sure your sister didn't take it personally. She knew how much you loved her deep down through the bitchy facade."

The reassurance helped Heather to dry up. "Thanks, mom. We better head home and ring dad."

The car pulled away from the curb, and they once again slipped into silence on the ten-minute drive home. As they pulled into the driveway, Heather shifted the car into park and watched her distraught mother stagger into the house.

With her father away on business in Phoenix until the next day, she prepared herself for another meltdown and emotional rollercoaster the next few weeks held. She looked up to the sky.

I can't believe you allowed this to happen, God.

***

DOWN THE BLOCK AT ALEX'S EVERYONE sprawled out in the living room and studied while the faint chatter from the television provided them a well-deserved distraction. Alex glanced at his watch, it was nearing three-thirty, and he slammed his laptop closed and sprang from the couch.

"Anyone else starving?"

John and Amy raised their hands.

"A snack sounds perfect," Amy said.

"Well, you know, my house is your house. Help yourself to the pantry."

Amy sprinted towards the kitchen while John remained propped against the couch. "Are you coming?"

"I'll stay here and study. Thanks for thinking about me though."

"Yeah, no problem."

Alex grinned and walked away. John's had his head in the books hard, more than ever to refuse food.

Alex almost crashed into Amy in the hallway. "Whoa. Looks like you found some goodies."

"Oatmeal raisin cookies are my favorite. Where's John?"

"Not sure what's going on with him. Whatever it is, one thing's for sure: he's overdoing it on studying."

"That's how he is. He said his parents ride his ass every day about keeping his grades high, getting into the right school. Leave it to me, I'll get him out of his shell."

"He could still be shaken up following this morning. I know I am."

"It's possible. Oh, while I got you here—you decided yet about staying in Colorado or going on my New York adventure with me?" Amy asked.

"I don't know yet. The main reason I wanted to stay in Colorado was for Mike…we both see how the plan worked out."

"Well, perhaps New York is the change of scenery you need?"

"I'll let you know in a few days."

Amy smiled at her and reached out for a hug. She was notorious for being an affectionate person, always giving out hugs instead of handshakes. They embraced, and Amy pulled away and looked Alex dead in the face.

"Promise me no matter where we end up in life, we'll always be best friends."

"I think I can keep that promise."

They ventured back to the living room, side-by-side. As Alex and Amy emerged around the corner, they found John with his legs planted on the coffee table. He swept his eyes up and down, catching sight of them, and he smiled. Amy, on the other hand, moved forward and shoved off his legs.

"Were you raised in a barn?"

"Maybe."

Amy scowled before she cozied up against the cushy tweed couch next to John. Right away, he scooted aside as Alex plopped down on the floor at his feet.

"So, studying hard or hardly studying?"

"Funny. I'm so frustrated."

"I'll bite; why are you frustrated?"

"It's this French class. Anything less than an A-minus and my parents will flip their shit."

"Wait. Weren't you already accepted to Yale? I doubt getting a 'B' will have them withdraw their offer. Right?"

"It's a conditional acceptance dependent on how this semester ends. I can't blow it."

Alex ruffled his hair. "You guys, we need to ease up. We're going to crush finals, blow this shitty town, and be trailblazers."

Amy chimed in. "Alex is right. Didn't someone publish a study which found cramming for finals made you *less* focused?"

Hesitant, John caved in. "Fine. I have straight A's so what's stopping me from keeping this momentum?"

"That's the way to look at it. Now, let's do something more low-key."

"Such as?" Amy asked.

"TV. And before you know it, it'll be time for dinner."

"Do I hear any objections?"

Amy and John looked at each other and in unison declared, "Nope."

Alex grabbed the remote from the coffee table and changed it over to Channel 9 in time to catch the end of *Leeza*. While the credits rolled the grandfather clock in the foyer chimed.

One, two, three, four.

"Just in time for the news," Alex said.

"Nope, change the channel. Not the 'low-key' I was looking for," Amy replied.

"How un-American to not keep up with the news."

"They could have an update about this morning. Come on, Amy, the first five minutes."

"Ugh, way to guilt trip me."

Even with no sound, Alex caught sight of the words scrolling across the bottom of the screen, *Violence in Ridgewood Hills*. The attention-grabbing headline obligated him to reach for the remote. With the volume up full-blast, the anchor swapped to a field reporter who stood in the parking lot of the same 7-Eleven where their terrible morning originated.

"Thanks, Ken. Two separate incidents this morning have rocked this peaceful Denver suburb. The first occurred around seven-forty-five this morning when three people were brutally slaughtered at this 7-Eleven behind me..."

"Two incidents? What else happened?" Amy asked.

John threw his hands up. "Shut up, and he'll tell us."

"Now, you mentioned two separate events."

"Correct. Two hours later Ridgewood Hills Police responded to Centennial Park where they located the mutilated body of a Ridgewood High School student in a bathroom stall. Captain Eric Reed revealed they are handling this as a homicide."

Alex lowered the volume, and the three exchanged dumbfounded glances at each other. "Okay, so we knew about the store, but someone from school? Murdered?

"Who could it be?"

"Guess we'll find out tomorrow."

The faint sound of the telephone rang from the kitchen, and Amy tapped Alex on the shoulder, but he couldn't take his eyes off of the television.

"Want me to grab it?"

"Yeah, thanks."

Amy hustled through the first floor and made it to the kitchen right before the call rolled over to voicemail.

"Jones residence."

A hoarse feminine voice cracked, "Amy?"

"Yeah, who's this?"

"It's Heather."

"Oh, hey, you sound awful. Wait. Have you been crying?"

"Maybe. I got some unsettling news."

"Hang on, let me find Alex. We both know he's better at handling these things."

Amy rushed back to the living room and handed the phone to Alex. "It's Heather, something's wrong."

Alex reached from the cordless phone, stood, and walked to the corner of the room away from prying ears. However, it didn't stop Amy or John from eyeballing his every move.

"Heather? Is everything okay?"

"It's Kelli."

"What about her? Is everything okay?"

"Yes. Well, not quite. The police—"

Alex didn't let her finish because he already knew the next sentence to come from her mouth. "She's the fourth victim. The one they found in Centennial Park?"

Heather sobbed and nothing else.

"Take a deep breath. Are you breathing?"

"I'm trying."

"Good enough. How do you know it was Kelli?"

"I identified her body downtown."

"Shit. What can we do to help? Do you need us to come over?"

"No, not the best idea. My mom needs me."

"Okay. You'll let us know if we can do anything?"

"I will. I also wanted you to know I won't be in classes the rest of this week and next."

"Yeah, school isn't a high priority. We'll make sure you get the notes you need."

"Thanks, Alex."

"Sure. And now you call me, or Amy if you need anything."

"I will. See you guys in a few days."

Alex hung up and dropped the phone into his lap. Amy and John's eyes never wavered from him the entire call. He stumbled in his mind on how to break the devastating news.

I guess the best way to do this is to be blunt.

Without filtering to put things delicately, Alex opened his mouth. "Kelli's dead."

The stunned expression on John and Amy's faces spoke more than words ever could. Once the initial shock wore off, they refocused on Alex who still concealed his mouth with his right hand.

"Come again? Don't joke about stuff like this," Amy said.

"I'm…I'm serious. I'm aware I joke around way too much, but you can't think I'd make up shit like *that?* Can you?"

Reality set in for John and his back slammed against the couch. "Damn, didn't see any of this coming."

"Yeah, me either. So, if Heather needs anything, we'll be there for her."

"Yeah, of course. I'll try my best," Amy said.

Alex looked to John who remained quiet. "You'll be there for her too, right?"

John gazed at the floor. "I mean, come on Alex, I'm not comfortable dealing with other people's emotions. Hell, I can't manage my own."

"She's our friend. I'm not asking you to provide her with a full-blown therapy session. Just be there to lend an ear or let her cry on your shoulder."

John folded his arms across his chest and rocked on his heels. "Can't do it, man, sorry. I don't know her *that* well."

Alex wasn't shocked, more disappointed. However, he couldn't fault John for his indifferent position. In eighteen years, John had never mourned the death of a loved one, yet Alex and Amy had.

Never being one to bite his tongue, Alex expressed his frustration. "I have to say this or I'll go to bed pissed."

John stood and puffed out his chest. "Say what?"

"I assumed you two would be compassionate, more worried about a friend. Instead, you're acting like it doesn't bother you."

"It's your prerogative to be disappointed, except I didn't know her. How can I be a weepy mess over someone I never met?"

"Exactly. Alex, you know, err, knew her. It's reasonable you'd be upset," Amy said.

"You don't have to be friends with people to have empathy," Alex replied.

John held his hand in front of his face. "You can argue as long as you'd like, it won't change our minds, so you should save your breath."

Ready to drop the subject, Alex proposed a compromise. "Let's say this; we'll be available to Heather, regardless."

"Duh. We're not heartless monsters, you know."

"I never used those words. I believe I called you uncompassionate."

"Okay, I'm over this. Next subject."

Alex dropped his head as the faint sound of the garage door opening caught his attention. He bolted to greet his mother.

His mother, Carol Jones, was a busy woman. As the chief neurosurgeon at a major hospital in Denver, spending time at home with her son was far and few between. After her promotion two years earlier, Alex grew accustomed to taking care of himself, nevertheless his love for her never diminished. Any time they could, they spend quality time together.

Alex's father died when he was five, and over the years, he concluded she worked so much to avoid dealing with the past. He never complained about it since her workaholic life gave him freedom.

He skidded across the floor into the kitchen in time to find his mother dropping her car keys on the counter. He rushed up and wrapped his arms around her. "Have a good rest of your day, mom?"

"Nothing special. Boy, what's gotten into you?"

"Nothing—can't I be glad to see my mother?"

"Depends—."

"On?" Alex asked.

"I've known you eighteen year. You either want something, or you're up to something."

"Well, I don't need anything, and we haven't done anything we shouldn't."

"I sense a story ahead, so spill it."

"We better sit down."

Carol looked perplexed. "I can't picture anything you'll tell me is more tragic than a triple homicide."

Alex lowered his head.

Carol reached out her hand. "It is serious, huh?"

"Yeah."

They walked a few feet to the dining room, and Carol slid out a chair and collapsed. Alex stood next to her and swallowed hard. "How do I begin?"

"Best place is at the beginning."

"Okay…it's about Heather."

"Is she in trouble?"

Alex remained quiet.

"Is she dead?"

Alex fidgeted with his sleeve.

"Tell me already."

"It's her sister. The police found her body in the park this morning."

Carol stood to her feet as Amy entered the room. "Alex Alan Jones, if you're lying, I swear——."

Amy interrupted. "He's telling the truth. She called us right after we saw it on the four o'clock news."

"I better call Wendy and check on her."

"Maybe tomorrow, mom."

Carol pulled out a chair. "Probably so. How are you guys holding up?"

"W—we're hanging in there," Alex said.

Alex tried to continue, but his cell phone interjected. He glanced at the display and covered his mouth.

Amy cocked her head. "Who is it?"

"I'll give you two guesses."

Amy crossed her arms across her chest. "Maybe after your emotional outburst this morning he's worried about you."

"What outburst? I told him not to touch me."

"Whatever. Downplay it all you like. Are you going to answer?"

After the fourth ring, Carol threw her hands up. "Answer the damn phone already."

In an evident rebellion, Alex slammed the phone on the counter. "I'll talk to him when I'm ready."

Amy stared at the phone, convinced he'd leave a voicemail. However, after a minute, the notification never came. Everyone made their way to the living room, and Amy had to have the final word. "At some point, you'll have to talk to him."

"Nope."

"This is Mike we're talking about. He'll find a way."

Everyone made themselves comfortable, and before long the room went mute. Alex's mind wafted back to the foggy evening three weeks earlier to the evening with led to the current melodramatic tension between him and his ex.

41

It started after Mike asked Alex out for a romantic dinner at their favorite place. Alex was so excited about the date it was all he could chat about for days. Then the day arrived, and he raced home, beaming from ear to ear. Then the moment he stepped out of the shower the phone rang. It was Mike calling to cancel their plans last minute. Mike deployed his go-to excuse—work.

Alex accepted from the moment he met Mike that dating a police officer wasn't all fun and games. There were plenty of late nights and countless broken promises. Still, none of it discouraged him from falling in love.

So, instead of sitting around moping he called Amy, and they took the dinner reservation. There they were, sitting in the window discussing prom, laughing, and having a fantastic time until Alex returned his gaze out the window. What his eyes saw soured the mellow atmosphere and their conversation.

"What's wrong?"

"The guy on the corner looks an awful lot like Mike. Don't you think?"

Amy slid to the window and took a glance. "It sure the hell is. Who's the guy though?"

"Never seen him before. I'll be right back."

Amy tugged the sleeve of his button-down. "Don't make a scene."

"I won't."

Amy scoffed. "Yeah, okay—don't say anything you can't take back later."

Mike stood on the corner and caught sight of Alex marching down the tree-lined sidewalk along Sixth Street. He swallowed past the lump in his throat.

I better come up with an excuse and fast.

Mike shooed the man away and prepared for an earful from his boyfriend. He faked a smile and held it as Alex grew closer. And as Alex's scrunched-up face came into focus, Mike wiped the phoniness from his face, and he paced on the corner.

"Alex, I can explain."

"Revising reports, huh?"

"It's related to work, I swear."

"Hmm. Kind of looks like something else."

"No, no, he's my informant. He called and needed to meet up."

Alex rolled his eyes. "Whatever you say."

"Besides, why in the world would I be sneak around with someone else when I'm in love with you?"

Alex crinkled his nose and tossed his hands in the air. "Sounds like whatever *that guy* had to say was more important than me."

"You know I can't tell you what we discussed. I've already shared more than I should have."

"Yeah, pretty convenient it's confidential. Listen, I'm going back to finish my dinner with Amy. When you're ready to be honest, you know where to find me."

Alex stormed away and back to the restaurant. Mike yelled down the busy street full of shoppers. "Alex, wait, don't leave mad."

People stopped and watched the two lovers quarrel, yet without missing a step in his stride, Alex ignored him and everyone else. He crossed the street, back into the restaurant, and tossed the linen napkin back into his lap.

"Fuck. I hate men."

***

HE POPPED BACK TO REALITY to Amy snapping her fingers and shouting his name. "Alex. Alex?"

"Yeah, hey."

"What's on your mind?" Carol asked.

"Nah, I'm good."

Alex leaned against the arm of the chair and gazed outside the picture window at the snow-covered mountains in the distance.

Amy leaned in. "It doesn't seem like everything is good."

"Okay, fine. I was thinking about Mike."

"And are you livid about what Mike did or worried he told the truth and you made a huge mistake."

Alex stuttered, "A bit of both. We've been together a year, and not once did he ever lie. Maybe everything bad I said can't be taken back?"

"You can always take stuff back. Let's face it, though, you're a loose cannon and go off without thinking."

Alex grinned. "It's one of my many shortcomings."

"So, if your such an expert on yourself, why are you sitting around here with us *instead* of calling him?"

Alex smirked and stood. It caught the attention of John, who looked up from his book. "What's going on?"

"Oh, I think Alex decided it's time to make up with Mike."

A shit-eating grin graced John's face. "About time. Maybe now you'll be less of an asshole to everyone."

Alex presented him with a stern glance as he walked past towards the staircase. At the base of the stairs, he swung around. "You guys mind getting dinner going?"

"No problem, now go and call him back."

Amy glanced out the window and watched the sun dipped below the mountainside. She faked a smile and stepped away from the beautiful scene before her. "I got this if you want to relax, Ms. J."

"And miss out on spending time catching up—nah."

They walked into the kitchen and Carol removed the pots and pans, setting each on the stove.

"Anything special you need me to do?" Amy asked.

"Are you any good at watching pasta boil?"

"You bet I am. In fact, I'm a pro at doing mundane tasks."

"Suppose it's your lucky day."

Amy laughed under her breath and steered the conversation back to the events of the day. "How are you holding up after this craziness today?"

"In shock still, I guess. What about you?"

Amy touched her black and blue cheek and winced. "Oh, you know, better than some. I can be honest with you, right?"

"Of course."

"I'm so ready to move to New York."

"Your parents still driving you insane?"

Amy scoffed. "You don't know the half of it."

"Well, I'm happy for you. Did my son make up his mind yet what he's doing?"

"You're joking, right? Alex is a master of many things, however making a final decision is not one of them."

Carol concurred and poured the sauce in the pan while Amy stood at the stove watching the water come to a boil.

***

WHILE THINGS DOWNSTAIRS WERE TAKING OFF, upstairs events were much different. Alex planted himself at his desk, and with one swift move lifted a four-by-six pewter frame. He stared at the photo, a recent ski trip to Vail with Mike and him, their arms wrapped around each other with huge grins scrawled across their faces. His cell phone rested in front of him, and his eyeballs shifted between the phone and photo, and a flood of happy memories brought a smile to his face for the first time in weeks. *He genuinely makes me happy. Calling him isn't giving in; it's the right thing to do.*

He set the frame down and grabbed the phone. His hand shook, and he hesitated to flip open the phone and dial the number he knew all-to-well. He bounced his foot under the desk, threw caution to the wind, and searched through his contact list.

45

With Mike's name highlighted, he closed his eyes, exhaled, and pressed the send key. After two rings a familiar, husky voice answered. "He-l-lo?"

"We need to talk."

Mike sighed, "Yes, we do."

"Where should we begin?"

"Well, the first thing I have to explain is what you saw the last time I saw you."

The line was idle.

"The man you saw is an undercover informant I deal with from time to time. He offered me some intel on organized crime which bled over from Denver."

Alex fidgeted in his chair. "Organized crime? Like the mafia?"

"There's no such thing as the mafia."

"Okay, whatever. Continue," Alex replied.

"I shouldn't tell you this, on the other hand, since it concerns you and your mother, I'm compelled."

"Affects us how?"

"The murders this morning—"

"What about them?"

"You and your mom might have a connection to them."

"What are you talking about?"

"Look, it's safer if we talk in person. Can I drive over?"

"Now I'm worried."

"Let me come over, and I promise you'll be fine once we talk."

Alex hesitated a few seconds. "Fine. Come over."

"Cool. Be there in ten."

Alex pressed end and stood from the chair. He slipped the cell phone back into his front pocket and strolled to the bedroom door. He stopped for a brief moment to gather his thoughts.

How am I going to explain this?

He stepped into the hallway and the floor groaned under his feet. Ten feet away was the dim stairwell and the closer he got, the louder the laughter from downstairs grew. He descended, afraid to tell everyone about Mike's impending arrival. He stepped onto the second tread, and a creaking sound echoed behind him. He swung around, and to his surprise, the hallway was empty.

Great. Now I'm hearing shit…just what I need.

He blew off the uneasiness and picked up his pace as he flew down the stairs to the foyer. He emerged into the hall where he found Amy and John sitting at the dining room table talking and laughing with Carol. Alex stepped into the archway, and they fell quiet and looked up with inquisitive stares on their faces.

Amy stood and moved towards Alex. "So? You two forgive each other?"

"Not quite. So, um, Mike says he has news to share and needs to come over."

"Okay? What news?"

"Amy, it's more than likely code for he wants to see him. Right, Alex?"

He threw his hands up. "With him, anything is possible. He did utter something about the murders and how my mom and I are somehow connected."

Carol perked up. "How?"

Alex shrugged. "No idea. Might be the reason he's coming over so he can explain everything."

Carol paced the dining room. "Should we be worried? Are we targets?"

"Mom let's calm down and wait for Mike."

The doorbell rang, and Alex stared at the door. "Looks like he miscalculated his arrival."

5

CAROL SHOOED HIM WITH HER HANDS, and Alex trotted to the front door, took in a deep breath before he gripped the handle. He flung open the door, and a cool breeze blew across his face. When his eyes glanced up, they met with his ex. Mike leaned in and endeavored to hug Alex. Instead of open arms welcoming him, Alex stepped back.

"Hey, not ready yet."

"I understand. May I come in?"

Alex stepped aside, allowing Mike to step in from the frigid air. He closed the door, and his mom and friends stepped into the archway, eager to hear this shocking news.

Carol stepped forward and rushed up and wrapped her arms around his neck. "Welcome back, Mike. Come. Dinner's getting cold."

"Thanks."

Everyone settled into their chairs and thanks to Amy, the table was set, and the food dished out. With Mike back in the house, there was a slight tension in the air, yet Alex tried to lessen the uneasiness. After all, it was Alex who blew things out of proportion, and the right thing to do was swallow his pride and apologize. Two things Alex was never any good at.

"So, shall we eat or hear this news first?" Alex asked the group.

"I'm starving, so the news will have to wait," Carol said.

"Fair enough."

The twenty-minute dinner was silent while everyone shoveled food in their mouths. Mike presumed everyone had finished; he stood and gathered plates to take to the kitchen.

Alex jumped from his chair. "Let me give you a hand with those."

Mike nodded and continued along.

With every plate and utensil in their hands, they disappeared into the kitchen. Alex set the dishes as quiet as he could on the counter and backed away.

Mike, on the other hand, dropped the utensils in the sink and turned around to face Alex. Before he allowed him the chance to squirm away, Mike extended his hand and clutched Alex's. "We need to talk…about us."

"Can we finish delivering the news first? Afterward, I promise I'll make time."

Mike ceded and let the topic go for the moment. He flipped the faucet on and waited for the water to warm. "I can wait."

They finished cleaning the kitchen and returned to a table full of impatient people. Alex pulled out the chair and made himself comfortable while Mike hovered. His hands trembled, so he hid them behind his back. "So, I've received some intel regarding the incident this morning."

Everyone's eyes fixated on the broad-shouldered man towering over them. "Don't keep us in suspense."

"So… an informant passed on some information about the murders and your last name came up."

"I don't understand," Carol said.

Alex's eyebrows furrowed. "How are we connected to criminal activity?"

"He didn't say it involved you. He said, 'tell your boyfriend to keep a low profile.'"

Carol glanced downward. "Do I need to hire security?"

"Not yet. Can either of you think of a reason this guy would say this?"

"Sorry, Mike. I got nothing for you," Alex said.

Mike glanced at Carol who had drifted off. "Carol. Anything?"

The heaviness of stares aroused her. "I'm sorry, what?"

"Why was Alex mentioned by my informant?"

"I can't do this right now." Her mind drifted off to whatever had pulled her away from the conversation in the first place.

John pointed to himself and Amy. "Should either of us worry?"

"Not sure…Alex appears to be the only one mentioned."

Amy lowered her head and rested her hands against her temples.

"What's important to do is keep your guard up for a while. This means paying closer attention to your surroundings, travel in groups."

"How long have you known about these maniacs?" Amy asked.

"They've been on our radar a few weeks. However, the destructive path they left today was not why we were keeping our eyes on them."

"What about school? Finals are next week."

"I'll see you make it safe to school."

The questions tapered off and everyone stared at each other, not sure what to say next. Mike extended his hand out to Alex. "You guys don't mind if I borrow him for a few minutes, do you?"

Amy and John nudged each other playfully, and Mike flashed a bright smile at Alex. "Okay. We'll be back soon."

Alex and Mike faded from sight when they stepped into the living room. They had a plethora to discuss, and Alex wasn't sure what he would say. Would he be his usual forgiving self, or throw manners to the wind and go full-blown hostile?

He melted into the couch, and Mike paced around like a nervous schoolboy on his first date. Watching it play out was far different from how Alex pictured this in his mind. His eyebrows raised, and he bit his lower lip. "Mike, for the love of God, sit down already."

Without hesitation, Mike plopped down and left a foot between them. He bent one leg up on the couch and situated himself to give Alex his undivided attention.

"I know this isn't where we saw ourselves a year ago," Alex began. "There's no excuse for my behavior, and I shouldn't have overreacted the way I did. There aren't words to express how sorry I am."

"It's okay. Your heart is in the right place, yet sometimes I don't know where your mind is. I'd never cheat on you. You're the love of my life."

Alex hung his head in shame. "I know. You're mine too. Can you ever forgive me for how I've acted in the past few weeks?"

"I'd be a shitty boyfriend if I didn't."

Alex scooted closer and rested his hand against Mike's leg. "Yeah, you would."

Alex leaned in and planted a gentle kiss on his plump lips. He lost himself in the sentiment of love, and he pulled away. He tried not to smile but failed.

"I was serious in there, ya know. These guys, the whole thing feels off."

Alex nodded.

"And I can't have you leaving for school without me at least escorting you there."

"I'm still confused how my mom or I fit into any of this. You sure your informant said nothing else?"

Mike yanked at his shirt and curled his lip. "I've told you everything he said."

"Okay. If you find anything else out, you'll let us know, right?"

The muted sound of the telephone ringing in the distance gave Mike the evasion he sought. However, Alex refused to let it go. "Don't worry, my mom will answer it. Don't avoid the question."

"I'm not. You'll be the first to know if anything comes up."

Alex smiled. From around the corner, his mother appeared in the foyer, her hand covered the telephone. "Alex, when was the last time you saw Heather?"

"I dropped her off around twelve. Spoke to her around four when she let us know about Kelli. Why? Is everything okay?"

"Mrs. Burgess says she left for a walk around four-thirty and hasn't returned."

"She's had a traumatic day; my guess is she's off somewhere gathering her thoughts. Did she check the pavilion?"

Carol announced, "She's already been there."

"If she's not there and not here, I'm fresh out of ideas. Don't worry, she'll show up. She just needs some space. Trust me."

Carol respected his assessment and disappeared into the kitchen. Mike stood and reached his hand out. "Well, now that we've cleared things up, we should rejoin everyone?"

Alex rubbed his arm as he pondered if he wanted to go back. "You're right. I don't want to subject them to my mom's torture any longer."

Alex walked into the kitchen while Mike returned to the dining room table. Alex stopped dead in his tracks as he witnessed his mom drop the phone on the cradle.

"Everything good?" he asked.

Her head tilted, and she tightened her lips together. "I—I'm concerned."

"Why?"

"Mrs. Burgess says Heather isn't generally gone this long. Plus her cell goes straight to voicemail."

"You want me to try?"

Carol grinned. "If you could."

Alex pulled the phone from his pocket and searched through his contacts until he found her name. He pressed send and raised the phone to his ear, and as Mrs. Burgess relayed to his mom…the call went straight to voicemail.

Her recording was loathsome, and he tapped his foot waiting for the beep. "Heather, it's Alex. Just calling to check on how you're doing. When you have a second can you please call your mother or me back? We just want to know you're safe."

He hung up, slipped the phone back in his pocket, and spoke to his mom. "Sorry."

"Thank for trying. You should return to your friends," Carol said.

"Are you coming?"

"Nah, I need to, uh…make a grocery list."

Alex knew she was giving him space to spend time catching up with Mike, and he loved her for it. He breezed through the archway and passed behind Mike stealthily. He reached down and wrapped his arms around him from behind.

Mike jerked. "Scare the shit out of me why don't you."

Alex pulled back. "Who else hugs you like me?"

"I mean, I knew it was you, I was in deep meditation. Heather—did she answer?"

"Straight to voicemail like her mom predicted. Maybe Mike and I should take a drive and see if we can find her?"

"Yeah, smart. I mean, Heather will come home, except she might need a nudge towards home."

"What about John and me? Should we stay? Go home?"

"Up to you guys. I have plenty of room if you want to stay."

John stood. "I'd love to stay, except my parents are expecting me any time. Besides, I'm pretty beat and should call it a night."

John approached Alex and slapped his hand against his back, shook Mike's hand, and hollered into the kitchen. "Ms. J, amazing dinner. Thanks again for having me over."

Alex pulled him close. "Please be careful, and I'll see you in the morning."

John pulled away and ran his hand through his hair. "Yup, see you then."

They watched as John grabbed his jacket and bag and walked through the front door. Alex didn't worry too much about a football jock like him. Besides, his house was at the end of the cul-de-sac. Alex directed his attention back to Amy at the head of the table. "You gonna stay over?"

"I should, huh? I'm worried about Heather, and it might be good for my sanity to have a night away from my psychotic parents."

"Your parents still at it? Mike asked.

"You have no idea. I'm sure any day now you'll be there for a domestic."

"Let's hope it doesn't progress that far," Mike joked.

"Enough about my family, can we refocus on Heather?"

"Right."

"Hear me out: what if she headed out for a walk and the same guys who murdered Kelli and those people at the 7-Eleven snatched her up?" Amy asked.

"Sounds far-fetched, wouldn't you say?" Alex asked.

"Maybe. Maybe not."

Alex and Mike glanced at each other.

"You know how my imagination runs wild. Just forget I mentioned anything."

Perhaps Amy's judgment was out of whack—Heather abducted by the same men who killed the convenience store clerk, two innocent bystanders, and Kelli. Alex was still uneasy about Heather's disappearing act, and it was still too early to involve more police. After Alex weighed the pros and cons, he opted to leave the resolution up to Mike.

"Well, shall we try to track her down?"

"Yeah, daylight is fading fast," Mike said.

Alex stuck his head into the kitchen where Carol was making a list she promised she would. "Mike and I are going out to search for Heather. You wouldn't mind giving Amy a ride to her house to pick up a change of clothes, would you?"

"Sure, sweetie, I don't mind one bit."

Alex smiled and grabbed Mike's jacket off the coat rack. The two left and walked down the gray paver walkway to the massive SUV parked behind Alex's BMW. Mike watched Alex rub his hands together as he tried to shake the cold.

"We're going to find her. You know it, and I know it," Mike said, flashing a smile.

"Let's hope so. I can't take any more death today."

"Trust me, no one else is going to die if I can help it."

6

ALEX AND MIKE SEARCHED FOR OVER an hour and a half and had no luck in locating her. They drove around the subdivision, the shopping center, and the football field at the high school. After the security guard at the main entrance to the development handed their IDs back, Alex rubbed his index fingers against his temples. Mike sensed the defeat in Alex's face, yet kept his mouth shut.

The SUV pulled into the driveway, and Alex opened the door, without saying a word, and stepped onto the concrete. Mike rushed around the front of the vehicle and grabbed ahold of him by the forearm.

"Hey, wait up."

Alex paused and lifted his head.

"She'll turn up."

"How can you be sure?"

"I'm not. Would it reassure you if by tomorrow morning she doesn't call I'll file a missing person's report on behalf of her parents?"

"A little, but let's hope it doesn't come to that."

"I hope it doesn't. You do realize I'm on your side."

"I do, and I appreciate it. Well, I better head inside and try to rest. Got a feeling I'll need it."

Mike leaned in and hugged Alex. "You rest and I'll see you in a few hours."

Alex didn't want him to let go, however, recognized he had to pull away at some point. He reached out his hand, smiled, and veered away towards the house. Mike stood in the mist and kept an eye on the love of his life until he was safe indoors.

Alex unbolted the front door and stepped into the foyer where, to his surprise, he found his mom and Amy camped out in the living room, watching TV.

"Shocked you two are still awake."

Amy stretched out her arms and yawned. "Waiting up for you; any luck?"

"No. We searched everywhere for her, no sign."

"She's gotta be hiding out somewhere, I'm sure she'll surface in the morning. It's so late; you two should get to sleep," Carol insisted, as she stood up from the couch.

"She's right. We have an early morning and a long day," Amy said.

"Yup. Night mom."

"Night."

***

IN THE MIDDLE OF THE NIGHT, dark storm clouds wandered into Ridgewood Hills. The light mist which fell over town earlier now grew into a moderate rain shower. A clap of thunder awoke Amy, who lied in the bedroom across the hall from Alex's room. She pulled the duvet closer to her face as the heftier raindrops pounded against the window. Amy shifted her head and watched the alarm clock change from two forty-four over to two forty-five and out fell a loud groan.

I'm never getting back to sleep now.

Across the hallway, things were different. Alex lay on his side, fast asleep. He wasn't the type of person to let some rain, storms or drama going on in his life to disturb his sleep.

Amy planted her feet onto the hardwood floor, opened the door and crept into the dark hallway. She couldn't help herself—a late-night snack sounded like the perfect idea to help her fall back to sleep.

She tried hard to be as quiet as possible. There wasn't any need to wake the entire house because she couldn't sleep. With each step she took, the floorboards beneath her feet creaked and echoed off the walls.

Shit.

She moved faster, hoping it would be like ripping off a bandage—it wasn't. She threw her hands up in defeat and continued down the stairs. *Not going back now.*

Amy opened the refrigerator and grabbed a small bag filled with turkey, a jar of mayonnaise, and a slice of mozzarella cheese. She left the door open to shed some light as she walked to the other side of the kitchen for the bread, knife and a plate.

In the distance, an unfamiliar noise rustled, and her hand trembled. She clutched the knife and set the plate onto the granite countertop as quiet as possible. Her back hugged the wall, and she tiptoed towards the noise.

Amy saw a figure moving near the staircase and without hesitation retreated. Her heart pounded, her palms grew clammier, and with each passing second, the footsteps grew louder and louder. She closed her eyes and raised the knife above her head. Thankfully, before she took her first downward jab, Alex flicked on the light switch and called out.

"Amy? You in there?"

She opened her eyes. "Alex?"

He rounded the corner. "Yeah. Um, why do you have a knife?"

"Scare the shit out of me why don't ya."

"It's okay, you're safe. You can let go of the knife now; it's only me. There's no one here except us."

"Okay—sorry. I got hungry."

"I see. Still doesn't explain the knife."

She looked down at her hand. "I needed it for the mayo, but I heard a noise and thought those guys from earlier were coming back to kill me."

Alex's eyebrows raised. "Honey, no one is coming in here to murder you. They'd have one hell of a time getting past security."

She loosened her grip on the handle. "Mike scared me earlier when he was talking about those guys."

"He scared me too, but how can we be scared when we have each other?"

"You're right. Why am I over-reacting?"

"You're not. You ready to return to school tomorrow?"

She stayed silent.

"I'm up for going. However, it's clear you aren't."

Amy bowed her head and fidgeted with her fingers. "I'm fine."

The rhythm in his voice sped up. "Oh, is that so? You tried to murder me a minute ago."

"Sorry, I'm a little on edge."

"Exactly. Why don't we take another day off? Tomorrow is Friday, and it'll give us the entire weekend to recuperate."

"Okay, let's do it."

Alex replied, and as soon as the first word fell from his mouth, a shadowy figure jolted past the living room window. "Hold on."

Amy tailed Alex into the living room at the slightest hint of weirdness. "What is it?"

"I swear there was a silhouette outside, just now," Alex said and pulled her closer to him.

"In the front yard?"

He nodded, and the two meandered into the unlit living room. They inched their way to the large picture window where nothing obstructed their view outdoors. Amy stared at Alex even though every ounce of his energy focused outside the window.

"Maybe it was a stray," Amy said.

"Ain't no damn animals around here walking on two legs."

"Could have been a bear?"

Alex cocked his head and in his typical sassy fashion shook his head. "Get real."

"Okay, I'm out of ideas. Could be our mind's playing tricks on us. Face the truth; we're both a disaster."

Alex ignored her rationale and continued towards the window. He pulled back the curtain, scanned the front lawn, and watched the raindrops fall from the sky. Without deliberation, he lowered the blinds and stepped away as soon as he could.

"Did you hear me?" she asked.

"Yeah, sorry. No, our minds aren't playing tricks on us. I know what I saw. Someone's out there."

"Well if it was a person who was it?"

"No clue. The only thing I saw was a bulky figure standing there, didn't see a face."

"Maybe someone's watching us?"

"Let's try to fall back asleep."

"You need to call Mike. He told you to call if anything came up."

Alex had to stop her before the hysteria got any more out of hand. "For Christ's sake, it's three in the morning. I'm not calling Mike."

She stood there, her body shaking.

"Listen, tell you what; there's some tequila hidden under my bed. After the day we both had we deserve a shot."

Amy pondered what to say. "Yeah, a shot sounds much better than food."

The two snuck up the stairs. Neither Alex nor Amy drank very often, however with unusual happenings around town, Alex deliberated. *What would one shot hurt?*

They reached his bedroom door, and Alex pushed the door inward. As Alex closed the door behind him, Amy plopped onto the bed, and Alex got on all fours and reached for the hidden bottle of *Jose Cuervo*. He stood, clutching the bottle in his left hand and Amy smiled.

He walked over to his desk and pulled out two shot glasses from the bottom drawer. He ran the opened bottle beneath his nose and inhaled, letting out a soft couch. "Shit's potent."

Amy laughed, and Alex poured an equal amount into each small glass. "Where are the limes? And salt?"

"Kid, you're gonna have to do this the old-fashioned way."

Amy crinkled her nose and threw caution to the wind. With one quick flick of her head, she let it flow down her throat. "Whoa, fuck."

"I told you," Alex threw his shot back. "Another?"

"Ah, what the hell, if Mr. Perfect can do two, so can I."

Alex let her comment slide. His friends were always saying off the wall shit to provoke him. How could Alex help it if everything in his life regularly went his way? Alex poured another round and handed Amy hers. "Well, bottoms up."

"Bottoms up."

They finished the second round, and Alex smiled at Amy, who stretched out her arms and yawned. "Well, back to sleep. We'll discuss our plan when we wake up."

"Yeah, this is just what I needed. Thanks again."

Alex climbed under the covers as Amy walked out the door. With his privacy back, he glanced at the clock: three forty-five.

Alex groaned at the thought of the alarm screeching at him in two hours. He fluffed his pillow, threw his head hard against it, and laid there, staring at the ceiling. He couldn't stop thinking about the shadowy figure. *What if Mike's right and someone is after us?*

With the adrenaline still coursing through his veins, the chances of him falling asleep were slim to none. He allowed the air to escape from his lungs and thought, *if I don't try tomorrow will be a shitty day.*

He continued for another ten minutes watching the ceiling, straining to conjure up his latest reason for not going to school. Even though his mother would hound his ass, he decided on using 'I'm still in shock from the robbery' excuse and was certain he'd score sympathy points with her.

With his decision made, he glanced around the creepy room once more, and the stillness drove a chill up his spine. Confident the room was free of he reached for the remote and switched on the TV.

That should help.

Not even a second later a bang outside the window shot him straight up in bed. He pulled his covers tighter. *It's only the storm outside, relax.*

He laid his head back down and shut his eyes. At last, the tequila kicked in, and in a matter of minutes, he was fast asleep.

***

A FEW HOURS LATER, LIKE CLOCKWORK, Alex's alarm blasted out a country song. He spun over and smashed his hand on the snooze. Same as last night, he found himself staring at the white ceiling, except now a few beams of sunlight peeked through his bedroom window. He smiled and allowed himself to drift off again. A soft knock at the door and Alex roused.

"Come in."

"Sorry. I didn't wake you...did I?"

"Nah, I've been up. Come in, come in."

"I might have fallen back asleep, but I couldn't swear to it. I worried the entire night someone was going to break in and murder us in our sleep. How did you sleep?" Amy asked.

"It wasn't as good as usual, but I was able to pass out twenty minutes after you left. I can say with certainty it wasn't the best night's sleep."

"Same. What'd we decide on what to do about school?"

"I'm with you. We'll tell my mom we're still traumatized, and she won't make us go."

Amy sprang onto the bed. "Let me call John and see if he wants to come over."

Alex dug his fingertips across his forehead. "Maybe we should let him go. We can take a day for just the two of us."

"If that's what you want."

Alex was unsure if missing another day of school was worth it, but for Amy's sanity, he figured it was the right thing to do. Amy walked out, and Alex reached over to swipe his cell phone from the nightstand. He scrolled through his contacts and called John.

The phone rang once, and John answered, his deafening music blared in the background. "What's up?"

"Are you going to school?"

"Yeah, why?"

"Amy and I are going to take the day off. Do you mind running by my place and handing in my paper during fifth period today?"

"Yeah, no problem. Be there around seven-thirty?"

"See you then."

Alex tossed the phone onto the bed and groaned at crawling out from under the warm covers. After several minutes of wrestling with his mind, he flung his legs from beneath the covers and planted his feet on the floor. But he was never one to let anybody except Amy see him unprepared and looking like shit.

He slammed his feet onto the floor and trudged to the closet to grab anything low-key to wear. With shirt, jeans, and underwear in hand, he hurried into the bathroom and when he caught a glimpse of himself in the mirror, and he dropped the clothes on the floor.

I'm so worn out. I need a spa day…soon.

Alex leaned over the sink. The warm water seeped through his fingers although he managed to cup some and splashed it across his face. Alex stared up again into the mirror as the water dripped from the tip of his nose, and he cracked a plastic smile.

Inside, his mind was exhausted, but no matter the circumstances, Alex always found the positives in anything. And while forgiving Mike brightened his mood, fear gnawed away in the back of his mind as he tried to figure out what caused the string of violence to rock the sleepy town.

The familiar ring tone chirped from the bedroom, and he ran, trying to make it in time.

"Hello?"

"Alex, good morning. It's Mrs. Burgess."

"Ah, good morning. Did Heather ever come home?"

"No. I keep trying to reach her, but—," Mrs. Burgess paused.

"Let me call Mike. It's not like her to disappear like this; not like her at all."

"She's never been gone this long without at least calling."

"Mike will have the magical answer on what to do. I'll have him call you, okay?"

Alex took notice of the tremble in Mrs. Burgess voice, "Okay. And if you hear from her—."

"You'll be the first person I call."

He hung up stepped into the hallway. He tapped against the guestroom door, and Amy yelled out, "just a minute." He waited patiently, and after about a minute she flung open the door.

"Mrs. Burgess called."

"And?"

"Heather didn't come home last night."

"Oh shit, she's been murdered too."

"Jesus, Amy, let's not go that far…yet."

"Well, have you called Mike?"

"Just about to, but I wanted to make sure you were aware first."

"Thanks. Now go."

Alex dashed across the hallway. Amy strolled behind him, and as Alex entered the room, the cell phone rang. He answered without checking the caller ID.

"Hello?"

"Alex?"

"Brandy? Is that you?"

"Yup. How are you?"

"Things could be better, but let's not dwell. God, it's been so long since I heard your voice."

"Too long. But I've got terrific news."

Alex remained silent.

"I'm going to be in Denver for some stupid training class for work. I was hoping if you're around, I could drop by."

"Yeah, I'll be around the entire day. Call and give a heads up in case we're out."

"No problem. Shall we say six o'clock?"

"Yeah, perfect time."

"And if you don't mind, I'd love to take you to dinner."

Alex chuckled. "I never say no to free food. Well, see you later."

"Yup. See ya."

Amy stepped behind Alex as he set the phone on the desk. "Who was on the phone?"

"Brandy. I met her in seventh grade when I spent the summer at orchestra camp in Colorado Springs."

"Ah, right. Now I remember," Amy said.

"Well, she's in town and wants to have dinner before she heads back to Colorado Springs."

"Sounds like fun. Could be a good distraction."

"Yeah, haven't seen her in over a year. Ooh, you have to come with us," Alex said.

"Nah, I don't want to intrude."

"You won't be intruding. You're my best friend," Alex began, "but enough about the evening ahead. We got a crisis which needs our urgent attention."

"Shit."

"What, shit?"

"You forgot to call Mike."

"Damnit. Be back."

Alex left the room and raced down the stairs. Meanwhile, Amy lounged at his desk and let her mind wander. She speculated about a reasonable explanation of what happened to Heather.

Maybe she couldn't take the pressure and ran away. Maybe she's staying with a friend we don't know—but who?

Amy brushed off the notion of Heather meeting with foul play, yet she continued to allow her overactive imagination to bombard her. She paced around the room, and when she caught a glimpse of the picture frame on his desk, she tilted her head and smiled. She pulled out the chair and took a seat as heavy footsteps creaked outside the door in the hallway.

Probably Ms. Jones heading to work.

Alex rounded the corner back into his bedroom, and an unexpecting Amy jumped as he raced in. Alex looked at her with an odd stare. "Did I scare you?"

"Not funny."

"Sorry," Alex said as he walked past her.

"Did you speak to Mike?"

Alex nodded. "In fact, he's so worried he's already given his sergeant an update last night."

"Well, it's a start," Amy said.

No more than thirty seconds later Carol rushed past the bedroom, and Alex stepped out into the hallway. "Whoa. Where's the fire?"

"I'm running behind, and I still need to eat," she stopped and gave him a look-over, "Why aren't you ready for school?"

"Well, neither of us slept well last night with the murders and Heather—you see where I'm going with this."

"Fine. I'll make Amy's mom aware and call in an excuse for you. But you have to go back on Monday. You have two weeks left, don't blow it."

"I won't. By the way, Heather still hasn't shown up."

"Add another name to the list. I better call Wendy on the way to work as well."

"Don't stress too much about calling her. I've already spoken with her this morning, and Mike filed the missing person's report. The cops searched throughout the night for her."

"I don't know where she could be. Of course, I don't understand why people commit crimes in the first place," Carol said. "Okay, sweetie, I have to go. You two stay out of trouble today and for God's sake, do something constructive."

Carol didn't wait around for a reply. She raced down the stairs and into the kitchen and filled her travel mug with the fresh coffee. Alex and Amy descended as the garage door slammed closed. Amy looked at Alex, "I'm—"

67

"You're what?"

"Apprehensive. Are you going to tell your mother about the person prowling around outside the window last night?"

"Why? We aren't sure it was a person. You must admit we've been under immense stress the past few weeks. Isn't it possible our overworked minds are playing tricks on us?"

"Eh, could be. At the very least, will you tell Mike about it?"

"Later, at lunch. He's better hearing unwelcome news after he's eaten."

She approved, and they ventured into the living room, and without hesitation, Alex reached for the remote, clicked on the television, and stretched out his feet. Amy chimed in.

"Is the channel nine news on?"

"Why? You hate the news."

"I used to. Now, with the drama going on around town, I find it attention-grabbing."

Alex leaned forward, shook his head, and searched through the channels until he came across what Amy was waiting for. The clock in the foyer chimed six times as the wind and rain pounded unyielding against the window.

After watching the lead story which updated them on where the police stood on the investigation—nowhere, Alex allowed his mind to drift outside the window. Violent crime was nothing new to the Jones family. Alex recalled a day, similar to the current one, thirteen years earlier which changed the course of his life forever.

They executed his father when he was five as he walked along the walkway to their Cherry Hill home. Alex forgot nothing about the day. The ominous sky. The rain falling obscuring his view of the mountains. He did as he would always do when the weather kept him inside: moped in his window seat wishing he could be outside with his friends.

The family station wagon pulled in the driveway, and Alex remembered being happier than ever. In 1985 his father spent a tremendous amount of time on the road, some hush-hush assignment, one he never learned about nor ever took the time to investigate.

Alex's joy flipped to horror as a masked man rushed out from the neighbor's front yard, taking his father by surprise. His father struggled the fight the man off, and Alex rushed to the staircase. He couldn't make a sound. Instead, Alex ripped through the house, and down the stairs. When he flung open the front door, the man pointed the gun at the back of his father's head. There was a bright flash from the barrel of the gun, and he remembered watching his father fall to the ground before everything went blank.

At that exact moment, Carol was in the kitchen preparing dinner. The loud blast surprised her, and she dropped the knife and ran to the front door. With neglect for her safety, Carol scooped up Alex and ran back inside and slammed the door with such force it knocked her favorite vase to the floor, shattering into a million pieces.

Carol ran to the phone and called the police, left Alex in the house, and rushed back outside to her husband's side. She held the phone with her shoulder and cradled her dying husband in her arms as he gurgled blood from his mouth. As he lay dying, he whispered with the little energy he had left, "I love you."

The gunman stood across the street watching her sob on the wet pavers, and she looked up to see him bend his fingers into the shape of a gun and point it towards her.

The feeling of Amy tapping his shoulder disturbed Alex from his flashback. He shuddered, trying to shake the memory. After the haze faded, Amy's face was inches from his.

"Hello…Alex… you with me?"

"Yeah, sorry. Sort of lost my train of thought. What were you saying?"

"Um, I wasn't saying anything. We were watching the news. I assumed you fell back asleep."

"No, no, I'm awake. Brandy's visit stirred up a memory from a long time ago. Nothing to be alarmed about."

Amy smiled, yet deep inside sensed Alex was withholding his feelings from her. She couldn't pinpoint why Alex wasn't comfortable enough to tell her what was on his mind when he never held back before. She shrugged off her disappointment and continued watching the news as if nothing happened.

Time passed by in silence, and once the news finished, Amy changed the TV over to an old rerun of some show. "I don't want you to take this the wrong way, but why are you so fascinated with these shows?"

Amy shrugged. "These people make it appear their lives were so simple back in those times. It's like no matter what you did, there was always a solution."

"You realize it's fictional."

"And it's a damn shame; I wish *real* life worked the same."

The mood lightened, and they both had a good laugh over it, but soon Alex reverted to his serious-minded self. "Was there anything you wanted to do today?"

"Can't we chill?"

"Well…about earlier. When I spaced out—"

Amy shifted her eyes away from the TV. "What about it?"

"How about a quick trip into Denver?"

"Denver? Why would we go there?" she asked.

"My conversation with Mike last night got me thinking."

"About?"

"He mentioned a possible connection to these guys. Maybe something to do with my father? It's all I want to say right now."

"Someone murdered your father thirteen years ago, so how could there be a link between the present and the past?"

"I don't know. It's a feeling in my gut. You trust me, right?"

Amy cocked her head. "Are you serious? I trust you more than anyone."

Alex smiled.

"Am I confused? You bet I am. Do I want to help? Yes."

"So, you'll go with me?"

"If this helps bring you closure, I can spend a few hours in Denver."

"Perfect. It's like I don't know what or who to believe anymore," Alex said as he stood. "I better shower."

Amy leaned back and watched Alex hurry towards the stairs. His cryptic ramblings about his father gave her reasons to be concerned. Although she trusted his intuition, she questioned if the thirteenth anniversary of his father's death was hurling his anxiety through the roof. She glanced again back to Alex as his feet disappeared into the dark stairwell.

The credits zoomed across the screen, and she shut off the TV. With one smooth move, she tossed the remote control onto the coffee table, and it made a thud as it landed.

Suppose I should shower too.

She ascended the stairs as the wooden floor creaked beneath her feet. She listened to the rain as it picked up in intensity and pounded against the roof. As she reached the top of the stairs, the wind howled, and a scratching sound at the end of the hallway stopped her in her tracks.

What the hell?

She advanced beyond Alex's room and towards the window at the end of the hall. Her hands trembled as she moved closer and the scraping increased. As Amy reached out her hand and drew the curtain, she clutched her chest when to her surprise it was a single tree branch causing the disturbance.

She chuckled at her overreaction and returned to Alex's door. With a soft knock, she shouted out. "You in there?"

"Yeah, what's up?"

"Can I come in?"

"Sure, I'm decent."

She reached for the doorknob and pushed against the door. The transition from pitch black to some light stung her eyes, and she took a moment to adjust. "What do you have against lights?"

"I'm trying to save the planet."

Amy smiled. "Everything good?"

"Just needed my phone. Was about to jump into the shower. What's up with you?"

"My show ended and figured I better primp myself if we're heading to the city."

He smiled, and his cell phone rang. "Hello?"

"Alex, it's Mom. Just checking on you. You were so peculiar this morning."

"Mom, I promise, everything's fine. I'm about to jump in the shower."

"Okay, sweetie. You worry me sometimes. What are you both planning today?"

"Homework. Pretty wild, huh?"

"Well, I'll let you go. Call me if you need anything."

"You know I will. Love you."

"Love you, too."

Alex hung up, and he faced Amy, who straddled the edge of his bed. With her head tilted, and brows furrowed, she had a few questions. "A quiet day at home? What happened to Denver?"

"Oh, we're going. My mom doesn't need to know though."

"Why?"

Alex sighed. "I don't need her upset seeing as I'm about to go dig into my dad's murder. Doubt she'd be supportive."

"Promise me what we're doing is safe."

"100 percent safe."

"And what will we do if we find stuff you don't want to know?"

"We'll deal with it when it happens. But for now, let's get ready. I'd like to make it there and back with time to have lunch with Mike."

Amy nodded and stood up from the bed. She walked into the hallway and closed the door behind her. Alex walked into the bedroom and slammed his hand against the door before locking it.

He stood at the mirror and tugged at the bags under his eyes. *I need a break.*

He paused before walking back into his bedroom to pick up his cell from the desk. The wind subsided outside, enough for him to hear Amy across the hallway shrieking as she attempted to sing-along to the radio. He snickered under his breath but soon revisited the bathroom.

He cracked the window to allow the cooling air to pass in. Unnerved, the white noise was the only way to drown out the stillness. He took in a deep breath, twisted the knobs of the shower, and an unbroken stream of water gushed. While Alex paused for the water to run hot, he stripped away his clothes and ditched them piece by piece onto the cold ceramic tile.

Alex stepped into the shower, closed his eyes, and his peacefulness vanished when his mind launched into worry-mode. Whenever things got too quiet for him his memories, and postponed decisions brawled around inside his head, wrangling for his attention. There were so many things to consider, but at the top of the list was what to do after graduation.

Alex loved the mountains and Colorado, and the idea of giving up everything to move away to New York with Amy scared him to death. Perhaps the apprehension came from letting go of a past he never healed from, or having to handle a long-distance relationship, or recognizing he'd now have to deal with crowds, paying bills, and being responsible for himself. Maybe growing up was his actual fear.

With one item confronted, his mind allowed him a moment of happiness when he remembered how amazing it was to see Mike again last night. Mike's love rippled through the embrace, and Alex calmed until he recalled the tumultuous day which kick-started a chain of events. Before he let his mind grow too ominous, he opened his eyes. The scalding water spattered against his golden-brown skin and gradually the morbid thoughts swimming about his mind dissipated.

Meanwhile, in the guest bathroom, Amy stepped out of the shower and reached for the crumpled towel resting on the floor. Her feet landed onto the cold ceramic tile, yet she continued to sing at the top of her lungs along with the radio. Just like Alex, the events from yesterday still fresh on her mind. After having a gun shoved in her face, watching her crush die in front of her eyes, and dealing with Heather disappearing, for her to keep her composure together was nothing short of a miracle.

As she stood at the foggy mirror, she couldn't help but feel an unspoken vibe between her and Alex that menacing shit was going down in Ridgewood Hills. To make matters worse, it was as if they were the only two in the entire town who recognized it. And the notion his theory could be right, concerned her.

With one quick swipe, she flung the moisture away and stared at herself in the foggy mirror. The past few months hadn't been kind to Amy. Her parents were on the verge of divorce, and she wasn't sure what she'd have done if Alex hadn't been there to lend a supportive hand. He kept her busy planning positive things in life; prom, graduation, and reinforcing the realization she was moving away from her psychotic family.

Any time she remembered how supportive he'd been for her waterworks would commence without delay. The fog crept up the mirror again, and she first wiped away her subtle tears before wiping the mirror.

Alex finished and stood in the middle of his bedroom in his underwear and undershirt. More than ever needed to figure out what led to his father's murder.

Before he had a chance to rummage through his closet, his cell phone rang. With a quick glance at the caller ID, he answered with some pep in his voice. "Good morning."

"Wait, who is this and what have you done with my boyfriend?"

Alex snickered. "I'm so happy to hear your voice. What's up?"

"Leaving my morning briefing. I'll give you two guesses what the top headline was."

"I'll go out on a limb and say the four unsolved murders and missing teenager?"

"How'd I land such a smart boyfriend like you?"

"Stop, you're making me blush. Let's get down to business. Do you have any updates?"

"We were able to identify one of the suspects. A Russian born man whose rap sheet is longer than Santa's naughty list. He's connected to crimes not only here, but in Germany and New York."

"Sounds like a dangerous guy," Alex said.

"FBI's had him under surveillance for years, yet never had enough evidence to go after him."

"Do you have enough now?"

"Not yet, we're getting there. And not to brag but since I'm *so,* what's the word I'm searching for—ahh — magnificent, Detective Scott asked me to help out on the case."

"That's huge."

"But hey, I gotta go for now. You'll be around the whole day?"

"Yeah, I mean, we're heading to Denver, but we'll be home in time for lunch."

Mike's mood shifted to confused in a matter of seconds. "Denver?"

"Need to do some research. I have a hunch.

"Please promise me you'll be careful, Alex. And if anything feels even the slightest bit off, promise me you'll call."

"Of course. You're on speed dial."

7

IT WAS CLOSING IN ON SEVEN fifteen, and Alex grew more anxious to make it to Denver after his conversation with Mike. He hurried and threw on some casual clothes, but the steam in the bathroom grabbed his attention. *Won't be leaving these windows open anymore.*

Alex tied his shoes and rushed into the bath. He reached into the shower, closed the window, and clicked the lock. A soft knock at the door scared him.

With his heart pounding, he raced to the door. He flung open the door to find Amy standing with her arm propped against the door frame. "You ready? Traffic is a bitch at this time of the morning."

"Ain't that the truth. Give me another minute or so."

"Is John still coming by to grab your paper?"

Alex glanced at his alarm clock. "Matter of fact, I expect him any time."

True to his word, John pulled up in front of the house five minutes early. He stepped out of his car as Amy and Alex walked out the front door. It closed behind them, making a loud thump. Alex stood there with his black backpack draped over his shoulder.

"John, you're a lifesaver. Thanks again."

"Anytime," he began. "Hey, I have a few minutes, and I'd love to hear about this hunch you have."

Alex's eyes narrowed as he didn't remember telling John about it. "How d'you—oh?" He twisted and stared at Amy.

She bowed her head. "I told him about Denver."

Alex pressed his lips tightly together. "Fine, come in."

Everyone bolted for the dryness of the foyer and waited for Alex to provide them a detailed explanation.

"I spoke with Mike this morning."

"Okay," John replied.

"As you both are aware, my father was murdered thirteen years ago. They caught the man who did it and come to find out he worked with some Russian guys."

John and Amy remained focused on the story.

"Mike told me they identified one of the men from the robbery and homicide yesterday. He's a Russian guy. What if my father was working on a case involving these guys and that's what got him killed?"

Amy shrugged. "Seems a bit out there, even for you. Isn't the man who killed your father in prison?"

"As far as I know. Maybe he got out and is hellbent on revenge?"

John grabbed his forearm. "Buddy, you need to relax."

He sighed. "It's just a hunch. I could be wrong, *but* I could be right."

"Suppose you gotta do what makes you comfortable."

Alex turned to Amy. "Enough with the dramatics, do you need anything dropped off at school?"

She flashed a proud smile. "Thanks, but I'm already ahead on my assignments."

"Well, I guess I won't keep you waiting from your trip. We're still on for tonight?"

"Yup. Oh, but my friend Brandy will be in town, and she'd love to meet you. I'm sure of it."

His face lit up. "Is she cute and single?"

Alex laughed. "She's all of the above."

"Well, damn, count me in."

They parted ways, and as John drove away, Alex and Amy continued along the walkway to the car. From the corner of his eye, Alex noticed his neighbor from across the street standing on the curb, holding a dog leash, wearing a see-through nightgown and an umbrella hung over her head.

He politely waved and whispered to Amy. "What a psycho."

They walked through the misty air. The car was a few feet away, covered in a pearly condensation. For May the weather was cooler than average, yet the one thing Alex craved was for the sun and warmth to return. With the click of a button, the doors unlocked, and when he slid behind the wheel, the cold leather seat sent a quiver up his spine. He slammed his door closed as he watched Amy have the exact reaction.

As Alex surveyed behind him in the rear-view mirror, what was meant to be an inner soliloquy leaked from his mouth. "Hell must have frozen over—this car is freezing."

"Something froze over. Can we go? The weather doesn't seem to be improving any time soon."

Stunned by the attitude, he swung his head and shot daggers. "Would you like to stop at the drugstore for some Midol, perhaps?"

"Hey, watch it. I'm going out on a limb and trying to be supportive. Do I want to spend the day in Denver? Nope. You do, so let's chill out a bit so I can watch my shows when we return."

"Shows? How can any of them interest you when you're in class every day?"

"Sometimes I stay home sick."

"Whatever. No offense, but you sound like an old woman."

Amy crossed her arms. "I'm not old. I just don't want to spend my entire day in a library. We both know the types who hang there; stalkers or bookworms with nothing better to do. The sole reason I'm going is I realize how important this is to you."

"Well, that's what best friends do."

"Yeah. I want to be there to offer support. When I told you we're in this together, I meant it."

Alex swerved to miss a mail truck parked along the street. Amy shrieked, "Watch out."

"Missed it by a mile. Now, let's take this time to discuss an important matter at hand—Heather."

"You want my opinion? With her bipolar ass, she's undoubtedly holed up somewhere keeping her distance. Would be awful for everyone to see her crack under pressure."

"Okay, but where? Where would she go?"

Amy shrugged.

"I hate to discount your opinion, but I don't see her running off anywhere. Who else does she hang with besides us?"

"Maybe she has other friends?"

"Not a chance in hell, we know everyone here. Maybe she's being held against her will and can't call for help."

"Who would want to kidnap her?"

Alex pondered a moment and shrugged. "Anything is possible."

"We have two possible scenarios: either she was kidnapped, or she ran away. Which one seems more plausible?" Amy asked before her head veered out the window at the dreary landscape.

Alex's mouth twisted, and he struggled to form a coherent response to her question. Instead, he kept his eyes on the road, and when the silence kicked in so came a million thoughts bouncing in his head. Was Amy pragmatic with her outlandish opinion? Could Heather be behaving like a spoiled brat since without notice the attention wasn't on her anymore? If Amy was right, and she skulked off to hide out, not alerting her friends and family was a shitty thing to do.

Alex sped along the drenched blacktop of Highway 36. The muteness was awkward, and his thoughts took over. He chose to fight it, so he stretched for the radio, cranked it up, and the little voice in his head subsided…for now.

Amy struggled to survive the unease, yet with Alex's mood swings, she imagined he had more complex thoughts drifting around his head than she did hers. Not that any of her worries were less critical. With locating an apartment in New York City, the need to obtain a prom dress before next week, and graduation right around the corner, Amy had a carefree attitude about everything. As she'd tell you, in the end, everything had a way of working itself out.

The weather deteriorated the closer Alex progressed to Denver, but his dedication to figure things out was strong, and no weather would stand in his way. For always being outgoing and never at a loss for words, Alex found it difficult to express his emotions about his father to Amy. He glanced in her direction and contemplated to himself.

The robbery, Kelli, and now Heather is missing. None of this adds up.

At eighteen years old the pressures of life encompassed him, shifting his comfortable existence into a world of chaos. His strong-willed personality was no match for the tough choices he faced. Yet tough decisions were nothing new, and still, Alex always needed to be the one in control of every situation. His belief something more sinister was going on created friction between him and Amy.

However, Alex was confident whatever was looming in Ridgewood Hills would blow over soon enough. And even if it was here to stay for a while, he was bound to uncover who was behind it.

8

THE SILENCE AND TENSION IN THE CAR reached a breaking point, and Amy clicked the radio off. She shouted, "I can't take this silence anymore. You sure everything's okay?"

Her tone and genuine concern snapped Alex out of his trance. "I can't express what to feel right now. There's so much rushing around in my head, and I wish I could connect the dots."

"In the entire time we've known each other, you've always been able to figure things out. Maybe if we put our heads together, we can do it."

Alex scoffed. "Easier said than done."

"You should be aware by now you can always tell me what's on your mind. You don't always need to be in control of every situation. I wish you'd let people help you every now and again."

"As always, I appreciate your help. It's just—we've lived through four murders, our close friend has gone AWOL, and we're behaving like covert agents sneaking off to Denver to dredge up stuff about my father's murder. Everything is messed up right now."

"Well, when you say it that way, it sounds shady."

Alex scoffed. "I don't expect you to empathize. Do I want to hear the truth right now, or not? Couldn't tell you."

Traffic ahead thickened, and Alex pumped the brakes. There was a tremble in Amy's laughter. "Let's try not to stress over this too much."

"'Suppose you're right. Besides, we're not all doom and gloom; I do have Mike back in my life and Brandy is coming to town for a visit."

"There you go. Every negative holds a silver lining."

"I hope we find nothing today and we can go back home. And let's not bring Brandy into this sordid mess."

"No problem. We should also keep a low profile, too."

"We should? Why?"

"Almost certain if we dig around into my past might it's possible, we'll unleash a plethora of crap neither of us has curiosity in."

Alex peeked in his rear-view mirror. "Damnit. I got more upsetting news."

Amy wrinkled her nose. "Huh?"

"Have a glance in your side mirror. Looks like we may have already drawn attention to ourselves."

"What am I looking for?"

"See the white van, two cars back?"

"Yeah. What about it?"

"I swear it's the same van we saw at the shopping center yesterday. They've been following us since we left Ridgewood Hills."

"You have such a vivid imagination. Let's not allow this to spiral out of hand."

"I didn't start it…they did."

"They who?"

Alex thumped his hands against the steering wheel. "Whoever these people are. It's not like we're besties or anything," Alex snapped back.

"Well, if you're right, we might be in grave danger, and we're sitting here talking about going with the flow. Are we having a bi-polar moment?"

"Calm down, Amy. We're going to a library. Have you ever heard of anything bad happening in a library full of people?"

She scoffed. "No, but that isn't the point. If this car *is* following us, we ought to worry, and you know why?"

Alex gave her a blank stare and verbalized nothing.

"It means they have your address…and if they know where you live, they know who we are."

"Maybe some undercover officers Mike sent to watch over us."

"Did he tell you he was doing that?" Amy asked.

Alex shook his head. "No. He'd have shared something like that, too."

After fifty-minutes stuck together in the car, their drive ended as Alex pulled up to the main library in downtown Denver. He located a vacant spot along Broadway and swung the car into the snug space.

Feeling confident about his parking skills, they exited, and Alex peered over his shoulder. The same white van stayed close, parking a half-block away.

Far enough so I might not notice, but close enough to keep an eye on us.

The entire situation was amiss, still, with no alternate choices, he brushed off the van and continued towards the main entrance. Alex interlinked his arm with Amy's and pulled her closer for her safety.

She beamed, and Alex peeked over his shoulder once more to ensure the men didn't follow. They didn't, yet he caught sight of them in their van, and a shiver climbed up Alex's spine for the second time that day.

Amy leaned in, "Why you keep looking back?"

"Oh, making sure we lost those creeps from earlier."

"You see 'em anywhere?"

"Nope. We're in the clear."

They maintained course along the freshly constructed sidewalk until they arrived at the main entrance. Amy leaned in again and whispered, "I'm not comfortable with this. The building is putting off a bad aura."

Alex overlooked Amy's concern and yanked against the glass door. As he approached the information desk a chirpy, youthful librarian waited. He stepped up to the counter and her southern accent made him melt. "May I help you?"

"Yes, I'm curious where I might find your newspaper archives?"

The librarian extended her hand and pointed. "See the escalator there, take it to the third floor and follow the signs for the reference section. If you can believe it, we've digitized everything, so find an available computer and click away."

"Yeah, thanks," Amy uttered in annoyance before Alex could respond.

Amy jerked Alex towards the moving stairs. He gripped her shaky arm, "Sort of rude, don't you think?"

"Oh, that? She's too perky for her own good. Besides, she was flirting with you."

"She was not."

Amy grinned as they stepped onto the escalator. "A woman knows."

"Whatever. Why are you shaking so bad?"

"I'm nervous, okay?"

"I won't let anything happen to you. You remain calm, let me do this, and we'll be out of here soon."

"With the level of trust, I'm giving you, this excursion better yield results."

The escalator arrived on the third floor and spilled them out into a large, open space filled with row after row of computers and bookcases. He scanned left and found an available computer and rushed for it, leaving Amy behind. Amy tossed her hair back and watched her best-friend slide into the empty chair. She stepped forward and took a load off in the seat next to him.

With a quick shake of the mouse, the hibernating computer awoke, and the darkened monitor came to life. Alex clicked on the web browser icon while Amy inspected the lofty space.

"What are we looking for exactly?"

"Since my mother has never talked about my father's death, I'm looking for anything that might tell me what he was working on before they murdered him."

"Wouldn't information like that be classified?"

"You know what I mean. I'm sure his name would be mentioned in court cases, an obituary, anything."

"Do you have the exact date he died?"

"May 1985. I was five, and now that I remember, I'll never forget the sight of that man shooting my father."

"You didn't say you saw it happen. Jesus."

"It's okay, let's find what we came here for, hmm?"

Amy pressed her fingers into a steeple and leaned against the counter. "Sure. What was his name?"

"Robert. Robert Jones."

Alex typed in the name and clicked search. The internet was slow, and he drummed his fingers across the desk as he waited. Amy cleared her throat and reached for Alex's hand to calm his nerves. "It's none of my business, but has what happened affected you?"

Alex hung his head and tried to keep his emotions in check. "Sometimes I have these vivid flashbacks, and the haunting nightmares keep getting stronger as more time passes," his eyes watered up. "I'm not sure if I'm recalling or creating false memories. Fuck, talking about him brings up so many repressed feelings."

"I didn't mean to—."

"It's okay, the search results are up, let's focus on that."

Alex wiped away the dampness across his face and scrolled through the results displayed on the screen. Of the twenty-six results, the first article jumped off the page. The headline read, "FBI Agent Murdered after Testimony."

A Denver FBI agent was slain today at his residence in Cherry Creek after his testimony imprisoned one of the nation's most-hunted criminal masterminds. Agent Robert Stahl was returning home from the Alfred A. Arraj Federal Courthouse in Denver where he testified to the inner workings of the Mogilevich, crime family. Agent Stahl leaves behind a five-year-old son and wife. Funeral services are still pending.

Confused, Amy glanced at Alex, "Who's Robert Stahl?"

Alex's eyes widened, and he froze staring at the screen. "It has to be him. But how could he have a different last name than me?"

"Is it possible you were Alex Stahl at some point and don't remember?"

He glared. "I'd remember a name change, wouldn't you?"

She looked downward and didn't respond. Alex printed the article and jumped from his seat.

"Where are you going?"

Alex snatched the two-page article from the printer and rushed back. "We're heading to the hospital to see my mother."

"Oh, Alex, we shouldn't make a scene at the hospital."

"Why not? She has some explaining to do."

Amy grabbed her jacket from the back of the chair and followed Alex towards the escalator. "Wait up. You're about to open up something traumatic. Are you sure that's what you want to do?"

"It is."

The escalator dumped them back onto the main floor, and they rushed past the information desk without so much as looking up. Alex couldn't distinguish between the ever-changing cycle of emotions, but one thing was for sure, deceit topped the list. However, the more the thoughts simmered, he wasn't sure if his mother kept quiet out of protection and love.

Amy studied his face, and when the veins in his forehead throbbed, she knew she had to spring into action. She got out in front of him, and with one smooth move pressed against his chest. "Hey, wait—why don't we take a deep breath, okay?"

Alex drowned her out. He was on a mission to locate answers to the persistent question in his mind: *who am I?* His unrelenting determination forced Amy to step aside and let him pass.

Alex stomped past her and Amy stopped and gazed up at the sky. The sun disappeared behind the dark, gathering storm clouds which encased the region for a second straight day. There was a slight, spine-chilling breeze blowing down the street and Amy pulled her hair into a ponytail to prevent having it hit her in the face.

Although the weather was gloomy, the trees along the boulevard swayed back and forth, and Amy watched as the new blooms of spring drifted through the air and crashed to the ground. Winter was ending soon, but not fast enough.

Alex remained consumed by his thoughts; so much he failed to realize the white van from earlier vanished. He stepped up to the driver's side door of the black BMW and flung open the door. There was a fire in his eyes as he cranked over the car and even before Amy buckled in, he sped off down Broadway. The force jerked her against the seat, and she let out a high-pitched laugh. "Slow down. I get it, you're upset, but let's not die before we arrive."

"Do you realize how pissed and confused I am right now?"

Amy lowered her face, "I have an idea."

Alex kept on. "This explains why my mother kept secrets from me over the years. Stahl? Who am I? Better question, who was my dad and what happened to him?"

"I bet there's a valid explanation to this. I need you to take a deep breath and reflect on positive thoughts."

Alex's voice raised an octave. "Positive thoughts? Positive thoughts? You're kidding me with this hippie, tree-hugger bullshit, right?"

"I mean, could it be your mom changed your last name for your protection? Didn't the article mention your father worked undercover and put away some Russian mobsters? Not sure about you, but I'd sure as hell change my name and move as far across the country as I could."

Alex bit his lip. "Suppose you're right."

"Exactly, so let's not fly off the handle. At least not until you hear the details from her. I have a hunch once the two of you talk, you'll have the answers you need."

"Wait—no. None of this makes any sense."

"What doesn't?"

"I was five. How much do you remember at that age?"

Amy lifted her eyes to the left. "Uh, not much."

"Every bit of this pisses me off for the simple fact more than half of my life has been a complete lie."

"Okay. Okay. I follow. It's not right you had to deal with this."

"You're damn right; it's not."

Amy let her authoritative voice free. "This whole tough, macho side of you isn't cute. Please swear when you talk to her, you won't say or do anything crazy. We've both seen what transpires when you bring up the past."

His eyebrows furrowed, and he gave her a stare of death. "I don't need a lecture…"

Amy continued to badger him. "For example, let's use what occurred between you and Mike; you presumed he was a lying, cheating dog when I fact it turns out he wasn't. You almost ruined everything you built over unsubstantiated allegations."

"Fine. You've made your point. I give you my word. I'll keep calm."

Alex relaxed his shoulders and veered onto Colfax Avenue headed towards Presbyterian Hospital near downtown where his mother spent most of her days. Not being the type of guy to ask rational questions, he struggled with bringing his emotions together instead of trying to wing it and bringing in his flair for the dramatic.

What am I going to say first? The opening line is the most critical.

After a moment of calm, rational thinking, it came to him.

Amy's right; if I ask straightforwardly, with any luck, she'll tell me the truth.

Amy interrupted him with a tap on the shoulder. He raised his head, "Why after thirteen years are you realizing this?"

"For as long as I can remember I've had the nightmares, an unexplained consciousness, and after yesterday with those gunshots, it triggered something. It was like I had an 'ah-ha' moment, you know?"

Amy listened, not wanting to interrupt her best friend as he disclosed his frame of mind, something he hadn't done in such a long time.

Alex continued. "When you're a kid, you go on with your life, pretend everything is fine, fake it 'til you make it. Am I right?"

"I get it."

"But now, I don't know, I get flickers of my past. A past which is full of holes. Some things I can explain, yet there are some things I can't."

"What sort of flickers?"

Alex hesitated to answer. "Watching my father being shot on our walkway."

"Wait…what? You saw it and didn't remember it until now?"

Alex's eyes wandered everywhere except at hers. "Not until a few months ago. After yesterday it's been at the forefront of my mind. It's hard to describe this to you, but you're my best friend—who better to understand me than you?"

"I'm doing my best, but until we hear what your mother has to say first before anything else."

Alex nodded.

He pulled up to the garage and snatched a ticket from the machine. After failing to retrieve more information from Alex, Amy sank in the passenger seat and deliberated whether to ask him to take the curves smoother. After contemplating she opted to allow him to vent his frustration before he saw his mother. She squeezed her eyes closed and conceded to the fact saying anything would annoy him more.

The car followed the upward spiral several times until Alex exited onto the sixth floor of the garage. The continuous corkscrew left him dizzy, and he spotted a spot close to the elevator and slipped the car into it. Amy opened her eyes and loosened her grip on the door handle. "Thank God I'm still alive."

Alex twisted the key, and the car shut off. "So dramatic. I've never endangered you."

"At least not intentionally," Amy began. "Figure out yet what you're going to say to your mom?"

"We'll see what happens."

Amy shook her head disapproving.

"What? I promised I'd keep my cool."

"Be nice if for once you kept your word."

They walked along the north side of the garage as the white van from earlier pulled up the ramp. Alex noticed the rickety vehicle approach and pulled Amy closer. The same hair-raising guys crept behind them, and Alex moved faster, his head twisted back and forth. On his final glance before they arrived at the elevator, he spotted the driver; a thirty-something with an overgrown beard, beady eyes and a beanie hat covering his hair. The man stared Alex up and down, top to bottom.

For the first time, everything sunk in and the feeling of dread bounced around in the pit of his stomach. All he could do was mull over if these brutes were undercover police sent by Mike to protect them. And if they were, his boyfriend sure did handpick the scariest people on the force. Alex stood at the elevator and watched the shorter, clean-cut passenger puff away at his cigarette. Alex wasn't sure where their home country was, but one thing was sure; they weren't from anywhere near Denver.

Amy stood by, oblivious to anything going on around her. The elevator bell chimed, and the door slid open. Alex kept calm and ushered her inside. Once out of their view, Alex pointed his back at Amy and retrieved his cell from the inner pocket of his jacket. He slid out the keyboard and tapped away a short text message to Mike.

Excellent job choosing the creepiest people to watch over us.

Alex hit send and snuck the phone back in his pocket. Amy caught this and gave him a glance. "What were you just doing?"

"Oh, that," he pointed at his chest and sniggered. "Checking in with Mike."

"Has he gotten in touch with you?"

"Nope. I'm sure he's busy trying to find Heather or those guys who killed those innocent people."

Amy remained expressionless but managed to nod her head. The elevator stopped on the third floor, and they stepped off. Alex, in a cavalier manner, approached the nurse's station where an unfamiliar, yet amiable, nurse greeted them.

"Good morning, may I help you?"

"I'm looking for Dr. Jones. I'm her son, Alex."

"Ah yes. Nice to put a face with a name," she said, picking up the phone. "Have a seat, and I'll tell her you're here."

"Thanks."

They left the station and walked down the hallway towards the tiny room where family members waited for their loved ones. They arrived and noticed it was half-full, and Alex searched for a place quiet to wait. Against the wall, Alex pointed when he spotted. Not the most comfortable he'd ever sat in, but much better than the ones at the police station.

Amy made herself as comfortable as possible and glanced at Alex. "These seats are worse than the police station."

Alex chuckled.

92

"I'll wait here."

Alex shrugged. "I don't want to bring you further into this mess. I'm sure the less you know, the better."

"I told you, Alex: we're in this together. I don't know what's going on, but there's no turning back now. Either we're in this 'til the end, or we stop, right here, say hello and return to our boring lives."

His eyes widened, and he mulled over her proposition. "For me, I need the truth. Sorry to say, but she's the only one who can provide it."

Alex hung his head and inhaled deeply. Amy slid her hand across his lap and squeezed his hand. "Let's uncover the truth, shall we?"

Alex bit at his nails and lifted his head right in time to spot his mom stroll into the waiting room. Amy pulled her hand away and leaned in to whisper in his ear. "Good luck and remember, don't say anything you can't take back."

Alex touched her shoulder lightly and approached Carol, who flashed a half-smile as he inched closer. She stood with an expression of guilt as if she already was aware of why Alex was there.

Stay calm, Alex. Don't make a scene. Listen to the facts and leave your emotions out of it.

Carol spread out her arms, and they embraced. "This is a surprise. Are you okay?"

He pulled away and gently but firmly grasped her forearm. "We need to talk. You got a few minutes to spare for me, right?"

"Oh, um sure. Do we need privacy?" she asked as Alex loosened his grip on her arm.

"Yeah. Not the kind of stuff I'd want anyone to overhear," he hinted as they walked down the sallow, sterilized hallway where the air smacked you in the face of disinfectant.

At the end of the hallway, they disappeared into her office. Alex followed her into the dimly lit office which was a stark contrast from the bright overhead fluorescent lights which illuminated the hall. Carol stepped behind her large, wooden desk and dropped into her swivel chair.

Alex leaned across the desk, opposite her. The white, thick cushioned armchair was comfier than the waiting room. He studied her body language; she fumbled with papers on her desk, every so often she bit her lower lip. Undoubtedly, she was jittery, still what Alex was about to drop on her might make her extra anxious. She finished with her obsessive compulsiveness and gave him her undivided attention.

"Are you sure everything is okay? You seem agitated."

His lower lip quivered. "I—I've spent the last half-hour driving, trying to calm myself down from the news."

Carol leaned across the desk. "What news?"

"Are you familiar with a man by the name of Robert Stahl?"

He watched the color in her face shift from a rosy red to a pale white in a matter of seconds. Her eyes bounced back and forth as she struggled to process the name. "Who?"

"Robert Stahl. You see, he too was an FBI agent in Denver, who happened to die on the exact day my father did. Funny thing; isn't dad's name Robert Jones?"

She remained silent, and Alex leaned in closer. "I mean, you see my confusion, right? We're the Jones', but I couldn't find any information about an FBI agent by the name Robert Jones."

She reclined back against her chair and rubbed her hands against her face. "I never imagined, in a million years, you'd connect the dots. I always presumed you'd take what I told you at face value and move on. I underestimated you."

Alex folded his arms across his chest and blurted out. "So, who was he? Better questions: who are you? Who am I? I demand answers, mom."

Carol glanced at the door before she spun her head back towards the wall. "I won't keep this from you anymore, Alex. Go ahead, sit back, and relax. There is a story behind this that is going to shock you."

She picked up a black fountain pen from her desk and twirled it between her fingers. She was hesitant to open Pandora's Box; merely speaking the truth could jeopardize their lives. She mustered up the courage, and after a few seconds of struggle, Carol began the story.

"As I always say, the best place is the beginning," she said. "First, your real name is Marshall Stahl."

"Where was I born?"

"In Colorado Springs, that's the one thing I told you that is the truth."

Alex relaxed and scooted back in his chair. "And I presume your name isn't Carol."

Her voice trembled, "Denise. Denise Stahl. You already discovered who your father really is."

"I don't get it. Why are we living under false names? Why the mystery?"

"We were placed in witness protection after your father's assassination. You have to believe me; this isn't the life I wanted for us."

Alex lowered his head and remained silent.

"We had an ordinary life in Denver. Safe neighborhood, you hadn't started kindergarten yet. A year earlier, your father graduated from the FBI academy, and his first assignment was to go undercover."

"Do you have any idea what he was working on?"

"At the time—no. But now, now I do."

"Are you able to tell me?"

"He was gathering intel on these Russian guys who set up shop in Denver. Mind you, these aren't the type of guys you double-cross."

"Russian? Like the men from the 7-Eleven yesterday?"

She bit her lip. "After some time, your father's loyalty paid off, and they trusted him more. Soon they divulged enough information, and he made enormous progress. More progress than anyone ever expected he would."

Alex interrupted, "Why would he do this? I mean, didn't he know the risks involved?"

Carol hung her head. "Sure, but he was doing what he swore to do— uphold the law. These men were corrupt—malicious to the core. They exposed every illegal thing they were doing: Drug smuggling, human trafficking, and murder. Your father took this information back to the bureau."

Alex sat mesmerized.

"As a result, the FBI raided them and shut down their criminal enterprise," Carol said.

"So, my father was a hero?"

"More than that. Your father was proud of what he accomplished. I remember him coming home right afterward and can you guess the first words out of his mouth?"

Alex shrugged. "What?"

"Justice wins. But—," she paused.

"Those men had him murdered?"

She held back tears but pushed on. "Yes. Do you remember anything about that day? The U.S. Marshal's told me you were so young, that the chances were good you wouldn't remember."

"I remember bits and pieces. The past few months I've had a few vivid nightmares…the kind that wakes you from a dead sleep. But with everything that happened yesterday—my mind snapped, and these emotions flooded my brain."

"Well, let me fill in those holes."

Alex leaned forward and rested his right elbow on the desk. "Please. I am so lost. I'm not even sure what I should believe anymore."

"It was a cold, rainy day in May 1985. A typical day for me. I stood at the kitchen counter when I noticed your footsteps were heavier than usual as they stomped against the stairs. Next thing I remember was a pop, pop. I dropped the knife into the sink and rushed to the front door. There you stood on the porch—."

"And there was a man wearing a ski mask with a gun, right?"

Carol nodded. "I scooped you up and rushed inside. I didn't consider myself or the danger, the only thing I worried about was getting you someplace safe."

Alex reached his hand across the table and grabbed his mother's hand. "Thank you."

She wiped away a stream of tears from her face and continued, "I ran back outside, and the man ran across the street. Your father lay there, shaking on the ground as the raindrops pounded him. I held him in my arms and stayed with him until he exhaled his final breath."

Alex squeezed her hand tighter. "We're going to survive this, mom. I can't imagine withholding any of this has been easy on you but thank you for revealing it."

Carol carried on crying.

"These flashbacks have me questioning my sanity."

"Oh, baby, you're not. I wish you'd come to me sooner with this and we could have worked through it."

"I wasn't sure if what I remembered was true or a creation of my wild imagination. So where do we go from here?"

Carol stiffened and paused. "Remember how I mentioned we're in the witness protection program?"

"Yeah, what about it?"

"It means you can never speak a word of this to anyone. Not Amy. And certainly not Mike."

"Wait. This means I must live as Alex Jones for the rest of my life? And worse, I can't share this information with my boyfriend?"

"No, I'm sorry. If these men ever find us, we're dead."

"Why? What'd we do to them?"

Carol cycled from crying to straight-faced. "Alex, I told you the whole truth. But—."

Alex stood and paced. "I can't breathe; this is so overwhelming. Do you have any idea how this makes me feel?"

Carol exhaled as Alex inched closer to the door. "Please, sit down."

"You sit there and disclose how my entire life is a lie and have the audacity to order me not to tell my best friend or boyfriend. I...I gotta go," he murmured and clutched the door handle.

Carol ran towards the door, slammed her hand, and grabbed him by the forearm, "Damn it, Alex, I did everything for us—do you want to die?"

The anger released and Alex broke down. His back slid down the wall, and he positioned himself on the floor, and he pulled his knees closer to his chest. "I don't want to die, yet, I can't live a lie either."

Carol crouched and pulled him in closer to her chest. A profound silence endured for several minutes. Carol pulled away. "I hear you. I don't enjoy living a lie either. I did it to keep us safe."

"You know, perhaps Amy's right."

"I don't understand, right about what?"

"A change of scenery might do me good."

Carol cocked her head.

"Maybe going to New York with her is exactly what I need."

"Alex, don't be this way. Why don't you head home, settle down, and we can hash this out later?"

"I won't be there. Brandy is coming over, and we're going out," he said as he rose to his feet. "Give me some space right now. I promise I won't stay mad at you forever."

"Well, that's a relief."

Alex returned to the chair. "You said those men would kill us?"

She bent her head. "Yeah?"

"Well, we may have a slight problem."

"How so?"

"There's been a white van tailing us since this morning."

"Are you sure?"

Alex bit his lower lip. "They followed us to the library, and they shadowed us in the parking garage here."

"Perhaps Mike has someone making sure you're protected?"

"Could be. I sent Mike a message earlier but still no word back."

"Now I'm concerned."

"Don't. I'm sure it's nothing life-threatening, but it is suspicious enough to bring up."

"Swear to me you'll be vigilant."

"Of course. Well, I've taken enough of your time away from your patients."

"Call me the minute you arrive at home. I'll have my cell on."

"Sure. Don't forget, I'm still pissed in case you forgot," he said reaching out for a hug.

Alex opened the door and stepped back into the vibrantly lit corridor. He walked back towards the waiting room where he left Amy to await his return. The thoughts in his mind wandered with visions and locked memories as he moseyed down the hall.

Everything about his predictable life now all seemed fabricated, like someone took his identity and tore it into pieces right before his eyes. Alex scanned the corridor, and with each happy face which zipped by, it drove him deeper into a haze. He stepped into the waiting room, and Amy stood to her feet.

"Everything okay?"

Alex fumbled with his jacket. "Let's talk in the car. Right now, I want to be someplace with fresh air. The stench of disinfectant is making my stomach churn."

They passed by the nurse's station, and the young nurse who first greeted them waved goodbye. Amy radiated with happiness and politely waved back, but Alex walked on past without as much as a simple, agreeable gesture. They advanced towards the elevator and Alex reached out and pressed the up arrow.

They stood impatiently on the elevator landing, waiting for what Alex deemed an eternity. The elevator chimed, and again the doors slid open. The entered the small, confined space and Alex stood there in a trance. Eventually, Amy pressed the P6 button, and the doors closed.

The ride up was silent. Amy wasn't sure what took place with his mother, but after studying his face for a few seconds, it was evident the discussion with his mother disquieted him. Amy assumed if he wanted to discuss it, she'd wait for him to make the first move.

The door opened, and the putrid odor of the garage smacked Amy in the face as she stepped into the garage. She glanced about unconcernedly, and eventually her eyes focused again on Alex. "You see that van anywhere?"

Her voice breached him free from the daze which consumed his mind. With a shaky voice, he asked, "How d'you know about the van?"

"I'm not an idiot. I spotted it earlier."

Alex scanned the area. "I don't see it anymore. Could we be in the clear?"

Amy shrugged. "Let's hope so. Now, what's our plan?"

"Head back to Ridgewood Hills," he said. "You up for some detective work?"

Amy slanted her head and grinned. "What d'you have in mind?"

"It's obvious my mother is keeping skeletons hidden from me. Whatever it is, there has to be a clue in her home office."

"You're so wrong. But count me in."

Alex genuinely looked happy for the first time that day. "Thanks. Right now, I'd enjoy some relaxing company."

Alex opened the car door and slid into the driver's seat. He took out his cell phone and checked for any messages he may have missed.

Zero. No missed calls, no response to the text he sent Mike.

He shifted into reverse and kept his eyes peeled for the white van as he drove toward the garage exit. Alex let out a sigh as the car descended to the level below. *Looks like they lost interest.*

He hung a right onto Colfax and headed back towards Ridgewood Hills. The car stopped at the traffic light at Wadsworth Boulevard, and his cell phone rang. He glanced at the telephone which rested in the cup holder; it was Brandy. He picked it up and flipped it open.

"Hey, what's up?"

"I wanted to tell you my class is being cut short."

"Oh, how short?"

"I'll be out to your place by two-ish," she replied.

"Ah, yeah. No problem. Amy and I are driving back home now from Denver."

"Denver? Why were you here?"

"My entire life was just flipped upside down. It will be a crazy story, and I do promise to fill you in more tonight. I can't be sure this line is secure," he said as an uninformed Amy threw him a puzzled glance.

"Sounds downright crazy yet mesmerizing. Can't wait to hear more about it when I arrive."

"You're in for a dynamic story," he scoffed. "Listen, I need to pay attention to the road. See you in a little while."

"Yup. Drive safe."

Alex ended the call and threw the phone back into the cup holder. The clock on the radio showed 10:56. The remainder of the half-hour drive home was quiet. Alex remained focused on the road and wasn't up for chit-chat. Amy, too, gazed off into the world in her head. It was the one place she could escape when things got rough.

She reflected on her friends, the new ones, the old ones and the ones she had lost. As hard as she tried, there was no way to shake the ominous feeling about Heather's whereabouts. Although they hadn't known each other a full school year, it seemed peculiar she'd vanish so soon after Kelli's murder.

She reverted to reality to discover they were three miles from home. Amy eyed Alex who remained engrossed on the road. He was more fixated than she had ever seen before.

Amy closed her eyes and interrupted the tranquility. "I'll be so happy when we are out of this car."

"Don't I know. It's as if we've been on the road forever, yet it's only been two hours."

"One thing is certain: I'm hungry. Food should be the first order of business when we return to your place."

"Agreed. I'm starving. But once we eat it's off to do some digging. I got a sense from my mother that she didn't quite answer my main question."

Amy, still in the dark about what transpired between Alex and his mother, finally asked, "And that question was?"

"Right. I haven't told you."

"Nope."

"For our protection, I'll keep much of the discussion to myself. I can say, though, my father betrayed some Russian mafia guys when he worked for the FBI. And according to her, these guys aren't the type you piss off."

"Russian mafia? Wait a minute—those guys from the robbery—they seemed like they could be Russian."

"Exactly. We need to connect them—on the down low."

"Of course. We don't need to draw attention to ourselves."

It was a quarter past eleven, and they arrived safely at Alex's. He pulled into the driveway and cut the engine. Amy was the first out, and she stood next to the passenger door waiting for Alex to walk around. A crack of thunder rumbled the earth, and she glanced upward to the cloudy sky. The storms clouds were gathering, growing darker with each passing minute. The weather was rather uncommon for this time of the year. Thunderstorms were not frequent in mid-May, but they also weren't out of the question.

She shivered as Alex stepped onto the driveway and fumbled with his keys. "Sorry, trying to pull my shit together."

"It's okay, I'm thinking about how over this weather I am. Guess we've got another rainy afternoon in store for us."

"Suppose so. Doesn't matter though—we've got an abundance of work ahead."

Amy chuckled.

"Besides, at least the thunderstorms enhance the suspense of our confidential sleuth work."

Alex unlocked the front door and rushed to disarm the alarm system. Amy dropped her bag onto the floor. "Yeah, it does improve the creepy vibe."

They rushed towards the back of the house so Alex could whip together a quick snack. Halfway there, Amy stopped and looked around the room. Unable to pinpoint exactly what was off, she brushed it aside. Why upset her best-friend who was already paranoid about the two men in the white van, she knew it best to keep this baseless sensation to herself. She reversed and moved for the couch to await Alex.

A couple of minutes passed, and Alex entered the living room and found Amy at the picture window staring aimlessly. Her demeanor told Alex she was reflecting, and so he sought to not surprise her.

"Lunch is ready," he whispered.

Amy flinched. "Scare the shit out of me why don't you."

"Sorry, wasn't my intention. You ready?"

"Yeah, give me a second," she said. "You shouldn't sneak up on me like that."

Alex snickered, and eventually, she too laughed it off. Lunch took no time, and after they finished, Alex and Amy washed up their dirty plates. As Alex dried off the final dish, Amy let out a brief grunt.

"What's wrong?"

Amy shrugged. "I think it's creepy prying into your mom's private things."

Alex brushed off her concern. "Eh, what she doesn't know won't hurt. You ready?"

"Do I have a choice?"

"Nope. Come on, let's go."

They walked from the kitchen to the long hallway that leads to the study. Truth be told, the house was more than Alex, and his mother needed. There were long hallways and oversized rooms in every corner of the two-story, brick Tudor. Alex flipped the light switch, illuminating the windowless hallway as they strolled towards the end.

Alex wasn't sure what he hoped to find but figured there must be something hidden in the house with a few more clues. There's no way possible so much chaos would erupt in his quaint town over nothing.

Alex was first to enter with Amy shadowing close behind. For being the least used room in the entire house, it was always in an immaculate state. No dust, everything in its place, and a slight hint of citrus saturated the air. Along the south wall towered three floor-to-ceiling bookcases which overflowed with copious volumes of books, decorations and picture frames from a life Alex did not recognize anymore. Alex stood for a moment and glanced around the room, taking in his surroundings before proceeding to the desk.

He yanked out the oversized black leather chair and carefully dropped into the seat and got busy snooping through the desk. Meanwhile, Amy rummaged through the bookcase.

Alex hoped he would hit a goldmine on the first drawer; instead, the only thing he found were loose papers, a passport and an abundance of office supplies—everything looked in order. This charade continued several more times, and as he reached the bottom left drawer, he discovered folders labeled cable, IRS, electric. Not the damning evidence he chased.

From across the room Amy called out, "Any luck?"

He slammed the bottom drawer closed. "Nope. Same crap you'd find in any office."

"Humph."

"Do me a favor though," Alex began, "can you check behind the photos, in the closet, and under the rug?"

"I'm sorry, do what?"

"She must have a safe hidden somewhere in this room."

"A safe? What is she a top-secret agent now?"

Alex shrugged. "She's private. Secret agent, oh how you make me laugh."

"Hey, you can never be too sure."

"Doubt it. I'd know something like that, wouldn't I? Let's get back to the task at hand, shall we?"

"Sure."

Amy executed her assignment and walked around the room, peeling back pictures, searching behind every one of them in hopes of finding this mysterious safe Alex insisted was there. Alas, as she peeked behind the last photo, there was nothing which resembled a safe or a secret hiding place.

Alex continued his hunt and when he unsealed the last drawer, resting on top was a manila folder labeled 'Private.' His eyebrows lifted and with one swoop he snatched the file and set it atop the desk. The word, *private*, piqued his interest, and he flipped through like a journalist who broke a mystery.

Inside he found several newspaper clippings and a few letters written in Russian. He jumped from the chair and scanned the room for Amy. "Hey, come take a look at this."

Amy released the carpet and glanced up. "What d'you find?"

"A bunch of newspaper clippings," Alex said as he spread them across the top of the desk.

Amy's voice trembled. "What the hell?"

"They're about my father's murder, the trial, and I found these letters written in Russian."

"Damn. Everything was right here this entire time. Wish we'd snooped around sooner."

"Would have saved us an entire day."

Amy scoffed.

"How's your Russian?"

Amy tilted her head. "What are these symbols? I can't make heads or tails of them."

"Me either."

The white, generic envelope had a strange feeling in his hand. His eyes studied the back. Sealed, dirty, and light. He flipped it over and scrawled in black ink were unfamiliar characters. *Для Denise Stahl.*

He aggressively ran his fingers through his hair—*what am I reading?* And it hit him—Denise Stahl—his mother. He slipped his finger beneath the flap and ran it carefully across. He peeled it open and removed the note shoved inside. He glanced briefly.

Jesus Christ, more Russian?

He bowed his head and massaged his temples. He exhaled forcefully before he crumpled the paper and hurled it onto the desk in defeat. He clenched his jaw and squeezed his eyes tightly closed.

How am I ever going to discover the truth?

He opened his eyes and written on the back of the letter was an English translation. He perked up in the chair, and his eyes scanned the document intensely.

You have something your husband stole from us long ago. We won't let you have a moment's rest until you give back what's rightfully ours. For you and your son's sake, I recommend you cooperate with us, or things will end badly for you.

Alex's eyes widened, and he slumped in the chair. What could his mother have to make these goons threaten her—and his life? And worse, what did his father poach from these people in the first place?

Amy closed the closet door and saw Alex sitting in the chair. His face was ghost-white, and his shoulders hunched forward. It was apparent something was wrong, and she ran to kneel at his side.

"What is it?"

Without saying a word, he handed over the letter.

Her eyes never gazed down before she handed it back. "Alex, I told you I don't read Russian."

Alex never looked up. "The English is on the back."

She snatched the paper from his hand and re-read the part Alex read. However, the letter contained another paragraph which Alex never got to.

Her eyes widened as she read aloud. "We know where you are, and we are watching your every move. You can't run and hide from us this time. We're everywhere. We might be your neighbors, your co-workers, or your closest friends. Give us back what we want, and your quiet life can go back to normal. Don't make me send this warning again."

Amy dropped the letter at her side and stared at Alex who remained motionless. "Uh, this is unsettling."

Alex slammed his fist against the desk. "This entire ordeal is unsettling."

She jumped back, shocked by his outburst. "I'm not the enemy here. You want my advice?"

Alex kept his mouth closed.

"Reach out to Mike—like now."

Alex stood and removed his cell phone from his front pocket. He flipped open the screen and dialed Mike's number from memory. It rang three times, and his gruff voice answered.

"Wow, we go three weeks without speaking, and now I've talked to you three times today. How'd I get so lucky?"

Hearing Mike's voice brought a sense of calm to Alex. "What can I say, I can't stay away from you."

Mike laughed.

"But a few things; first, why haven't replied to me about the van from this morning? And second, we got a situation here."

"Alex, slow down and speak slowly so I can understand you. Why are you so hyper?"

"Answer my questions."

"Okay, straight to the point in typical Alex fashion. Well, I've been in and out of cell service, and I never got a text about anyone following you. And what do you mean a situation? Are you hurt? Did something happen to Amy? Tell me what's going on before I freak out."

"Please don't. That's my job. And yes, a white van with two scary guys stalked us most of the morning. But we've got bigger issues."

"Bigger than two guys stalking you. Fuck, let me sit down."

"Amy and I snooped through my mom's office and came across a letter in her desk."

"Don't keep me in suspense here—spit it out. What'd the letter say? Should I send someone to keep a watch out front?"

"Don't. I'd prefer to deal with only you at this point. You see, I'm not sure who I can trust or if this phone line is secure. When can you be over?"

"Alex, you're scaring me. I'm doing a prisoner transfer to Golden Ridge right now. Can I offer a suggestion?"

"Sure."

"I'm advising you stop prodding into the past, go back to school tomorrow, study for your finals, and let me do my job so I can keep you guys safe." He took in a breath, and continued, "Also, stop snooping through your mother's private stuff. What do you think she's going to do when she finds out?"

The line went quiet for a moment. "Sorry, Mike…I won't stop. I'm in too deep now to give up. I have to find out what's going on here—not for my friends, not my mother, but for me."

"Why?"

"My world as I know it was turned upside down these last two days, and now my boyfriend has the nerve to tell me to stop investigating. I assumed we were a team? Aren't you expected to reinforce my decisions?"

"Not when they involve doing crazy stuff which you could die from. As your boyfriend, and as a law enforcement officer, I'm telling you to back down."

Alex tapped his foot and clenched his jaw. "No. We'll talk about this when you arrive. For now, you go find these goons, and I'll see how my father factors into this."

Before Mike could reply, Alex angrily closed his phone. He shoved the cell phone in his pocket, composed himself, and slumped at the desk. He reread the letter, over and over: Give us what we want. What was *it*? And better yet, did his mother know what *it* was?

While Alex was on the phone, Amy searched non-stop through the drawers, lending an extra set of eyes to the hunt. After ending the call, Alex returned his attention to Amy and discovered the contents of the drawer scattered across the floor. He gasped and rushed over.

"What the hell, Amy? She'll know we rummaged through her office for sure now."

"But I found something."

"Aw, screw it. What d'you find?"

"Two more letters and this coin envelope taped to the bottom of the drawer. Should we open them?"

"You bet your ass we should. If she hid it, it probably means it's important."

They stood at the desk reading the two unsigned letters. Each contained a repeated pattern of intimidations without a mention of what it was they were looking for. Alex reached for the coin envelope and peeled back the flap. He shook the contents and out fell a thin silver key into his hand.

"What could this go to?" he asked.

"Oh, I've seen those before. My dad has one exactly like it."

"Care to share?"

"His is for a safe deposit box at the bank. Do you think whatever it is she has hidden away?"

Alex raised his eyebrow. "Could be. Except there's no way we can walk into every bank in town and try to gain access."

"True. What do we do with it?"

"Put it back where you found it. If we need it again, we can find it easier."

While Amy straightened up the mess she created, Alex walked towards the window, paced around, and considered what his next steps would be. Outside the rain fell at a steadier pace than earlier and with the day half over Alex crossed his arms across his chest at the progress they had made. *Trying to figure this out is fruitless.*

Unquestionably, Alex concluded he was on his own if anything happened, but what hurt, even more, was that his mother wasn't as upfront as she could have been about the level of danger they were in.

Alex stepped away from the window and walked back to the desk. Everything was reasonably close to the way he found it, but the two letters remained on the desk.

"You forgot something," he said, waving the letters around in the air.

"Shit."

"No worries. Which drawer did you find this in?"

Amy pointed, and Alex slide the drawer out, and Amy taped everything back as she found it. "You think she'll notice we were in here?"

Alex shrugged. "Hard to say. We'll deal with the ramifications when they happen."

"I've never seen her heated, and I'm confident I don't want to either"

"You got that right," Alex muttered under his breath as they walked towards the door.

The time was closing in on one-thirty in the afternoon, and they chilled on the couch awaiting Brandy's arrival. Amy watched a campy soap opera while Alex did the responsible thing and studied for his Chemistry final the following week. He curled up on the couch and pulled a blanket over his legs, doing his best to ignore Amy and her new obsession.

His eyes grew tired of staring at equations, and he glanced out the window and moped. The enduring rain had dwindled into a subtle mist that fell from the lifeless afternoon sky.

So much for a barbeque. Looks like we'll be going out to dinner instead.

His mind fixated on seeing Brandy again. The last time he'd seen her was about this time last year. While she hadn't always been in his life, she was a constant ever since the two met at an orchestra camp in the summer of 1992.

It was his first time away from his mother in his entire life, and with unfamiliar faces surrounding him, when Brandy approached and introduced herself the two sparked an instant friendship. For once, Alex had someone he could spend quality time with whom shared many of the same passions in life as he did.

As high school continued, the two hung out every year at camp. Except everything changed after his junior year when he deemed it time to retire the cello and devote his energy in getting into college.

Although Brandy was two years older and graduated in 1996, they both still tried to see each other as often as they could. The past year had been the most difficult to make plans together. Brandy had taken on a full course load at the University of Colorado and took a new job to help pay for her off-campus apartment.

Every time Alex reminisced about their friendship, a smile donned his face. Even with the chaos in the backdrop, her familiarity would help alleviate some of the anxiety.

Alex looked out the front window. "Look, the rain let up. I don't know about you, but I sure could benefit from some fresh air."

Amy scratched her neck. "I need a smoke."

"With my shot nerves, I could use one myself."

"Always so dramatic."

They stepped outside onto the wooden deck which wrapped around the house through the French doors in the dining room. Alex hadn't moved fifteen steps before his phone dinged. He groaned and reluctantly pulled his phone out, opened it, and read the text message.

I'm sorry about earlier. I still love you, and I'm heading back now. See you soon.

In disbelief at Mike's nonchalant attitude, Alex chucked his phone onto the glass patio table as the text dredged up the phone conversation from earlier. As Alex mulled over it, he grew more frustrated, and the stress forced him to pace at the pool's edge.

The fact his boyfriend, the one he should count on for help and guidance, declared he drop everything and go on with life as if nothing happened, was the worst part of it all.

Little by little Alex was getting somewhere, connecting the dots. And whatever was about to resurface from his family's past would be huge.

Still, he couldn't shake the why. *Perhaps Mike has a legitimate justification for why he doesn't want me interfering… or he doesn't want me to overshadow him when he breaks the case?*

His pep-talk to himself hurt more than it helped. Alex stopped pacing and let out a huge sigh before he walked into Amy's cancerous cloud of smoke. He looked into her eyes. "Give me one."

"Give you one what?"

He pointed at her cigarette.

"But you don't smoke."

"Observant. But with everything I've been dealing with, I figure what do I have to lose?"

She pulled out her pack and handed it and a lighter over to Alex. "Please don't get hooked."

"Why? You always appear calm and composed when you have one; why shouldn't it do the same for me?"

Amy threw her hands up. "Just don't, okay."

Alex lit the cigarette and took in a deep puff. He let out a massive cough and spewed out a few words. "Fine. I won't."

They stood around puffing away as the wind blew through the towering pine trees surrounding the house. For the third time that day an awkward silence fell between them, but Alex would not let it stay that way for long.

"Hey, can I ask you a serious question?" he asked.

"Yeah."

"No bullshit either."

"Of course."

"Do you think I'm crazy? I've always believed I had my life in perfect order but is it possible I'm reading too much into this? Could these recent events have nothing in common?"

"You're not crazy; that much I am certain of. What I don't get is if any of this is connected."

"It has to be."

"I'm following your lead and intuition. If your brain is telling you something is wrong, it is."

"But is it my place to get involved?"

She shrugged again. "If this were me, I'd pack my shit and flee as far away from here as I could."

"Mike asked me to drop the whole thing, go back to school tomorrow, and finish finals."

"He's worried something bad might happen, and I hate to admit, but he isn't unreasonable."

"You think he's reasonable?"

Amy tossed her cigarette into the yard and snapped around at Alex. "He's doing his best to keep us safe. He's a cop—do you think for a second he'll tolerate you putting yourself in danger?"

Alex hung his head. "No, I suppose not."

"You need to relax and leave the dangerous stuff to him. I'm drowning in emotions: the murders, Heather, you, and us. This has all been stressful on me too."

Alex hung his head. "I'm sorry you got drawn into this mess."

"It's okay, I didn't mean to yell at you. Why don't we go back inside and take it easy?"

Alex overheard the clock inside chime while he stood underneath the patio umbrella in the moist, spring air. He stood, tossed his cigarette butt, and advanced for the French doors.

As he stepped into the house, the overpowering scent of citrus struck him in the face. As he continued further into the room, the aroma weakened, and in its place was a peculiar, pungent odor. The stench was so foreign to him; it was impossible for him to describe.

He ran his fingers through his short hair. "Amy, come here."

"What?"

"Did you spray anything before we walked outside?"

"Nope. Why?"

"You don't smell that musty odor in the air?

"I smell nothing."

"I swear it's there."

"You smoked a cigarette for what, the first…no, wait, the second time in your life? Might be you smell yourself?"

"No, it's not that. I'm always around you; I've adapted to the smell of smoke."

She grabbed him by the arm and tugged him towards the living room. "Let's relax and wait for Brandy."

"Sure, but can we watch anything else other than soap operas? They're giving me a headache."

She chuckled, "Of course. We don't need the television on."

Alex found himself back at his usual place: the couch. The offensive smell left him miffed, but he brushed it off. Could be his mind was playing tricks on him. After all, they were there the entire time, and it wasn't likely someone else was in the house.

The sound of the landline ringing in the kitchen interrupted his overactive imagination. He sprang to his feet and rushed to reach it before voicemail picked up. He made it by the third ring and looked at the caller ID; security from the front gate was calling.

"Jones residence."

"Mr. Jones, there's a Brandy O'Connor here at the entrance requesting access. Are you acquainted?"

"I am. You can let her in."

"Fantastic. Can I have your access code?"

"It's five-four-eight-one."

"Thanks. Have a good day, Mr. Jones," the guard said.

Every bit of anxiety melted away as he rushed back into the living room. "She's here."

Amy stood and flung the magazine she was perusing onto the couch. "Excellent. Let's hope with her here you'll calm down."

9

THEY STRUTTED TOWARDS THE FRONT DOOR, and Alex's appearance changed from defeated to ecstatic in less than five seconds. Amy questioned herself, *does he do this when I'm coming over?* Alex watched as Brandy's car pulled up to the curb, but as he was about to open the door, his cell phone rang again.

Amy glanced over, "Okay, Mr. Popular."

"I know, right. I never receive these many calls in a day."

He looked at the caller ID before he answered. 'Unknown' displayed across the screen. He hesitated to answer but went ahead.

"Hello?"

"Alex…help me."

"Heather? Is that you? Where are you?"

"Alex, please, they will kill me."

It was difficult to absorb everything that came out of her mouth over the static, but one thing he didn't forget was the deafening scream and the line dying. He signaled to Amy who stood on the front porch waiting for Brandy to exit her car.

She didn't see him, and Alex couldn't muster up words. He stood there with the phone in his hand. Absorbed by what just occurred he was oblivious that Amy had walked out to the driveway to greet Brandy. A few seconds later, after the shock wore off, he glanced up and standing before him was Brandy with a bright smile painted across her face.

She approached and opened her arms. "Well, don't stand there, give me a hug stranger."

Brandy stopped in her tracks, and Amy grabbed Alex by the forearm. "Who was that on the phone?"

"I think it was Heather."

"What? Are you sure?"

"I can't be certain; there was so much static, but whoever it was, believed they would kill her," he replied with a slight tremble in his voice.

Brandy's jaw dropped, and she reached out her hand. "You mentioned earlier some sketchy shit was going on…so, instead of catching up about our boring lives, we should discuss the details of the chaos."

"Well, grab a stiff drink, we got shit to fill you in on."

Amy and Brandy took Alex by the arms and slammed the front door closed behind them as they ventured into the living room. They helped Alex to the couch, and Amy rushed to the kitchen to fetch him a bottle of water.

Amy peeked around the corner, "Brandy, you need anything?"

"Well, it sounds like I need a drink. If there's red wine in the house, I'll take that."

Amy flashed her bright white teeth. "You got it."

She came back a few moments later, a bottle under her armpit and two glasses of red wine. Finally, comfortable enough, Alex set off into story mode. The two ladies anchored the ends of the couch leaving Alex smack-dab between them. It was as if an interrogation was about to commence, so he jumped to his feet and paced in front of the window.

Outside the trees blew forcefully as the strong wind sailed down the mountain slope into Ridgewood Hills. A moment passed, and when his interest in the storm faded, he noticed Amy and Brandy leaning in, eager for more information.

Brandy was eager to learn what she was getting herself into. "Will somebody please tell me what's going on around here. I appreciate how you love to build suspense, but I don't think this is the right time."

"Well, guess I should begin at the beginning. It was yesterday morning, and it was like any normal day, except Amy and John fighting—."

Amy interrupted and laid her hand on Brandy's shoulder. "He's an asshole which I'm sure you'll find out later."

Alex ran his fingers through his hair and continued. "We stopped at the 7-Eleven down the street like we do every morning."

"I need snacks and smokes—the essentials."

Brandy acknowledged Amy before she returned her attention to Alex.

"I stayed in the car with John while Amy and Heather were inside. I remember seeing these two guys walk inside, but I paid no attention to them. I suppose two minutes later, and the store turned into a war zone. Bullets zipped past my car, glass shattered over the parking lot. When they fled, three people were dead, and they left six of us left to tell the tale."

"I saw this on the news last night down in Colorado Springs. But if this is the same story I'm thinking of, didn't they find four dead bodies?" Brandy asked.

"Ah, which brings me to the next item. After spending the better part of the morning with Ridgewood Hills finest, later Heather called to tell us they had found Kelli murdered in Centennial Park."

"Heather…the girl you thought called. Have I ever met her?"

"I don't think so. She moved here in August last year."

"That's awful to hear about her sister. Am I going to meet them?"

"Well, I'm sure John will stop by after school. But Heather, well, how do I say this?"

Amy jumped in. "She's missing."

"Missing?"

"You heard her right. Heather's been missing since last night, and now my worst fears have been confirmed—someone kidnapped her, and she's in grave danger."

"And we're sitting around talking about it when you should be on the phone with the police."

"Mike's on his way, I'd rather deal with him."

"Am I safe here with you guys?"

Alex and Amy swapped glances at one another. "You're here now—and with Mike here you're in the safest house in town."

"Yeah, don't worry."

Brandy's lower lip quivered, but after a minute she smiled. "It's been so long since I last saw him. You guys are the cutest couple. But convince me again that staying here is a good idea."

"I'm a hundred percent sure you're safe. I mean, didn't the nosy guard interrogate you to let you in here to see us?"

"You have a point—they have this neighborhood on lock-down, that's for sure," Brandy said as Alex's cell phone rang again.

"Damn it, who now? Hello?"

"How are things?" Mike asked.

"Brandy arrived, so we finished filling her in on everything. Hey, can you do me a favor?"

He answered, "Depends."

"Can someone at the station run a trace on my last incoming call?"

"What? Why?"

"I'm not sure, but I have this feeling it was Heather. Mike, she sounds like she's in trouble."

"Be more specific?"

"She said they would kill her. The line sat silent for a few seconds, and there was a loud scream."

"And?"

"And nothing, the call dropped."

"Damn. You were right this whole time. It appears like someone kidnapped her. Okay, let me go so I can call the station. How long ago did she call?"

"Ten minutes ago."

"Was there a number on your caller ID?"

"Unknown."

"I hate that. Okay, I'll do my best to rush it but dealing with the phone company and trying to get a waiver annoys me because it's so time-consuming. There's too damn much red tape these days—people's privacy and shit."

"Screw their privacy. They've got my friend."

"I hear you, Alex. But there are laws in place, and I can't circumvent them on the grounds you say so."

Alex grunted. "Yeah, it's what people like this love: being able to remain anonymous on account of some lawmakers in Washington."

"Um, don't want to kick off an argument, but it's written in the Bill of Rights. Just saying."

"Whatever. Are you on your way?"

"Almost to the station. Tell you what, I'll have someone in forensics get on the phone trace and I'll head over when I'm done. Deal?"

With deflation in his voice, Alex replied. "Deal. I love you and see you soon."

Alex ended the call, huffed, and slid his cell in his front pocket. Brandy and Amy had eavesdropped on the one-sided conversation to learn as much as necessary to establish a conclusion.

"So, he will trace it?"

"He promised he would, although it might take a while. I guess you can't give that information out freely with no reason."

"Alex, why don't we help Brandy settle in. Might help calm your nerves while we wait for Mike."

"Sounds like a plan."

Everybody worked their way to the staircase. The entire way up the stairs his mind raced, and he asked himself whether allowing Brandy to stay was the right thing and could he keep her safe. That gut feeling of his kicked at the moment she pulled up and nothing he did could shake the gnawing dread. If anything went down and she got hurt, he'd never forgive himself.

The ascent up the stairs lugging two bags behind him was daunting. *I can't wait 'til I reach the top so I can drop this shit.*

As Alex reached the top of the stairs, the girls were already standing at the door to the second guest bedroom further down the hall from Alex's bedroom. He shuffled along and reached the room where he set the bags on the floor.

Brandy joined Amy on the edge of the bed, and she glanced up at Alex. "Are you sure I should be here? I'm weirded out now."

"Brandy, everything will be fine. Neither me, nor Amy, nor Mike will let anything happen to you. If you'd be more comfortable you and Amy can bunk up tonight?"

"Yeah, come on Brandy, we'll be fine if we stick together."

"Let me think about it."

"Besides, we're going out to dinner. We should try not to worry so much and have fun," Amy said as she nudged Brandy, "And you can answer me later about sharing a room."

"Yeah. I'm with you, Amy. If we stay together, no one in their right mind will try to take us all on," Brandy replied.

After spending a few more minutes reassuring Brandy, they found themselves back on the living room couch. Outside, the weather took an ominous turn, and the wind moaned as it blew past the window. If anything, it added an element of mystery to the day. The mahogany grandfather clock tolled four times, and the noise interrupted his concentration. Alex flinched and clutched at his chest. *For fuck's sake clock.*

He stood and deliberated if they'd need to cancel going out considering the lashing storm. However, he recognized everyone needed a night out to chill, so Alex settled that no matter how unkind things were outside he'd see to it the plans remained unbroken.

Alex twisted around and stared at Amy, who was right in the middle of picking up the remote from the coffee table to flip off the television. He gasped, and she turned around, giving him the side-eye.

"Don't look at me like that."

"I'm not looking any kind of way."

"Yes, you are. Let's do something more productive than watching this crap all day. Any ideas?"

"Hmm, nothing comes to mind. And going outside right now is out of the question; have you witnessed the hurricane conditions out there?"

Brandy stood and stopped next to Alex. "I did—treacherous."

As she rested her head on Alex's shoulder, a few hailstones dropped from the sky and plummeted the earth. "I loathe this shit. Destroys the fun we could be having."

"Well, I say we still go out. I can't stay cooped up in this house forever," Alex complained as he let his head fall against Brandy's.

"I'm with Alex; this house feels like a prison. We're here non-stop either studying or fearing for our lives. A night out on the town is exactly what we need."

They exchanged glances. Brandy interlinked her arm with Alex's. "So, what to do while we wait?"

"We could go search for the safe," Alex mentioned.

Amy shook her head disapprovingly. "We've done everything we can in there. Yet I have lingering questions about those letters."

"I'm listening."

"Does your mother know Russian? I mean did she translate it into English, or did someone else?"

"I don't think so. Maybe the people who sent them translated them for her?"

"Seems to defeat the purpose of writing them in Russian, doesn't it?" Amy asked.

His eyes danced up and to the left. "Yeah, it does. Damn, now I'm more baffled than before. We're overlooking something. What are we missing?"

Brandy chimed in after letting the information settle for a moment. "Hang on. What are these letters you two are going on about?"

"While we were being nosy earlier and combing through my mom's files, we came across them. There were three in total—each one typed in Russian. However, somebody handwrote the English translation on the back," Alex explained.

"That seems odd. And you're positive she isn't the one who did it?" Brandy probed.

"I'm about ninety-nine percent sure my mother doesn't speak, read, or write Russian. However, she could have had them translated. Perhaps by someone she trusts?"

"Here's the real question we should try to answer—who did it, and why?" Amy urged as she rose from the sofa.

"True, but let's move past the letters: there's a safe in here somewhere, and we will find it."

Brandy shrugged her shoulders and glanced at Amy, who had crossed her arms across her chest. "Alex, your mother could be home any minute."

"Nah, she's never home before seven. Come on."

They trudged down the dark hallway back to the study. Alex was hell-bent on locating what other things his mother hid from him. They reached the door, and Alex twisted the knob. As he entered the same smell from earlier crept into his nostrils.

I know I'm not crazy. Earlier it smelled like lemon in here, now this.

He stuttered. "There's, that, that smell again."

"Alex, enough about the smell."

Brandy inhaled deeply. "He's telling the truth. You can't smell that?"

Amy sniffed around. "Wait. I smell it now. It's, eh, what's the word— musty."

"Someone's been in here," Alex exclaimed.

"That's crazy. No one except the two of us has been in here. How would they have gotten in?"

"Let's back out of here, pretend none of this ever happened, and return to the living room."

"Not a chance in hell. I'm not scared of whoever these people are."

"But—," Alex attempted to make a case.

"We came in here to hunt down a safe, and I'm not leaving this room until we find it. Besides, who in their right mind would hang around a house they broke into?"

"Amy you must not watch enough horror movies."

"What makes you assume that?"

"If you did, you'd recognize people who say things like that are the first ones the predators kill," Brandy joked.

"No killer is going to 'take me out' as you say. Now let's get what we came in here for before Mike arrives."

Alex, Amy, and Brandy each picked a corner of the room to explore. They peered behind pictures, behind books overstuffed in the bookcase, and in the closet again. And yet again the quest generated nothing. It was in that moment it struck Alex: *maybe it's concealed under the desk?*

He rushed to the desk and pushed. "Help me move this out of the way."

Amy and Brandy glanced at each other with blank stares written across their faces. However, they watched Alex struggle and rushed over to help.

Amy spoke up. "Sure, why didn't I think to check under there? I mean who hides a safe under a desk?"

"An ounce less sarcasm and instead more pushing."

The three of them pushed, and there it was, plain as day, right in front of them: a floor safe. Alex bent forward to catch his breath.

"I told you she had one here. Now comes the hard part; the combination."

"Don't look at us. She's your mom."

Alex crouched to the floor and scanned through his mind. "Well, it'd have to be a combination she could remember."

"Your birthday?" Amy asked.

"Nah. Way too easy. Why don't we try the day they killed my father?"

Brandy bent her knee. "So morbid."

He typed in the code: 05-12-85. The electronic lock beeped and made an audible click. It worked. It worked.

Alex twisted the handle and pulled the massive door upward. When he looked inside, it became unmistakable what his mother tried to hide over the years. Alex was now one step closer to figuring out who his father was and what led to his own demise long ago.

10

THEY STOOD OVER THE HOLE in the floor eyeballing the insides of the safe. To everyone's disbelief within coexisted piles of bank-strapped cash, diamonds, and more envelopes.

Alex's voice shuddered. "What in the hell have we stumbled upon?"

"I'm going with something we never should have seen," Amy uttered as Brandy concurred.

To Alex, the most interesting item was the envelopes. For all he knew the money and jewelry were things passed down from his grandparents or stuff his mom wanted to keep secure. Alex reached inside and grabbed the stack of envelopes and handed them over to Amy and Brandy.

He remained crouched over the safe, and he counted each strap of cash: seventy-thousand. He lowered his head and pinched his thumb and ring finger together against the bridge of his nose.

That's a shit-ton of money. There's no way everything came from my grandparents.

Alex retreated to the leather chair and grabbed a few letters from the stack. After a few minutes, Brandy interrupted his in-depth reading.

"Alex, you'll never believe this," Brandy shouted.

Alex set the letter in his hand on the desk. "What is it?"

"I'm no Russian expert, but on the other hand, I did take two years in high school."

"Spit it out."

"These people have been looking for your mother for some time. Check out the date," she pointed at the letter.

Alex looked closer. "That was last Saturday. What about it?"

"It says she had until Monday to comply or face the consequences."

Amy jumped back, and a coldness fell over Alex. "Shit. They have to be the ones behind the murders. Let's assess what we've learned: she didn't comply, and Tuesday morning there's a quadruple homicide in Ridgewood Hills."

"And don't forget they've kidnapped Heather," Amy chimed in.

"Right. Murder and kidnapping. I don't have a good vibe for a happy outcome. Do they know where we live?" Alex asked.

"I don't have an answer. They sent the letters to a hospital in Denver. Come to think of it, your mom works in the city, doesn't she?"

Alex swallowed hard. "She does. I better make sure she doesn't leave the hospital without an escort until someone resolves this."

"Shit. Shit. I'm more worried about her," Amy said.

Alex grasped for his cell and dialed. He had to warn her; but what would he give as the reason for how he uncovered this knowledge? He needed to concoct a story quick to conceal his intrusiveness.

The phone never rang; instead, voicemail answered right away. In these instances, Alex took it as a sign she was with patients and not receiving calls. Alex strolled in circles waiting for the beep.

After her rambling greeting, the beep he awaited came, and he spoke. "Mom, I have a serious favor to ask, and it involves your safety. Please don't leave the hospital unless someone from security escorts you. If no one is available, you call me, and we'll drive down and pick you up. I can't quite put my finger on it yet, but I'm worried enough for your safety. I love you."

He ended the call and prayed she'd hear his message before leaving the building. Familiar with her day-to-day life, Alex was sure she'd check in the car on the drive home. Alex stepped back into the study and Brandy reading a letter aloud interrupted his train of thought.

"What? I missed most of it," Alex said.

"Um. About your father—how much do you remember about him?"

"To be honest; not much. Everything from my childhood is such a blur. Sporadically I have these flashbacks of his murder, yet there's not enough there to discern if it's real or made-up. What brought that up?"

She waved the letter in her hand around. "This letter mentions wanting their money and documents back. They flat out accuse your father of being a thief."

"They suspect his father stole their money?" Amy gasped.

"From the sound of this letter, someone believes it. They claim your father stole money, drugs and something important to them."

"Did they say what the important thing was?"

She shook her head. "No. It seems he crossed them, had their headquarters raided, and they were all arrested."

In the distance, a deafening crash of thunder vibrated the house, and the power flickered. It was now a full-blown storm outdoors, and it grew more ferocious as the hours crept by. Alex had a shocking revelation about his father that disturbed him to the core. He had undeniably pissed off the Russian mafia, and he paid with his life for it. From the sounds of these letters whoever these guys were from the 1980s had come back, devoted on vengeance.

An onslaught of feelings inundated his mind, and each one made him reexamine his whole life. *He must have stolen the money. How could we afford the house were in, and the luxury of buying new cars every two years?* It became more apparent to Alex about what sort of person his father was.

Alex dropped into the chair, and the room spun. Every drop of blood in his system emptied from his upper extremities, and he turned whiter than fresh bed linens. He shielded his face, and when the adrenaline surging through his veins achieved its peak, he exploded into tears.

Amy rushed to his side and stroked his hand with hers. "What's wrong?"

"I have confirmed my worst suspicions."

Amy cocked her head. "What suspicions?"

"What these letters say. It has to be true. There's no way my mother could have afforded to live in this exclusive neighborhood, both of us drive luxury cars, and how? From stolen mafia money."

Amy grabbed his hand. "What a wild imagination you have. Your mom is a neurosurgeon, and last I checked, they made somewhat decent money."

Brandy crouched next to Alex. "You must be exhausted after such an intense day. Are you sure you want to go out tonight?"

Alex lifted his head.

Amy released her hold on his hand. "The weather will get worse, and I don't sense your frame of mind is up for fun. Maybe we should keep sifting through these letters and brainstorm."

Alex sucked back the mucus which dripped from his nose. "I'll be okay. I won't ruin everyone's night. Besides, I want—no, I need a distraction."

"We'll support your decision as long as you're sure it's what you want."

"I mean I can't let psychopaths alter my life over crap my dad did all those years ago. If I stay in this house like a prisoner, it confirms one thing: they've won."

Alex stood, and Amy shouted. "They won't win. Besides, Mike will be here soon, and nothing will happen to us with him around."

**

THE THREE LEFT THE STUDY, AND Alex flipped off the lights before he shut the door. His mom was sure to know he snooped around once she checked her voicemail, yet Alex didn't care. And even though she would be more pissed than he had ever seen, everyone else's well-being was far more important than her privacy at that moment.

It was approaching four in the afternoon as they emerged into the living room yet again. In the back of Alex's mind, he had hesitations about heading out later, but he would not make it an issue. His family's sordid mess was not the drama his friends deserved to find themselves drawn into. What they deserved was to enjoy the last few weeks before they moved on with their lives. His pesky gut instinct would need to take a back seat for the evening. He was going out; mafia or not, they would not stop him from living his life.

As Alex rounded the corner from the foyer into the living room, an unnerving sensation forced its way up his spine. The chill trembled his body, and it brought him to a standstill in the archway. It had been at least a year since he experienced such a reaction, the last time being the night him and Mike had their first date. It was as if his life was out of his control, and there was nothing he could do to stop what was about to occur. Amy, who was about to sit on the couch, found Alex standing with a blank expression plastered across his face.

"Are you coming?"

"In a sec. I had this dreadful feeling come over me."

Amy smirked. "Seems to be the popular theme today."

"So, it does. It's undeniably nothing more than residual shock wearing off."

Amy passed her hand across the empty cushion next to her. "Come, sit and relax."

Alex hunched forward his shoulders and forced the uneasiness from his mind. As he sat next to Amy, he tried to unwind, yet his persistent worry refused to loosen its grip. Amy turned to the side and slid her leg underneath his thigh. He slouched against the back cushion.

Amy sighed. "It's like we keep coming back to this room. Is there a reason?"

He looked around. "Feels more comfortable in here. This is the happy place I sometimes go when the world around me feels like it's crumbling down."

"Understandable. My spot is the loft in the garage. It's serene, isolated, and better yet, no one would ever think to look for me there," Brandy replied.

Alex stood. "Can I show you guys something?"

"Of course."

He walked towards the entertainment center against the far wall, bent over, and opened a drawer. He fumbled with several items inside, scattering them about. Eventually, he heaved a sizeable black scrapbook out and flipped it open to a specific page.

"No one has ever seen this before, not my mom or Mike. You two are the first."

Brandy adjusted her posture and leaned in closer. "What is it?"

"It's a book I made several years ago of some photos I came across when looking through some boxes in the attic. They are of my father, mother, and myself from back in the Denver days."

"Wow, let's look."

Alex sat between them and placed the open book in his lap. An upbeat smile graced his face as he flipped each page. Everyone studied the photos intensely, and when Alex got to the page with a picture of his father from the FBI academy, Brandy smiled and pointed.

"You look just like him here."

"You think? My mom and I never talked about him. Now, sitting here with you two, looking through these photos give me optimism he's still here, watching over me."

"He's got to be proud of who you've become."

Amy nodded in agreement. "Thank you for trusting us enough to share this."

"You're both amazing friends, and if I'd trust anyone, it'd be the both of you."

They continued exploring the photo book, and to Alex, it was immediately apparent he changed somewhere along the way. The Alex in the photos didn't represent the guy he was now. The days of carefree happiness faded, and orderliness and melancholy superseded it. He agonized too much, yet somehow, he did an incredible job of projecting to everyone how happy he was. Deep down the facade he'd built over the years slowly chipped away, and the real Alex Jones shone through.

After they finished thumbing through the book, they spent the better part of the next half hour lazing in the living room, reminiscing about the old days. Alex opened up to his best friends about his true feelings about graduation, Mike, and whether he'd join her in New York at the end of summer.

Amy glanced away and stuttered, "Alex…"

"What's up?"

"Promise me we'll always be friends."

"Why would you say that?"

"I've read these stories of people who move away from home drifting apart from their lifelong friends. I don't know what I'd do if that happened to us."

"It won't; ask Brandy. We've stayed friends this entire time. We may not see each other every day, yet we make it work. Isn't that right?"

"I can appreciate what Amy's saying, though. She's moving across the country. It's nowhere near the same."

"Exactly. You can drive an hour to see her anytime. When I move to New York, we'll be a three-day drive apart."

"Trust me, the two of you will always be friends."

"How can you be sure?"

"I just am. Besides, they have these magical things called airplane now. Alex could hop a flight and be in New York in a few hours."

Alex's phone rang again, and he excused himself from the conversation. He shoved his hand into his front pocket to quell the screeching phone. As he stepped into the foyer, he expected to see Mike's name on the caller ID. Instead, he saw John's. He flipped open the cover and pressed the phone against his ear. "You still coming over?"

"I'm leaving school. You two sure missed a weird day. Everyone and I do mean everyone, was abuzz with what happened to Kelli."

"Not surprised. Its huge news."

"Before lunch, I revealed Heather was missing to a close friend—next thing I know she's told everyone, and by the time I walked out the doors it had ballooned into someone kidnapped her."

Alex shook his head in frustration. "What did you expect would happen? You know everyone at our school are gossipmongers. While we're talking about Heather, she didn't by chance call you today, did she?"

"Nope. Received a text from Amy talking about she needed help to translate some Russian letter. I haven't replied yet."

"Oh, don't worry about that—problem solved. You remember my friend, Brandy?"

"Vaguely."

"Well, she took care of it. I can't wait for you to meet her."

"Oh, right. She is staying over tonight?"

"She is."

"Perfect. Well, gotta go. This parking lot is crazy."

"Sounds good. When you arrive, we'll decide where to eat."

"Oh, we're going out?"

"Yeah, all five of us."

"Count me in. Suppose I should stop home and change first. Guess I'll see you soon. Later."

***

JOHN INDEED HAD A TOUGH day at school. He devoted the better part of the pre-lunch hours worried about Heather, then around second period came a bombardment of questions about what it was like to survive a robbery and listening to everyone run their mouths about Kelli's murder. It was as if the student body figured he had some insider information into the working of a police investigation. After lunch, it got worse once news spread about Heather going off the radar.

After about five minutes of waiting in the line of cars to exit campus, he pulled out onto the tree-lined boulevard and headed towards home. The rainstorm lashed out and made it difficult to see twenty feet in front of him. He chugged through traffic, and after about fifteen minutes he arrived at the main entrance to their subdivision. He hung a right and pulled into his driveway.

Emotionally drained from having to juggle assignments, worrying about his friends, and harassment the entire day from classmates, he shook his head before he pushed open the front door. John tossed his backpack to the floor of the foyer and rushed upstairs to his room, removing his polo shirt, and exposing his tanned skin and ripped stomach. He raced into his closet and grabbed a blue and white striped button-down along with a pair of dark-colored Levi jeans. Once John finished, he removed his pants, tossed them onto his bed, and set out to change.

John was meticulous about his outward appearance. Any outsider would imagine John was straight out of GQ magazine. John was always stylish when it came to fashion. And tonight, was no different, as he wanted to look his best for whatever reason. After he buttoned his jeans, he walked into his bathroom to give himself one last check-over before he left for the evening.

Confident about his choice in attire, he casually walked towards his bedroom door and switched the overhead light off. As he stepped into the hallway, he picked up the pace, rushing past his mother on his way towards the front door. She interjected into his hurried state. "Where are you off to in such a hurry?"

"I'm going out with Alex and Amy tonight. Alex wants to introduce me to his friend from Colorado Springs. Could be love at first sight?"

"Oh, well, have fun. We can chat more about Yale when you come home," she uttered with hesitation in her voice.

"Everything okay?"

"It's fine. It's that your father and I are also going out tonight, and I was going to ask if you would stay in tonight and watch your brother and sister."

"Oh, I wish I knew earlier."

"It's all good, sweetie. Go out and have fun. Adam's old enough to stay home for a few hours alone."

"I would surely think so; he's fourteen. I'm confident he's competent enough to hold down the fort while you guys go out."

"When you're right, you're right. Go and have a marvelous time tonight. You deserve to spend some time with your friends before you graduate," she expressed as she reached out and gave him a hug.

He wrapped his arms around her shoulders, hugging her back tightly as he jokingly asked, "You're not dying, are you?"

"Heavens no, why would you ask that?"

"I'm joking. It's odd for you to hug me out of the blue these days. Threw me off for a moment."

"You're too much; skedaddle before you're late."

"I should be home no later than midnight. Don't wait up."

Mrs. Davidson stood there in the frame of the front door and focused on her son as he walked towards the driveway. In her mind, these were the last few weeks she'd have her children under one roof. John was growing up, and she couldn't be prouder of him for everything he had accomplished in the past few years. She continued to watch as he backed out onto the street and disappeared into the distance. She closed the front door, snickered, and returned to the kitchen to finish with the dishes.

He finished up and hopped back into the car. He backed down the driveway and drove until he arrived at Old Orchard Boulevard. As he went to make the right, the radio interrupted his favorite song with a weather bulletin.

This radio station better be reporting an apocalypse for this interruption.

The weather bulletin yet again warned of severe flooding in the area, and the overkill made John utter under his breath, "No shit, Sherlock. It's been raining for days; I'm surprised no one's built an arc yet."

He sped along the rain-soaked asphalt towards Alex's on the opposite side of the subdivision. However, the trip took less than four minutes, and John pulled in behind Brandy.

He reached for his hoodie crumbled in the passenger seat, and before he opened the door, he pulled it over his head and raised the hood. He took a calming breath and flung the door open, darting across the front lawn. Luckily for John, his wide-stride minimized the amount of splash-back against his clothes. However, it didn't matter since the torrential rain pelted him across the face.

After what seemed an eternity, he reached the front door, inundated from head to toe. After he rang the doorbell, he stood patiently waiting at the large wooden door, and a drop of water dripped from his nose and splashed against the concrete patio.

Alex answered after a couple of minutes and furrowed his brow as John bypassed his typical friendly greeting and stepped inside without a word.

"Damn, it's getting worse out there…isn't it?"

"You think?" John sarcastically replied. "I don't remember the last time we had rain like this."

"Around five years ago," Alex replied before he disappeared to fetch John a towel from the powder room.

Brandy overheard their conversation at the front door and agreed. "This could be one of the worst storms I've ever experienced. Are we sure it's still a bright idea to go out? In this—?"

Alex cut in on her question. "Absolutely."

John chuckled. "I bet we're going to Casa Grille."

"You bet right. They have valet, a covered path to the door—what's not to love?"

"You have enough umbrellas for everyone?" Brandy asked.

"We have plenty to go around."

Amy reached out her hand when she detected Brandy's hesitancy to go out. "You seem unsure about tonight. You sure everything's good?"

"A bit nervous about the scenario Alex paints."

"I get why you'd be nervous. We did drop a ton of information on you in a short amount of time."

Brandy reacted with a slight nod and remained silent.

"Besides, Mike will be with us, and he's not the type of guy to let anything happen to us. Okay?"

The words jolted from Brandy's throat. "I trust every one of you. Alex has been one of my closest friends…he'd never do anything to put my safety at risk."

"Never."

They watched John dry himself off from the dining room table. Brandy had relaxed and told crazy stories about the wild things her and Alex did at camp. They were outlandish enough to have everyone, including Alex, laughing hysterically.

In between jokes Alex glanced at his watch. Five to five. Worry set in. It'd been hours since he spoke with Mike and the drive from Golden Ridge shouldn't have taken this long.

Not wanting to appear alarmist, he refocused his attention to his friends and tried to join in. However, Brandy dominated the conversation as she divulged tales, each one more embarrassing than the previous. The doorbell rang, and the room once filled with laughter fell silent.

Amy nudged Alex in the shoulder with her finger. "Go check the door."

"Geesh, why don't you go?"

Her eyes narrowed. "I'm not going. It's your house. Besides, what if it's…*them?*"

"Stop being paranoid. It's only Mike."

"The guards never called. How can you be sure?"

Alex stood and stepped away. "He probably flashed his badge, and they let him in. That's how I'm sure."

Secretly he looked through the spyhole and confirmed it was Mike standing on the other side—drenched from the rain. He opened the door and walked out, wrapping his arms around his soggy boyfriend was the most important thing at the moment. Mike flashed the killer smile which stole Alex's heart and pulled him closer, the beads of rain dropped onto Alex's neck, yet he never flinched. They embraced for a minute on the front porch before Mike pulled away.

"Let's not give the neighbors a show."

"Screw them and their small-minded ways."

Mike smirked. Their love was resilient enough, and neither of them would ever allow anything to come between them. "I'm soaked. Let's go inside where it's warm."

He grabbed Mike's hand and led him into the house. After closing the door, he stood on his tip-toes, reaching to plant a kiss on his cheek. "You had me worried."

"Why? I told you I'd be late."

"Never mind, I'm glad you're here. We have tons to fill you in on."

Mike removed his water-logged jacket and draped it on the banister. When he left, the room was full of chatter, yet upon his return with Mike in tow, low-level whispers replaced the laughter.

Amy caught sight of Mike and stood. "You're finally here."

"Yeah, traffic is pretty rough."

Amy spun towards John. "Hey, Einstein, can you share your towel?"

John stopped speaking. "Uh…sure. Sorry about that, Mike."

Mike stepped away and rubbed the damp towel through his hair and across his face. "So the rumor is true, you got slightly bored and chose to be nosy."

"We stopped our snooping a while ago. For the last hour we've listened to Brandy and Alex regale stories about their summers at orchestra camp. Did he ever tell you the crazy things these two got into?"

"I've heard a few stories. I'm personally holding Brandy accountable to fill me in on the ones he left out."

Brandy leaned in. "I've got the juicy scoop."

"Well, glad to see you've been keeping yourselves entertained and less absorbed by the chaos."

"I'll forever find something fun to divert my attention away from drama," Amy said.

Mike pulled out a chair. "Good to hear. However, we have a significant amount of information to cover prior to dinner. Does anyone object if we start?"

Everyone exchanged looks, and it didn't seem as if anyone had a problem. Everyone acknowledged the need to assess the risks which existed before they proceeded. Mike concentrated as Alex and Amy discussed everything uncovered in the study; however, neither of them kept to a timeline, which caused Mike's head to spin.

Lost from their zig-zagging, Mike butted in. "Hold on...hold on. Can we go back to how we got to this point? What happened in Denver?"

"Amy and I drove to the main library downtown this morning. I had a suspicion everything occurring had to do with my father and his murder. I did some research on it."

"Okay, I gathered that much. What I want to hear more about are these two men and their white van. Where were you when you first noticed them following you?"

"At the intersection where the 7-Eleven is. We drove past, and I noticed them pull out of the parking lot right away."

"And were they directly behind you the entire time?"

"Not the entire time. But..."

"But?"

"They were there when we got to the library."

"Odd. Did you catch a plate number or anything? Surely you had to see it in your rearview mirror."

Alex closed his eyes, trying to recall. "There wasn't a front plate, and I wasn't about to walk around the back to check for one."

"Interesting. Either they removed it, or it's not registered in Colorado. Either way, excellent observation."

Alex continued. "Everything went fine at the library until I had a bombshell dropped on me."

"Bombshell?"

"I'm getting to that. When we left the library, the van had vanished. My worry subsided and my anger built."

John tapped his fingers across the table. "Anger from what? You're talking in code."

"There's a build-up to it. Hang tight."

John slouched back in the chair and crossed his arms over his chest.

Mike continued asking questions. "So, you left the library. Where did you go next?"

"The hospital to visit my mother."

"And what happened once you arrived there?"

"When we got out of the car on the sixth floor of the parking garage, the white van from earlier crept behind us, followed us like prey. We walked to the elevator, and they waited. And watched."

A teasing smile crossed Amy's face. "Hard to miss a rust bucket like that."

"Okay, I think we've covered the men in the van. You mentioned discovering upsetting news at the library, so you drove to the hospital to see your mom about it?"

"Yes."

"And do you mind sharing with the group exactly what news pissed you off?"

His hands grew sweaty and a cold chill swept over his body. "My entire life has been one colossal lie."

"I'm confused; what do you mean by 'a lie'?"

"I'm not Alex Jones."

Mike hesitated, without a response.

"My name is Marshall Stahl. I can't disclose any more for reasons beyond my control."

As the words spewed from Alex's mouth, Brandy's phone interrupted. She glanced down and stood. "Sorry, it's my boss—be right back."

She unlocked the patio door and vanished into the hammering rain before Alex could recommend a better place to go if she needed privacy.

"What do you mean you're not Alex Jones?"

Alex stuttered. "I can't say any more. Let's move on."

"Fine. I'll remember we didn't exhaust that topic," Mike pointed his finger. "I assume you came home and snooped. Right?"

Amy hung her head. "We did."

"And in the course you came across some letters?"

"More like threats targeted at my mother."

Amy continued. "Russian script on the front, on the flip-side, the handwritten English translation. Who translated it? No clue."

Mike massaged his temples with his fingers. "And you're positive they were threatening her?"

Amy concurred. "They warned if she didn't give back what Alex's father took from them, she'd bear the consequences."

"Did they give a cutoff date?"

The two best-friends swapped glances and responded in sync. "Monday."

Mike cracked his knuckles and leaned back. "It's making sense. Monday was the deadline. Wednesday, they shoot up a convenience store, murder Kelli, and kidnap Heather. Then today they mess with you."

"Yes. Finally, we're on the same page."

"Seems like whatever it is you can't tell me about lead you to this conclusion."

"Now you're caught up. The question we need an answer for is what we're having for dinner?" Amy asked.

"I was thinking-." Before Alex could drop the name of the restaurant, Brandy returned. She lingered in the doorway, drenched from head to toe and her body shivered from the inhospitable outdoors.

"For the love of God. If you wanted privacy, you could have slipped into the study or my bedroom. Let me grab you a fresh towel?"

Alex ran up the stairs, and Amy rushed into the kitchen to grab the closest thing to wipe the droplets of water from her face.

Amy returned and passed a fresh dishtowel. "Here, it's not much. With luck, it will suffice until Alex comes back."

"Thanks."

"Everything okay at work?"

Brandy looked up. "What?"

"Work. Wasn't that your boss on the phone?"

"Oh, that—it's all good. Had to resolve a scheduling conflict next week. Did we decide on tonight?"

Mike drummed his fingers against the tabletop. "Alex is gonna drag us out to Casa Grille...again."

Brandy wrinkled her nose. "Is the food terrible?"

"Quite the opposite; the place is amazing. I imagine with numerous choices he'd want to taste something new."

Brandy wagged her finger. "Isn't this the same restaurant you two had your first date?"

"Yeah, it is. Damn, your recollection is remarkable. Look, when he gets back let's pretend we're content with whatever he picks."

With everyone chatting downstairs, Alex hunted upstairs for a clean towel. He sifted through the linen closet ultimately settling on a gray, Egyptian cotton one. He closed the door and rushed to return to his friends.

As he reached the first step, an icy breeze blew throughout the hallway, and he stopped dead in his tracks. He calmly glanced over his shoulder down the dim hallway. It laid empty except for a side table with a bouquet of fresh tulips which swayed back and forth. He lingered near the stairs, petrified to take one more step. Down below the uproar of laughter from his gave him confidence, so he mustered up the courage to step back into the darkness.

Did I forget to close a window?

He arrived at his bedroom door and pressed against it softly. The creaky hinges whined as it opened inward and Alex poked his head inside to check for the source of the draft—and found zilch. He shrugged it off, closed the door, and worked his way back towards the staircase.

He emerged at the foot of the stairs with a towel in hand, and Mike cracked a crooked smile as he passed the hand towel over to Brandy.

"What took so long?"

"Had to grab something out of my bedroom, sorry."

"Everyone is waiting to hear where you've chosen."

"Well, my first choice was Casa Grille-."

Mike clapped his hands. "See, what'd I tell you."

Alex raised his hand and talked over his boyfriend. "However, with everything we've stomached these past few days I sensed we needed a change."

Jaws around the table fell at his unexpected announcement. Alex laughed to himself as everyone exchanged vacant gazes. "I know, I know. You guys assume I'm *so* predictable. So, I elected to step out of character for once."

"So, where are we going?"

"I want to be adventurous tonight. How about we try that new Mediterranean place, Felix's?"

"Any objections?" Mike asked.

With jaws agape, everyone glanced around the table at one another in silence. "Since I hear no objections let's head out."

Mike stood and pulled Alex aside. "Impressive."

"How so?"

"You're stepping out of your comfort zone and trying new things."

"Maybe. Or is it possible I remembered Mediterranean is your favorite?"

Mike smiled and pulled Alex closer. "I'm glad you remembered. Besides, Casa Grille has unhappy memories. I want to build happy, healthy memories with you from here on out."

Alex leaned in and kissed Mike. As he pulled away, he whispered, "This is the reason I fell in love with you."

After five minutes everyone was making their way towards the front door. Alex glanced at his cell phone again; still no call from his mother. He told himself if he hadn't received word from her by the time dinner ended, he would call the security team at the hospital and have them keep an eye on her.

Mike opened the front door, and the fierce wind blew the rain inward, soaking the tile floor beneath their feet. A bolt of lightning struck the earth, close enough to make the hair on Alex's arm stand on end.

Mike rested his hand on his shoulder. "Last chance to change your mind."

"Not a chance in hell. If we run, we can make it."

They dashed for the dark, four-door Escalade parked behind Alex's car. The SUV was capable of transporting everyone and the perfect vehicle to trek out into the storm with. Mike pressed the unlock button on the key fob and John, Amy and Brandy piled into the backseat while the lovebirds got into the front. With everyone buckled in, Mike threw it into reverse and backed onto the roadway. Before Mike shifted into drive, Alex had his finger on the radio scanning through the channels.

Mike intervened, "What are you doing?"

"What do you think? I'm changing the station. You guys are good with this for ten minutes?"

"He's right. I've listened to that song way too much, and it's driving me mad," John said.

Mike retreated his hand. "I'm giving in for the simple reason it's you. Only this once though."

Alex had grown accustomed to getting his way when it came to Mike. It was amazing how a disappointing frown would make Mike immediately give in to anything he wanted. However, Alex was head-over-heels in love with Mike and never took advantage of the situation often.

They drove past the security checkpoint, and the guard nonchalantly waved to them from the shelter of his shack as the SUV zoomed by. The sun retired thirty minutes earlier, and the streaks of lightning crisscrossing the blackened sky caught Alex's attention. On a typical spring night, you'd find everyone camped out on the back deck watching the sun set behind the mountains. However, on nights like this, the safest place Alex could be was inside a warm house or car.

Traffic was lighter than usual as most residents of Ridgewood Hills had battened down indoors for the evening. The music filled the otherwise quiet car ride into town. Any time things got quiet, Alex let his mind wander to places it shouldn't.

How could Heather be missing for over twenty-four hours and no one have a clue where she was? And how is my father tied to these people? Is my entire life built on Russian drug money?

He snapped back and the caress of Mike's fingers interlocking with his brought out a half-smile, even though on the inside his heart was dying.

Keep your shit together—only for this evening. Tomorrow's another day, and you can lose your shit then.

11

THE DRIVE TOOK TEN MINUTES, as Alex predicted, and Mike pulled the Escalade up to the covered valet stand. He parked, and a middle-aged valet greeted him and handed him a parking stub.

Mike jumped from the driver's seat and ran around the back of the vehicle towards the passenger side. Always the gentlemen, he wanted to make sure he opened the car door for Alex. However, by the time he reached the passenger side, Alex stood with everyone under two large umbrellas. Everyone glanced up and gawked.

"Mike, you're soaked," Amy stated as Mike stood there in the rain and ran his fingers through his short brown hair.

"I'll be fine; I'm not going to melt."

They scurried indoors like drowned rats struggling to flee the attack from the rain smacking their faces. Mike shook off the wet and approached the hostess stand while everyone else waited near the door. A blonde, slender woman welcomed him immediately.

She glanced at Mike. "Good evening. Do you have a reservation?"

Mike hesitated. "We don't. Do you have a table for five?"

He sour face switched into a laugh as she counted out menus. "I'm only messing with you."

Mike exhaled. "Oh, thank God. I would never hear the end of it if you didn't."

"If everyone can follow me."

And everyone did as she asked. The restaurant was a ghost town, and the lack of people sent off alarms in his mind. That was until she placed them at the biggest table near the window. *I love window seats.*

A passerby in the storm caught his attention as their server arrived at the table. She towered over them in her tight white shirt and black pants. "Good evening everyone. My name is Katie, and I'll be taking care of you this evening. Would anyone care for something other than water?"

Everyone exchanged glances, but no one spoke a word. Except, as usual, Alex opened his mouth at the last minute. "I'll have a Coke, please."

She jotted it down in her notepad. "You need more time to decide on food?"

"I guess another five minutes, and we'll be ready."

She smiled, walked away, and disappeared into the kitchen.

Brandy rapped her fingers across the table, doing her best to grab their attention. "I have to say thanks for having me here. Granted, I wish none of the craziness was happening."

"We're glad you're here with us too," Amy said.

"I'm so happy I finally met Amy and John. It's about time I place a face with a name. In all seriousness, I feel as though I've known you both forever and thank you for keeping Alex fun-loving over the years."

Alex lifted his glass of water and launched into an impromptu speech. "Tonight, I toast those who I trust most: the four of you. Without you guys, I don't believe I'd have handled the drama in the background. For now: friendships first, bullshit later."

A few moments later, Katie returned with the Coke and jotted down their food orders. The conversation around the table was onto happier topics such as graduation and summer plans. Precisely what Alex desired to take his mind off of murder, mayhem, and lies for at least a little while.

An hour passed and everyone ate, laughed, and let go of their anxieties and enjoyed a fun night away from the boundaries of Alex's house. When the bill arrived at the table, Alex snatched it from his boyfriends' hand.

"You are not paying for this. I invited you guys out tonight. Therefore dinner is on me."

Amy hesitated, "Are you sure?"

"100 percent. This dinner is my way of thanking each of you for your support and reassurance these past two days. Dinner is the least I can do to pay you back."

"Well, thank you. That's sweet of you to pick up the tab. Next time it's on me," Amy promised.

Alex reached across the table and grabbed Amy's hand. "I insist. You save your money for the move. Remember, the moment the movers show up at your door, mommy and daddy will cut you off like that."

"You make a good point; my parents are a mess. They're cutting me off considering my father has to replace the stuff my mom breaks every week."

After Alex paid the bill, everyone congregated around the table and slipped on their jackets in preparation to re-enter the storm. The large meal weighed heavy on their stomachs and moving was slower than usual. They eventually made it to the main door where Mike approached the valet stand to retrieve his car.

Night had fallen on the sleepy suburban town, and with the unusual weather, the streets were eerily calm for a Thursday night. The natural scene of happy couples strolling along the avenue gawking at the shop windows replaced by flashes of lightning and ferocious winds that whipped down Fifth Avenue. The somberness garnered the attention of Alex who was already on heightened alert. *Something will happen; I can feel it.*

The valet driver pulled up in front of the restaurant and stepped out of the vehicle, dropping the keys in the palm of Mike's hand as he slipped the driver a five-dollar bill for his trouble. They piled one by one into the car. The storm reminded everyone it had no plans to end anytime soon with a thunderous clap of thunder. The lightning flashed so vibrantly they could make out the outline of the mountain range a few miles west. Once everyone buckled in, Mike peeled out and headed back towards Alex's house. The rain pounded the windshield as the wipers barely kept up with the flow of water that poured down upon them. Alex glanced over at the speedometer and grabbed ahold of the door handle.

"Slow down, Mike. How is it possible you can see far enough to be driving this fast?"

"Alex, I'm a trained professional at this. You realize I do this for a living. So, sit back and relax, we'll be ok. You worry way too much."

Alex tightened the seatbelt around his chest and stuck out his tongue. "I'm more worried about an animal darting out in front of you. You'd never intentionally hurt us."

As they waited at the traffic light at the corner of Mountain Pass and Valley View Boulevard, Alex gazed out the window to his right towards the 7-Eleven store. The same store which had injected a massive ripple in his life. The light changed to green, and Mike floored it through the intersection. Out of the corner of his eye, Alex saw the 7-Eleven and became entranced to the point he could focus on nothing else.

Eventually, the store faded from sight, and when he snapped to, the shimmering lights of their beautiful subdivision a quarter of a mile down the road came into view. A sense of relief rippled through his head knowing the safety of his home was imminent. The only thing they had to do was make it there in one piece, and everything would be fine.

The vehicle slowed as they approached the corner and when Mike hung the right-hand turn, Alex noticed the guard hadn't stepped out to greet them.

He touched Mike's hand. "Where's the guard? He's usually on it as soon a car turns in."

"He could be waiting for us to get closer. In case you missed it, it's pouring, and if I were him, I wouldn't stand out in this if I didn't have to."

"Excellent point."

The SUV came to a stop at the shack, and Mike prudently surveyed the window of the insignificant, brick building. There were no signs of movement, and Mike slowly reversed and stopped. The young officer reached across Alex's lap and unlatched the glove box.

"What's going on?" Alex asked.

Mike didn't reply and instead withdrew his service weapon. Alex gasped in fear.

"What the hell is that for?"

"Shh. Stay in this car, lock the doors, and whatever happens, do not unlock these doors except for me."

Alex reached his shaky hand across and grabbed ahold of Mike's forearm. "This doesn't feel right."

"I agree," Mike replied as he rested his free hand on top of Alex's, "but I have to go check."

Mike squeezed the door handle and propped the door open. The rain beat against his head as he exited the vehicle and he quickly lifted the hood of his jacket to block the wetness. He slammed the door shut and Alex pressed the lock button.

Amy tapped Alex on the shoulder. "He's probably in there sleeping."

"He's about to have one hell of a rude wake-up call when Mike shows up with a gun," John replied.

Alex ignored their attempt at defusing the tense situation with humor and kept his eyes fixated on his boyfriend.

12

WITH HIS GUN DRAWN, MIKE SLOWLY stepped from the vehicle and approached the guard shack. It didn't take long to see why the guard hadn't greeted them as he typically would. With a quick peek into the window, Mike found the older gentlemen's lifeless body face-down on the floor in a pool of blood.

Mike gently twisted the doorknob and poked his head in the building. With no sign of the attacker in sight, he moved attentively inside. His eyes wandered the blood-spattered walls and a drip from above plopped against his jacket. His fingers reached for the wet spot, and as Mike glanced down he jumped back; it was blood. His eyes shifted upward, and he gasped in disbelief at the volume of gore that coated the ceiling.

He carefully tip-toed into an adjacent room and sprawled out across the floor was the lifeless body of the guard. He stepped closer, crouched down, and squeezed his eyes shut as he reached for the guard's wrist to check for a pulse. Nothing. Mike pulled his hand away and opened his eyes before retreating as quickly as possible.

Without hesitation, he reached for his cell phone and called for help. He paced around the room as the phone rang. After the third ring, a nonchalant colleague answered. "Ridgewood Hills Police, Sergeant Rivers."

Mike's voice trembled, and he struggled to speak. The words fell from his mouth. "Rivers...it's Temple."

"Ah, Mikey. You seem off. Everything okay?"

Mike rambled without taking a breath. "We got a situation over here at the Apple Valley subdivision."

"Need a bit more information."

"There's been another murder. The guard's throat...it's gashed from side-to-side. Send help...now."

The mellow sergeant perked up right away. "Shit. I'll send help out right away...don't leave the scene unattended."

"Got it."

He fled the copper-filled air and once outside Mike bent forward, resting the palm of his hands against his knees. The rain pounded against his perfectly styled hair, and he drew in a few deep breaths. Once he collected his thoughts, he retreated to the Escalade and beat hard against the driver's side window.

Alex glanced up to discover his boyfriend, white as a ghost, running for the vehicle. He unlocked the door, and without speaking a word, Mike threw the SUV into drive, dodged the gate arm, and sped down the street.

"Where's the guard?"

Mike avoided glancing in his direction and continued driving. When he took the first corner, everyone shifted from one side of the car to the other.

"What's wrong—tell me what's going on."

"I need you to reach someplace where they won't find you."

Amy whimpered from the backseat. However, Alex was hell-bent on finding out details. "Where's the guard? Why aren't we safe?"

Mike slowed the vehicle and looked over at Alex. "The guard's dead. The police are on their way. I'm already breaking protocol by leaving the scene unattended. You guys are my number one priority right now."

The tires screeched against the wet pavement below, and Brandy asked, "How did he die?"

Mike found her question bizarre and didn't hold back when he answered. "Someone slit his throat from ear to ear. Looks like they tried to decapitate him."

The SUV screeched to a halt at the end of Alex's driveway, and everybody fled into the rain. John ushered Amy and Brandy to the front door, yet Alex hung back staring into his boyfriend's unnerved eyes. "Now what?"

"Go inside, set the alarm, and wait for me to come back," he began. "Do not, under any circumstances, open the door for anyone—you understand?"

"Yeah, I gotcha," Alex said.

He tried to walk away from the car until Mike grabbed his arm. "I love you."

Alex stopped and swung around. "I love you, too. Now go."

Mike remained at the edge of the driveway until everyone safely entered the darkened house and when everyone disappeared from sight, he whipped the SUV around and sped towards the crime scene. He should have stayed on the scene instead of driving Alex home. However, it was the right thing to do, and now there'd be hell to pay for his defiance of a direct order.

Inside, Amy dead bolted the door while Alex messed with the alarm. Oddly, it didn't beep when he walked in as it usually would. "I set the alarm when we left? Right?"

"Of course—I stood next to you when you did. Is it disarmed?"

"Yeah."

John approached the alarm panel. "The storm could have knocked out the power?"

Alex rubbed the back of his wet neck. "Wouldn't matter. Alarms on a back-up system for that exact reason."

Everyone gave the nearby rooms a look-over, and Brandy pointed out one critical flaw in John's theory. "Digital clocks aren't blinking. Sorry to kill your idea."

Panic set in. Alex paced around the foyer in wide circles. "Right. John and Amy, make sure every door, every window is locked."

The two who only yesterday wanted to kill each other exchanged glances and did what was necessary. Alex continued to pace.

Sensing they were leaving her out, Brandy cocked her hip to one side. "What can I do?"

"Help me by flipping on every light in this house."

She shadowed Alex as he first checked the foyer, then the living room. They inspected every access point between both spaces and found everything intact and secure.

"Looks okay in here," she said.

Alex, however, wasn't confident about that. "Looks can be deceiving."

Amy yelled from the kitchen, "Garage door and window are locked."

A second later John shouted, "Dining room is good as well."

Frantic with emotion, Brandy snapped and shouted, "I knew staying here was a terrible idea. Now here I am…trapped with the three of you while some psycho is on the loose murdering people."

Alex grabbed her and shook. "Get ahold of yourself."

But Brandy didn't calm down, and John also got in on the hysterics. "She's right. I refuse to stay here—I need to go home right now. If I stay, I'm as good as dead."

"You're both crazy," Amy said. "Let's sit down and talk this out."

John scoffed and stomped in the direction of the door. With both hands extended out, Alex jumped in front of John and blocked his passage. John charged, and Alex pressed hard against his chest. "Hold it. No one's leaving."

John disregarded his pleas, smacked Alex's hand away, and brushed past. "Whatever. I'm out."

"Isn't any safer out there than in here. There's no guard at the main gate, the police are probably taking their sweet time coming."

"I'll risk it."

Amy hurried to Alex's side. "Don't go. Stay. For me, please."

John paused and staggered back a step. "You promise me, right here, right now, nothing will happen to us in this house, and I'll stay."

Amy crept towards John who trembled. "I can't promise anything. What I can express is safety in numbers."

John stood unmoved.

Amy softly touched his shoulder. "Now, can we count on you to help us sweep the upstairs?"

"I can't go up there. It gives me the creeps."

"Fine. Brandy and John stay here, and we'll go check. If you hear us scream—run."

They tiptoed up the wooden staircase and disappeared into the blackness of the second floor. With each step, the floor beneath creaked, and when Alex reached the sixth step, a gust of air chilled the warm house. Paralyzed, they stopped, and Alex cocked his head slightly. "You feel that?"

With shaky knees, Amy bit at her usually polished fingernails. "No way in hell am I going up there. Sorry."

"Agree. Let's wait downstairs."

They scrambled downstairs faster than it took them to climb. Amy latched on to his arm and pulled him closer to her. "What do we do?"

Alex glanced up and saw John and Brandy whispering to one another in the brightly lit dining room. The rain pelting against the French doors muffled their footsteps as they approached the duo. A bright flash of lightning and rumble of the thunder scared John, and he glanced up to discover Amy and Alex in the archway.

Alex stepped into the dining room. "You find anything?"

"It's clear down here. What d'you find up there?"

"A draft."

John bit his lower lip. "Come again?"

"Air. The shit you breathe. It blew past while we were on the stairs. If someone's in this house, they're upstairs."

"Umm, why the hell are we still here?"

Alex shrugged. "Where else is there to go?"

"Anywhere except here. My house seems safer."

"Mike told us to stay *here*. Keep an eye on the staircase, so we aren't caught off-guard."

None of them spoke a word, instead focused their concentration on the flight of steps, expecting some masked intruder to leap out at the first chance they had. Yet, several minutes ticked by with zilch. That was until the grandfather clock sliced through the stillness and Amy jumped to her feet as it struck eight.

With everyone on edge, Alex employed one last-ditch effort to slow everyone's adrenaline coursing through their veins. "Here's the plan—we should stay, wait on Mike, and try to take our mind off of things. Dumb idea?"

John chimed in. "Completely dumb. I mean, is Mike even returning?"

Alex forced a fake smile. "Of course. Why wouldn't he?"

"Things could take a while is what I'm sayin'."

"Believe me—," Alex's phone rang mid-sentence. He glanced down, turned his back to his friends, and flipped open the phone immediately whispering into the receiver. "How's it going over there?"

"A disaster, as you'd expect."

"Has anyone shown up?"

"Crime scene unit and Detective Scott are here."

"Sweet! This means you'll be on your way back soon?"

"Yeah. I ought to drive home and change clothes though."

"Why?"

"The moment I touched the body I became evidence. Damn lab rats took my clothes, and I'm standing here in a jumpsuit."

Alex pictured him stripping down at the crime scene, but Mike's deep voice interrupted his image. "Are you guys safe?"

"Safe as we're gonna be."

"Not the right time to be sarcastic, Alex."

"I need to make a confession."

"Now? I should come back and protect you."

"Mike, it's serious. When I walked upstairs a few minutes ago a breeze blew past. I'm worried someone might be up there. Tell me I'm paranoid."

Another voice intruded, and after a few seconds passed Alex coughed to remind him he was still on the line.

"Sorry. Were you aware you have a second phone line in your house?"

"A what?"

"A second line. You had me trace the call you alleged was Heather."

"Right. Was it her?"

"Who knows? I can say with certainty is it came from a landline registered to your mother. The call came from inside your house."

The realization someone had been in the house swept over Alex, and his heart thumped in his chest. "I was here when the call came in. It was just me and Amy in the house. How can this be? Could someone in Forensics have made an error?"

"Our guys don't make errors. It is possible someone was in there."

Alex paced and his voice octave changed. "I can't stay in this house. Come rescue us."

"I'll be there in a few. You'll be safer at my apartment."

Goosebumps spread up Alex's arms, and he struggled to repress his escalating fear. His voice crackled. "Yeah, you think? Hurry."

Alex was about to end the call when a bright flash of lightning illuminated the sky and thunder shook the foundation of the house. The lights flickered, and the house went pitch-black.

"Shit."

"What?"

"We lost power."

Panic overtook Mike, and he raced for the SUV. "Yeah, we still have power here. Go grab a weapon, anything you can use to protect yourself."

"Mike…. I'm scared. Please—."

His plea ended mid-sentence and an earsplitting gun blast resonated through the house. Alex's breathing grew heavier and faster, but he kept quiet.

Mike shouted into the phone, however not another recognizable word crossed the line, instead only stifled cries. He stopped and listened closer. Two distinct masculine voices whispered in an unfamiliar language, and it was in that split-second, it dawned on him he should make haste.

Mike placed his free hand against his exposed ear and pressed the phone closer. The final thing he caught before the line died, was glass shattering across the floor.

Unsure what he'd find when he arrived, he closed his phone and continued running for this SUV. He raced past the detective and never spoke a single word.

He reached the vehicle and flung open the driver's side door, hopped in, and pulled forward. However, he slammed the SUV into drive, however, didn't make it far. Detective Scott stepped out into the street and blocked his path. Mike slammed on the brakes and lowered the window. "Move out of my way. I have to save Alex."

The detective approached the SUV. "Temple, what the hell?"

"Alex and his friends—they're in danger."

"How?"

"I was on the phone with Alex, I think he's in danger."

"How so?"

"There was a gunshot. Now move."

Detective Scott stepped aside and fumbled in his pocket to grab his keys. "I'll follow. Go."

Mike floored the gas pedal. He wasn't concerned that his over-sized gas guzzler ripped through the waterlogged lawns of the residents. With Detective Scott closer behind his sole concern was reaching Alex at whatever cost.

13

MIKE RACED ALONG OLD ORCHARD BOULEVARD. Given the flooding conditions, driving was more difficult than usual. He skidded to a stop, barely missing the rear of Alex's BMW in the driveway. Without hesitation, he stomped through the mud on the way to the back of the house. He reached the back corner as Detective Scott pulled up.

Mike reached around and drew his gun from his waistband. He sneaked a quick peek around the corner—no one in sight. He leaned against the brick exterior and paused until the detective caught up.

"Go. I'll cover your back."

Mike grunted, his eyes darting from side-to-side, and without warning, he swung around and shuffled, with his back pressed tight against the rear of the house. He remained as close and near to the ground as possible. There was an eerie calmness, yet as he reached the back gate, it changed.

Without hesitation, Mike charged the gate at full speed. With Detective Scott was fast on his tail he ignored their safety and proceeded without checking his surroundings.

Detective Scott's booming voice ripped through the still night. "Temple. Stop."

Mike stopped barely three feet inside the enclosure and curved his head around. "Jesus, I've fully lost my mind."

He pushed his hand hard against Mike's chest. "Fall behind before your emotions get us killed."

The detective stole the front-runner position, and they inched closer to the deck. With a quick flick of his wrist, Mike shined his flashlight in the direction of the French doors where tiny shards of glass shimmered in the moonless night.

"It doesn't look good," Mike whispered.

"Stay back."

Detective Scott headed for the house while Mike spun around to investigate an anomaly in the grass outside the fence. A fresh set of tire impressions led away and across the golf course.

"Scott. Wait."

The detective stopped and illuminated Mike's face with his flashlight. "What is it?"

Mike signaled with nothing more than a finger point.

"Appears we're too late," Detective Scott said.

They stepped closer to the imprints, undeterred with the fact Alex may well be dead on the floor inside until an excruciating scream disrupted their attention. They shifted around and without hesitation extended the barrels of their guns towards the house.

"The hell was that?" Mike asked.

No reply, instead, he watched Detective Scott advance up the small staircase, onto the deck, and before Mike understood what was happening, the detective was shining his flashlight inside the house from the French doors.

A voice cried out, "Please, somebody, help me."

Mike recognized it immediately and was confident the attackers were long gone. He stepped next to Detective Scott. "I know that voice."

"Who is it?"

"John Davidson. I think it's safe to enter."

With flashlights and guns drawn, they rushed into the room. The beams of light scanned the dark room and propped against the dining room wall was John, bleeding immensely from his shoulder.

Mike rushed to John's side. "Hang in there. Where's everyone else?"

"They're gone."

"Someone took them?"

John corroborated as Detective Scott removed his necktie and wrapped it above the wound as a tourniquet to lessen the bleeding.

"Did you catch a look at them?"

"No. It happened so fast. I remember the lights went out, and someone grabbed Amy. I tried to help—."

"Instead you took a bullet for your efforts?"

"Something like that."

Detective Scott pulled tightly as John yelled out in pain. "This should cut down the bleeding."

"Good. Can you call for help?"

"Yeah, I'll be right back."

Mike crouched next to John and did whatever he could to keep him distracted yet alert. "We'll find them; don't worry. I need you to relax until help arrives. Can you do that for me?"

John clenched his jaw together. "I'll try. Oh God, I don't want to die."

Mike squeezed his hand. "I'm not going to let you."

A moment later Detective Scott returned with the phone in his hand. "It's Hector, he wants to talk to you."

Mike lifted himself to his feet and took the phone from Scott. "Keep an eye on him, okay?"

Scott nodded and took over Mike's place on the floor so he could speak someplace more private. "Hector, what's up?"

"I've got paramedics en route. However, I need more information about the abducted individuals."

"Sure."

"Age, height, eye color, hair color."

"Yup. Alex is eighteen, six-two, brown hair, green eyes. Amy is also eighteen, approximately five-six, blonde hair, blue eyes. The other girl, Brandy, age unknown, is about five-four, brown hair, blue eyes."

"Got it. How's your shooting victim?"

Mike peeked around the corner. "He's alert and talking. However, he's lost a lot of blood. I'm worried he may go into shock soon."

"The medics should be there soon. I've left word to contact Captain Reed of the situation, so chances are good he may be heading your way."

"Thanks. I'm going to head back to John until help arrives."

"I hope it works out."

"Me too."

Mike ended the call. In the distance, the subdued sirens screamed noisier as the seconds elapsed. Mike returned to the floor on the opposite side and squeezed John's hand.

"I'm back. You still with me?"

John could barely form words. "Yeah…is help on the way? I feel dizzy."

"Stay with me. I realize you're in pain, but is there anything you can tell me about who took them?"

"Two men and a woman."

"Anything special about them? Did they say anything?"

John slumped forward in pain. "Yeah. I suppose they figured I was dead, and they spoke freely. They had Russian accents, like the people who perpetrated the 7-Eleven attack."

"Any idea about where they were going?"

"The girl mentioned a cabin in the mountains where no one would ever find them."

"Come on buddy. Anything else?"

John went out and back into consciousness. He picked up as if nothing happened. "One guy asked the woman how they'd escape with the cops around."

"Okay. How?"

"She mentioned a secret route and said she had a van waiting."

"A secret route? Scott, you know of any other exit out of here?"

"Nope."

John tugged at Mike's shirt. "I've heard her voice before. I don't remember where though. Damn, it was so familiar."

Before Mike could reply there was a thud at the front door. "Helps here."

Mike picked himself off the floor and dashed to the front door to allow the paramedics access. Two of them rushed in, kneeled next to John, and worked to stabilize him before they moved him to the awaiting ambulance outside.

After the initial assessment, the paramedics inserted an IV, hoisted John onto a stretcher, and wheeled him out the front door. Mike remained at his side the entire way to the ambulance which attracted unwanted attention from several of the neighbors.

Mike scanned the street, hopeful a face might stick out. Nothing. Mike stepped aside while they worked on preparing him for transport. And when the rear doors closed, a lightbulb went off in Mike's head on exactly how the suspects fled.

A year earlier the subdivision broke ground on another access point, however, after numerous residents filed lawsuits, construction halted, and the site lingered unstaffed. Mike, familiar with the shoddiness of the security company, figured it meant the spot went unpatrolled.

Sneaky bastards. These people must have been watching Alex for a while.

Once the ambulance pulled away from the scene, Mike ran up to Detective Scott. "I need to check something. Can you go back to the main entrance?"

"Where are you going?"

"Chasing a hunch."

Detective Scott sighed. "Fine. Go. I'll wait here for someone to secure this crime scene."

Mike hopped into the Escalade, cranked over the engine, and flew at full speed along flooded Old Orchard Boulevard. With one hand on the steering wheel, his free hand clung to his cell phone. He dialed his captain's number as the car curved sharply onto Cherry Lane.

A few rings later and the captain answered with gruff in his voice. "Temple? This better be damn good to call so late."

Mike stuttered. "You haven't heard?"

"What?"

"There's been a murder and three students abducted from the Evergreen Gardens Subdivision."

"Not possible."

"Oh, extremely possible. Though, I believe I uncovered how the abductors avoided detection. I'm en route to follow a hunch."

"A hunch? Hold on, Temple, I got another call—."

The captain swapped over, and Mike tightened his eyes, battling to catch sight of the roadway through the blinding rain. Seconds ticked by and at last, the boss returned.

Straight to the point, Captain Reed dug in. "You failed to mention one of them was your boyfriend."

"Didn't see how it made a difference. But, yes, Alex was kidnapped."

Captain Reed exercised restraint in lashing out. "Where are you now?"

"Heading to the unfinished entrance they were building off Apache Center. If my instinct is correct, that's where they eluded us."

"Good. Evaluate the scene and when you've finished, report to the main entrance of the subdivision in twenty minutes."

"Yes, sir. Twenty minutes."

The captain cut off the call, and Mike threw his phone into the cup holder. Determined, he applied harder pressure against the gas pedal and when the asphalt change over to gravel, he knew he was closer.

The unfinished frame of a new guard building grew nearer, and before he drove too much further into the evidence, he stomped hard on the brake, shifted the car into park, and left the high-beams on. He snatched his flashlight from the passenger seat and departed the Escalade. After a few strides, he discovered tire treads which were similar to those found at Alex's trailing off into the uninhabited horizon.

I was right. Son of a bitch.

Mike reverted to the vehicle and fetched a camera from the glove box. He snapped a few shots of the tracks, considering the rain would ultimately wash away any trace they were ever there.

With a few photos taken, Mike drove towards the main entrance. The entire way he reflected on the clues Alex dropped over the previous thirty-six hours. The 7-Eleven, Kelli Burgess, the white van, and the unexplained Russian letters he discovered—while none of it added up at the time, Mike grasped if he had any chance of rescuing Alex, he'd have to decipher how everything connected on a larger scale.

Mike found his mind consumed with wicked thoughts the entire seven-minute drive to the main entrance. He reached his breaking point and slammed both hands against the steering wheel. With the one person he loved more than life itself in danger, his predictable imperturbable mood changed to one of aggravation in a matter of seconds.

He came up to the point where his nightmarish night originated and found the mobile command post established and a hive of commotion. Mike parked behind an unmarked squad car and hoped Detective Scott hadn't left for the hospital yet. The unrelenting rain hadn't let up, and as he stepped onto the flooded pavement, Mike pulled his waterproof hood over his head.

He caught sight of Detective Scott speaking with the crime scene supervisor under the canopy and made a bee-line in his direction before Captain Reed got to him first.

Detective Scott lifted his head. "What the hell, Temple? Where have you been?"

"I found their escape route."

Scott's eyes widened. "How? Where?"

"Apache Center. Found the same tire treads we saw in the yard."

Detective Scott smacked his hand against the table. "Damn. And from that point, they could be anywhere by now."

Mike paced. "They've got at least a good thirty-minute head start."

"The Davidson boy mentioned a cabin in the mountains."

"Yeah, and since the mountains are to the left, it's reasonable to guess they're traveling west."

"I'll have forensics order a GPS trace on their phones. We won't have their exact location; however the cell towers they ping off can help narrow it down."

Their conversation withered when Mike spotted a tall, lean, older gentleman exiting an unmarked black SUV. He nudged Detective Scott, and the two men fidgeted as the man approached.

"Good evening, gentlemen. Officer Temple, a moment?"

Detective Scott raised both hands in front of him and backed away, leaving Mike alone with the captain.

"First, sir, I'm sorry I didn't call earlier—"

The man raised his index finger to his lips, motioning for Mike to stop talking. "Two questions."

Mike remained motionless and allowed the man to continue.

"We've had five murders in two days, that's more than we usually have in a year. Can you tell me what the hell is happening around here?"

"Sir—."

The captain shook his head disapprovingly. "Let me finish. Second, how long have you known any details?"

With smugness in his face, Mike replied. "Can I answer now?"

"Don't be a smart-ass. Just answer the questions."

"I have no idea what's going on. And, yes, Alex revealed yesterday about a white van like the one used in the 7-Eleven homicides following him around."

"And you didn't think that was enough of a reason to—."

Detective Scott interrupted. "Captain, with all due respect, sir, you can't fault Temple."

"And why not?"

"He's done an excellent job providing me with information. Yet, sir, you can't expect us to take four teenagers at their word. Hell, for all we know they concocted some fantasy story in their minds."

"I guess not, Scott, though a heads-up would have been nice."

Mike stuttered. "Sir, I had no idea any of it was linked until tonight at dinner. C'mon, captain, you've known me long enough to discern I relay information when I'm confident it's true. How was I to know any of these events would lead up to tonight's main event?"

Scott placed his hand on Mike's shoulder. "No one would have."

Captain Reed pointed his finger sternly at both of them. "We'll discuss this later. Right now, we've got four missing teenagers to find."

Mike moved to follow him, and Detective Scott yanked on his jacket sleeve. "Man, let it go. Don't poke the bear unless you're prepared for the bite."

Mike exhaled. "You're right. Will you do me a favor?"

"Sure."

"Will you fill him in on everything John explained to us?"

"Of course. And mention how he recognized the female kidnapper's voice."

Captain Reed overheard Mike giving details to the detective, and he swung around and snapped. "How does any of this help us now, Temple?"

"For the fact, a witness told us where they were taking them."

The captain pinched the bridge of his nose. "Go home, change, take a breather, and be back in an hour."

"I don't need a break, sir. We need to find them."

"No excuses. You're a mess, and with the media on the way, I need my officers to look fresh."

"But. I should be up in the chopper searching."

The captain choked on a laugh. "With this weather? Temple, it'll be hours before we get one up."

Without argument, Mike gave in. "Yes, sir, I'll be back."

He stomped away and piled into his Escalade. Before he drove away, Mike twisted the knob to the radio and immediately a well-known *Faith Hill* song blared from the country station Alex left it on. It took every ounce he had to keep it together, so he pressed his back firmly against the leather seat, rested his head, and listened to the lyrics. Tears welled in his eyes, however, sucked back the mucus as it dripped from his nose and wiped away the wetness from his face. There was no time to sulk, not while Alex was missing.

He pulled away and drove until he reached the end where it intersected with Valley View Boulevard. With the road deserted, he hung a left and zoomed off into the darkness.

Time was critical and following the speed limit was out of the question. The bright lights of the city limits came into view, and he stopped at the traffic light with the 7-Eleven off to his left.

His eyes fixated on a single fragment of yellow crime scene tape and as it flapped in the wind, and his mind revisited yesterday morning when he reconnected with Alex after such an extended break.

He lowered the music and shouted. "They knew he'd be there and waited until the right moment to strike. How'd I miss this?"

The traffic light changed, and he veered right. Two minutes later he pulled into his assigned parking space at his apartment complex. He yanked back the emergency brake, opened the door, and sprinted for his front door.

After he inserted his key, the deadbolt unlocked, and he pressed the door open. Once inside, he stripped away his soaked clothes and tossed them next to the washer. Alex reached for the light switch in his bedroom as he stood in nothing except his underwear and undershirt. The first thing to catch his eye was a photo of him and Alex from Vail sitting in a four-by-six frame on his desk.

He reached down and picked it up with both hands. He ran his right hand across the smooth glass and struggled to keep his emotions in check.

"I realize I'll never win 'boyfriend of the year,' but I'll do whatever it takes to bring you home safely."

He set the frame down and moved into the closet to grab a fresh uniform. He tossed it onto the bed and stopped and stared. "I need to stop giving work more priority over everything in my life."

With his emotions expressed, he stepped into the bathroom and cranked the shower to the hottest setting. "Wherever you are, Alex, I'm coming for you."

14

MILES AWAY, CAROL JONES PACKED UP to head home. After Alex left her earlier, she spent the rest of her day checking on patients, which left no time to check voicemails. Dr. Jones locked her office door and walked along the calm corridor towards the elevator. As she passed the nurse's station, the overnight RN waved. "See you in the morning."

She flicked her wrist and checked her watch. "So soon?"

The nurse replied. "I hate being the bearer of crappy news."

Carol lifted her head and sighed as the elevator door opened. "Don't we all. Well, have a wonderful night, Julie."

She pressed P5 on the keypad and the doors closed. *I'm so lazy.*

The elevator doors opened onto the fifth floor of the parking garage, and an eerie sensation fell upon her. She scanned the empty garage and clutched her purse tighter against her body. Her high-heels clacked against the concrete. Still, she couldn't shake the uneasiness like someone stalked her every move. Carol paused, did a three-sixty, and found nothing to give her cause for alarm. Her SUV was a mere thirty-feet away, and she moved quicker towards safety.

She rummaged through her purse, pulled out her keys, and her hand trembled as she rubbed her finger across the key fob in search for the unlock button. The car beeped, lights flashed, and she flung open the door. Tossing her purse into the passenger seat, Carol locked the doors and rested her head against the back of the seat.

With her eyes closed, Carol took a few calming breaths before she cranked over the car. She slumped in the leather seat and relished the solace of comfort for the first time in hours. Her fleeting moment of pleasure ended when the barrel of cold metal pressed against her face.

She opened her eyes; the sound of metal-on-metal clanking kept her frozen in the seat. A soft female voice whispered from the backseat. "Do what I say, and I won't kill you."

Carol kept both hands on the steering wheel. "I'll do whatever you say. Please don't hurt me, I have a son at home."

"I'm aware. We've been looking for both of you for a long time."

Carol's voice quivered. "Why are you searching for us?"

"For vengeance. You can thank your piece of a shit husband for everything."

Carol glanced up in the rearview mirror and could distinguish a black mask, the attacker was white, had blue eyes, and bright white teeth. "He's been dead for thirteen years. Why now?"

"Keep your eyes forward. You believe you lost someone important—well, I lost someone more important. Now get us the hell out of here."

"Okay. Okay. If I were you, I'd fade. Security sees you with a gun to my head, he'll alert the police."

The intruder lowered the gun and warned, "I'm watching you. No sudden moves or you and the security guard will regret it."

Carol drove down the ramps and arrived on the ground level. She pulled up to the gate where a young, attractive guard in his mid-twenties stood at the flashing gate arm. Before she arrived, he stepped out of the tiny building and waved. She lowered the window and stopped inches from the barrier.

"Good to see you, Dr. Jones. Late night, huh?"

"You have no idea, Joe. Unfortunately, it's not over yet."

"Sorry to hear that. Well, I won't hold you up. Can I get you to input your code, so I can get you on your way?"

Carol reached out the window and typed in her six-digit code. "Thanks, Joe. I'll see you tomorrow night."

"Drive safe."

Carol drove through the exit and regained her composure. The reality of an assailant behind her weighed as their piercing eyes studied her every move. Her palms clammed up as each silent second passed. Once a safe distance from the hospital, the muzzle of the gun tapped her against the neck, and an all too familiar voice resonated from the backseat.

"At least you were honest about one thing, Denise—it will be a long night for you *and* Marshall."

Her mouth gaped open. "How do you know our names? What do you want with us?"

"Robert Stahl, your husband, sent my father to jail many years ago. Yeah, sure, I had visitation privileges at the federal pen. You tell me what sort of life is that for a child? Huh?"

Carol stayed silent and listened.

"I was barely old enough to remember him. Then your husband lies in court, and they convict my father for things he didn't do."

"Your father is Yerik Smirnov?"

The silence in the car persisted until the kidnapper spoke. "*Was* my father. An inmate from a rival gang murdered him a year into his thirty-year sentence."

In a hushed tone, Carol reacted, "I'm so sorry. I didn't know."

"You're not sorry. While my father rotted away in prison, you and your son lived a posh life. New names, new identities, new everything. And for poor me, you ask; first I lose my father, and eighteen days later I lost my mother to suicide. I had to spend my entire childhood in the foster care system until I ended up in Ridgewood Hills."

Carol gasped. "Jesus. I don't know what to say, except it was the government's decision, not mine. Whatever my husband did, or didn't do, that's in the past. Not once did I ask questions, for the simple fact, I never wanted any of this to catch up with us."

"You're using the 'I didn't know' card, huh?"

Carol bit her lip and paced back-and-forth. "I'm not. I never once questioned what Robert was into."

The hooded-figure scoffed. "Well, now I got you, and there's not a damn thing you can do. You have two choices to end this. One, give us what we asked for weeks ago, or two, we'll kill you, your son, and anyone who tries to stop us. It's your decision."

Without warning the abductor scrambled over the center console and plopped in the passenger seat. She kept her face concealed with the mask and hood; however, her voice was something Carol knew although she couldn't pinpoint where from.

Carol tensed up with having a gun pointed at her while she zoomed through the green lights. Every few minutes she glanced into the passenger seat, praying for a peek at the unsettled soul next to her. The moment she waited for came. Her abductor pulled back her hood and yanked off the mask obscuring her face. And it hit her. The person holding her hostage was no stranger. In fact, it was someone she never imagined in a million years capable of this.

Now unmasked, she whispered. "Surprise, bitch."

Carol gripped the steering wheel tighter and swerved out of her lane. "You'll never get away with this."

15

MIKE STEPPED OUT OF THE SHOWER. A quick five-minutes was the refreshment he needed. Unlike Alex, who spent at least ten minutes fixing his hair, Mike never required over ten to do everything. He wiped his bare hand across the mirror and strained to glimpse his reflection through the fogginess. Worn-out and disheveled were perhaps the friendliest way his captain could have described his appearance. How he looked was by far the least of his worries at the moment.

Where do I even look for them?

After applying lotion, he strutted naked into the bedroom and threw on fresh undergarments before suiting up.

He finished and walked out the door within fifteen minutes after his shower. Not knowing who was out there, he double-checked under the frame and in the backseat of the SUV before he unlocked the doors.

He slipped back into the warm seat, backed out of his space, and trepidation filled his mind at the long, grueling evening looking for Alex.

The rain fizzled into a light mist, and Mike glanced up at the sky. "Maybe now we can send up a helicopter?"

His continuous journey soon ended when he found himself caught at the dreaded stoplight in town which forever switched to red when he approached. Other than the purr of the engine, at the moment, life was peaceable. The calmness ceased when his cell phone rang from the passenger seat. Worried it might be Alex he reached over, picked it up, and without checking answered. "Alex?"

"Ah, the renowned Mike Temple, I suppose?"

"Who's this?"

"Let me cut to the chase—I have your precious boyfriend, and if you ever want to see him again, you'll do what I say."

"What have you done with them?"

"They're safe…for now. If you tell anyone about this conversation, they'll die. If you deviate from the route, they're dead. Understand?"

"Why are you doing this?"

"You'll find out soon enough. We're tracking your location, and we've cloned your cell phone to guarantee you're not speaking to anyone."

Mike pulled onto the gravel shoulder. "Who the hell is this?"

"I know you're going back to the crime scene, don't. Stay on Valley View until the road dead-ends at Highway 36. Take a left, drive into Lyons, and await further instructions."

"No way will I take you at your word. I want proof they're still alive."

"Not possible. I'm not someone you want to cross. Now drive and contact no one. Their lives rest in your hands."

Mike conceded. "Fine, I'm on the way."

Mike threw the phone back into the passenger seat and churned up gravel as he whipped back onto the asphalt. He turned his head as he drove past the subdivision headed into the dark Colorado night towards Highway 36.

The lonesome car ride gave him time to rethink leaving Alex alone in his house, and the belief this was his fault made him angrier at himself than the kidnappers. The anonymous called left him on edge, yet when he boiled it down, what other choice did he have in the matter?

ONE HOUR AND EIGHTY MILES LATER, Alex lifted his head and struggled to open his swollen eyes. His head ached, and as he went to touch his forehead, he discovered his hands bound to an unknown chair. Alex wiggled his extremities until he exerted what drop of energy he had left and then gave up.

He about missed the blurry figure in the distance walking straight at him. The closer they came, the heavier his breathing got. He turned his head away, hoping to avoid eye contact.

The man reached down, clenched his fingers around Alex's cheeks, and rotated him until their eyes met. The stench of stale tobacco radiated from him and Alex coughed.

"Your boyfriend better show; otherwise you and your friend won't see tomorrow's sunrise."

A droplet of blood fell onto Alex's button-down shirt, and his bottled-up anxiety unleashed. "What do you want from me? I can't help if I have no clue what you want."

"Payback."

"For what?"

The man walked around, wielding the gun like a plaything. "Do you have any idea how your father fucked us over?"

Alex stuttered, "I—I don't."

The man pressed the gun to the side of Alex's head. "I lost everything thanks to him."

The tension grew, and without holding back, Alex blurted out. "He's been dead for over half of my life. Besides, he did what he considered right. You ever consider if you weren't doing those illegal dealings, your life might have had a different outcome?"

The man gritted his teeth, glanced away, and without warning struck Alex across the face with the butt of the gun. "You're not running the show here. I am."

Alex exhaled in short bursts and unleashed a slew of profanities. "Fine, you're in charge. Got it."

The man yanked at his black leather jacket and stomped away without saying one more word. The door thumped shut, and the adrenaline pumped through his veins, Alex attempted to break free again from the restraints.

A fleeting five seconds was what he had in him before he exhaled in defeat. He hung his head, and a sweet, recognizable voice whispered from behind. "Save your strength, Alex. I tried for thirty minutes and nothing. We're stuck."

"Amy? Is that you?"

"Yeah. Are you hurt?"

"Um, there's blood running down my face, so I'll go out on a limb and say yes."

"Not the right time to be a smart ass. Help me come up with a plan on how we're getting out of this one."

Alex remained silent and allowed himself time to focus on how they'd escape this one. Several scenarios raced through his mind, none of which seemed possible given he wasn't confident he'd get past the thug.

He cocked his head to the left and whispered. "I'm sorry for getting you mixed up in this. I don't know how, but I'm getting us out of here alive."

His vision adjusted and off to his right, he glimpsed an unlit fireplace along the wall.

Alex remembered. "Have you seen Brandy? Or John?"

"Now that you mention it…I haven't."

"Shit. They're most likely dead. Whoever these people are, they aren't playing."

"Ya think?" Amy asked.

"There's no way my father did anything to rationalize any of this killing and kidnapping."

"And you swear you have no idea what they want?"

"If I did, I doubt we'd be in this predicament."

"Fair enough."

The man reentered the room, and they remained still as the man gave them a look-over. He grunted and walked away, and Alex hindered his exit. "Excuse me."

"What?"

"I wanted to say sorry about earlier. I'm not sure what my father did, or took from you, but can I ask a favor?"

The man advanced closer yet didn't speak.

"I'm freezing, and I hoped you had concern enough to build a fire for us."

"Why would I do anything for you?"

"You don't have to. I leave you with this. You are mad at my father, not me or her. When I watched my father's assassination, I was five—what could a five-year-old have done to deserve this? You don't want us to die of hypothermia...do you?"

The man weighed Alex's argument and without saying a word walked to the fireplace and threw a few logs in. "You make a valid point. I shouldn't do this since...eh, what the hell. I suppose you should feel comfortable in your final hours on earth."

The man kneeled down at the fireplace, and within a few moments, it roared to life. He huffed as stepped towards the door. "You're welcome."

After the door closed, and the deadbolt clanked, the heat from the fireplace melted away his shakes. Instead of worry about whether the Russian goons or the hypothermia would kill him first, he could now redirect his energy into finding a way out of the jam he was in.

Think...think.

An idea came to him. "I need your help."

"What?"

"When I say go, lift your chair off the ground with your legs and move towards the fireplace."

"How hard did that guy hit you? No way—they'll kill us."

"Trust me."

She moved her head up and down like a bobblehead. "Psh, you see where trusting you got me. Besides, didn't he say Mike is coming?"

Her utterance prodded his last nerve. "I'm not gonna wait for them to return and do God knows what to us. Nope. I'm going out with a fight."

"We should wait for Mike. He could bring back-up with him."

"They're lying. He's not coming to save us. If you want to live to see New York, I suggest you stop being naïve and help me."

Reluctant, Amy spoke. "I hope you know what you're doing."

Skeptical about his plan, Alex counted down from ten. He needed to make this work given the limited amount of options at his disposal.

"Three…two…one."

They labored to ascend on the first go, yet Alex had to make his plan work. "Again."

And again, they counted down, and on the second attempt, they inched closer to the hearth where the intense fire blazed only a few feet away.

"I hope whatever thoughts going through your head will save us," she moaned.

"You've always trusted me, and right now I need you to give me every ounce of trust you can give."

Twenty seconds passed, and they made it to the hearth. They lowered the legs of the chair onto the ground as quiet as possible.

Amy exhaled. "We did it…we actually did it."

"I told you we would."

CAPTAIN REED STOOD BENEATH THE CANOPY and searched the surrounding area for Detective Scott. Within the mist, he spotted him talking with a crime scene tech in the distance. He moved a few steps forward and shouted. "Scott. Can I see you for a second?"

The detective raised his finger and finished the conversation. With swift strut, he trotted over. "Sir?"

"Not to sound panicky, but has Temple reached out to you?"

Scott cocked his head and drummed his index finger against his lips. "In fact, no, I haven't spoken with him in a while."

"This isn't like him."

Scott shook his head in agreement.

The captain dug into his pocket and retrieved his phone. A few taps and he brought the phone against his ear. Voicemail. He pressed end and paused a few seconds before dialing once more. Again, straight away to voicemail.

Confused he squinted at the detective. "I've got an awful feeling about this."

"About what?"

Captain Reed pretended he didn't hear the dumb question. "Do me a favor. Take a ride over to his place and see what's going on. Okay?"

"10-4, captain."

Detective Scott rushed away to the unmarked Crown Vic, and after a minute he revved the engine and sped away.

As Captain Reed watched the car drive out of sight, he looked down at the phone in his hand and dialed again. Not to Mike, instead, he called the station house. Two rings and a familiar, masculine voice answered.

"Ridgewood Hills Police, Robert speaking."

"Damn, you're still there?"

"Yeah, with everything going on I'm pulling a double. Is there something I can help with?"

"There is. I hope there's someone from the crime lab around. It's urgent."

Robert stuttered. "I'm, n-not sure, sir. Give me a sec, and I'll take a look."

"Thanks."

A trendy, upbeat pop song performed in elevator style traded places with the quietness, and in disgust, Reed yanked the phone away from his ear.

Three minutes passed, and the gruff voice came back to the line. "Sir, Director Stevens is in his office. I'll transfer you if that's okay."

"Perfect. And hey, don't stay too late."

"I won't. Hang tight a minute."

The phone rang once. "Stevens."

"Stevens, it's Captain Reed. I need a favor."

He sighed. "Kind of tied up right now."

"Aren't we all? Officer Mike Temple isn't answering his phone, and I hoped you would run a trace."

"I can't promise anything."

"And why not?"

"I mean, if he's still on the analog system, it's a different story. What's his number?"

Reed spewed out the ten-digit number and caught the sound of the pen scratching against the paper. The line remained silent for a few seconds.

"Sir, don't we need a warrant? I mean, we're invading his privacy."

"If I wanted a sermon on Fourth Amendment violations, I'd have called a lawyer. I'm calling you since we don't have time for red-tape. Can you run the damn trace or not?"

Stevens murmured. "Of course, I can."

"Then do it; I'll take the heat later."

"It'll take time. I'll call back the moment I have an update."

Frustrated, he scoffed. "I'll be waiting."

The moment he ended the call his phone rang in his hand. Annoyed he answered with disdain. "Reed."

"Captain Reed?"

"Yeah, who's this?"

"Ah, this is Sergeant Simpson from the Denver Police."

"Denver? And you need me?"

"Yes, sir. Are you acquainted with Dr. Carol Jones from Ridgewood Hills?"

"I am. We're working a crime scene at her house right now."

"Well, hospital security called to inform us she used her distress code when she left this evening."

Captain Reed paced in a small circle. "First someone kidnaps her son, now she's using her distress code. Did hospital security give you anything worthwhile?"

"Nope. The guy claimed she was normal, calm, and the two chatted like it was a typical evening."

"Have you issued a BOLO on her vehicle?"

"We have, however, no sightings yet."

"And have you clarified that if someone spots the car not to stop it? I need no one else to lose their life."

"Captain, I made it crystal-clear; officers are to follow and report, nothing more."

"Good. We need not spook anyone."

"Indeed. If I hear anything I'll be in touch or if you need additional resources, call me."

"Sounds like a plan. We're good on manpower, now if that changes, you'll be the first call I make."

Reed closed the cover of his Nextel two-way and stopped in time to catch the medical examiner zip closed the body bag which held the corpse of the evening's first victim.

16

MIKE'S SUV ROLLED TO A STOP at the junction of Colorado 66 and U.S. 36. He waited for the light to change, and as he predicted, his cell phone rang on cue.

Right on time. "Yeah?"

"I guess you *can* follow instructions."

"I'm tired of playing games. Let me talk to Alex."

"Eh, he's still out."

"Out of it?"

"We had to drug him. I mean, how else could we move three teenagers and keep them quiet?"

"I swear to God if you'd hurt him in any—."

"Don't make idle threats. I will slash his throat in a heartbeat."

Mike took a deep breath, exhaled, and continued. "No, shit, I'm sorry…okay? Just tell me what my next move is."

"Take a left onto sixty-six, drive for thirty minutes. I'll call back when you're on the outskirts of Estes Park."

The anonymous caller ended the call as the light changed to green. Alone on the road, Mike stared at the phone until a motorist pulled up behind him and laid on the horn. With no other option, Mike swung left onto the dark two-lane highway heading into Lyons.

He couldn't shake away the unsettled belief the unknown left in his mind. With no clue what he was driving into, he kept one hand on the wheel, and with his free hand retrieved his service weapon strapped to his ankle.

With the cold steel in his hand, he set it beside his phone in the passenger seat. Learning in the academy how to handle this exact situation, Mike knew they'd search him the moment he arrived. The last thing he wanted was to provide the kidnappers with his weapon.

He reached across the center console, unlatched the glove box., and slid the Glock inside. Without taking his eyes off the road, he slammed the flap closed and exhaled.

I sure hope somebody realizes I'm missing. Otherwise, this won't end well.

***

BACK IN RIDGEWOOD HILLS, CAPTAIN REED'S fumbled to grab his ringing cell phone from his pocket. It was Detective Scott.

"About time. Anything?"

"I can't tell if he's been here. Every light in the apartment are off, and I've knocked and knocked, but there's no answer."

"Any signs of foul play? Forced entry?"

"None, sir. Do you want me to break the door in?"

"Stand down, detective. I need you back here."

"You have an update?"

"Denver P.D. called."

"Denver? This can't be good."

"They believe someone has kidnapped Dr. Jones or is forcing her to do something against her will."

"How would they know?"

"Sergeant Simpson said she punched in her distress code when she left the hospital."

"Wait. Distress code? I'm so confused."

"Scott, she works in one of the securest hospitals in the area. For the safety of the staff, every doctor must enter a code when they leave each day for incidents such as this."

The dots lined up in the detective's mind. "Shit—guess this means they have Mike too."

"Glad to see we're on the same page. See you in a few."

Detective Scott stood at the doorway of Mike's apartment in disbelief. He sprinted to the Crown Vic and peeled out of the parking lot toward Apple Valley Country Club.

***

A SHORT TEN MILES AHEAD on the same desolate mountainous road, Carol and her kidnapper drove along in utter silence. Carol peeked to her right in the exact moment the street light illuminated the gun, a reminder from above it was still there, pointed at her.

Tired of the quiet, Carol dug deep for the courage to speak. "You realize you'll never go scot-free."

"I've calculated this down to the last detail over the last year. Oh, trust me, I'll walk away, and do you know why?"

Carol shook her head.

"You're going to give me what I want, or everyone will die. It's as simple as that. I've read enough forensic books to appreciate how to murder each of you and never leave a trace."

"Everyone? What do you mean?"

"Oh, didn't I mention we have Alex, his friends, and there'll be a surprise visit from Officer Temple?"

"You cold-hearted bitch. They have nothing to do with any of this. Leave them alone."

"Too late—the wheels of revenge are already in motion."

"I can't believe I worried about you. We're you safe? I hoped you hadn't met the same fate as the others."

"Awe. You did?"

"Yeah, but boy was I wrong. Shit, you deserve a Golden Globe for your stellar performance in this drama."

"Just playing a part. I had to gain Alex's trust so I could get close to—." The kidnapper's cell phone rang.

She tried hard not to eavesdrop, but with her captor screaming in Russian, it was hard to drown it out. Carol exhaled and channeled her energy on her late husband. What would he have done in this situation? Although it was his job to be a mean, ruthless, son-of-a-bitch, none of it should have ever got her into the mess she found herself. Ultimately, his hard-heartedness thrust her into the twisted life of the FBI, and a year later it also consumed Alex.

Somewhere along the line, the Marshal Service failed them considering Carol found herself alongside the spawn of a Russian mobster, a reality thirteen years ago she never imagined she'd deal with again.

Thoughts shuffled in her head, and she considered her options on how to break away. She was unsure since any abrupt move placed not just her life in danger, but Alex's too. The risk was too much and downright insane. There was no need to make a dire situation any graver.

***

CAPTAIN REED OVERSAW EVIDENCE COLLECTION, AS he stood beside the guard shack. The fast-moving clouds whizzed by and sidetracked his concentration. As he glanced up at the sky, the full moon peeked through the broken clouds. In the distance, the sound of squealing tires disrupted his focus, and as he turned his head, Detective Scott drove erratic down the lane.

Christ, he's back.

He flicked his wrist and glanced at his watch. With no word from Stevens, his impatience grew, and as his nostrils flared, his cell phone buzzed. He dug into his pocket, pulled out the phone, and looked at the caller ID. His face relaxed, and he answered.

"About damn time, Stevens. You got good news for me?"

"With all due respect, sir, it takes time to retrieve this information. You recognize this isn't an episode of *Law & Order.*"

"Thanks for the reminder. Now tell me what you found out before I lose my cool."

"I've located Officer Temple."

"Yeah? And? Where is he?"

"Outside of Lyons."

"Lyons? Lyons? Isn't that thirty minutes north of here?"

"It is."

"Why would he be up there?" Captain Reed asked.

"Can't answer that. I gave you what you needed, what you do with it is up to you. Anything else, sir? I got evidence piling up and won't process—."

Captain Reed interrupted. "I need the same for Dr. Jones."

"I assume Dr. Carol Jones?"

"Yes, smart ass. Call once you have an answer."

He ended the call without a goodbye and walked back inside the trailer. Once inside officers and detectives were standing around a large table with a regional map sprawled out.

"Can I have your attention? We've been able to place Temple in Lyons fifteen minutes ago. If my hunch is right, I imagine he'll drive into Estes Park fifteen minutes from now."

Detective Scott spoke up. "I'll speak with the locals and get them out in full-force."

"No. Wilson, you call the locals. Scott, you're with me."

Everyone whipped into action and Reed, and Scott stepped out of the trailer into the nippy air.

"I'm waiting on Stevens to call back."

"You are?"

"He's running a trace on Dr. Jones. Once it comes back, I need you ready to go."

Scott pulled his jacket collar closer to his neck. "Yes, sir. I can do that."

Captain Reed stood under the canopy while Detective Scott walked away to take a call. From the corner of his eye, Captain Reed saw headlights shine down the lane. He detected a glossy-black, unmarked SUV with U.S. Government plates creep along and hunted for Detective Scott. He found him engrossed in a heated conversation, so he refocused on the approaching SUV.

It stopped shy of the gate, and two tall, broad-shouldered, corn-fed Midwestern men dressed in black wool trench coats stepped out. The taller man was white, middle-aged, no older than forty-five. His counterpart was younger, late-twenties max.

The grew closer, and Captain Reed processed scenarios in his head. *Who are these guys? Why are they at our crime scene?*

He squeezed his eyes closed, twice, hopeful if this were some gruesome dream he'd wake up. But after ten seconds, he opened them to find the agents flashing their badges at one of his officers handling the sign-in roster.

Detective Scott glanced up, saw the two men, and finished his phone conversation. He rushed to his superiors' side in time for the older man to display his badge. "United States Marshal Service. Who's in charge?"

Captain Reed stepped forward and pointed at himself. "That would be me."

The older man slid his badge into his pocket, stepped closer, yet didn't say another word.

"You guys seem lost," Scott said.

"Are you investigating a crime scene at the Jones residence?" the younger agent asked.

"Let's try this; I'm Captain Reed, and this is Detective Scott. And you are?"

The two men exchanged glances before answering. "Sorry, I'm Special Agent Tanner, and this is Special Agent Miller."

"Now that we got that clear, why are you interested in the Jones'?"

"Carol and Alex Jones are our responsibility."

"How so?" Detective Scott asked.

"That's classified, sir."

"Since they're both missing, I'd disclose what you have knowledge of, and if you're lucky, we'll do the same. How does that sound?"

The older agent spoke. "Um, is there someplace more secure?"

Captain Reed stepped aside and waved his hand towards the trailer. The agents walked ahead of Reed and Scott, opened the door, and stepped inside. As the last one to enter, Reed slammed the door closed, and the buzz of activity screeched to a halt.

"I need everyone to vacate. I'm Agent Tanner with the U.S. Marshals. And we need to hold a confidential conversation."

The support staff gathered their belongings, and without a word, marched for the door. When the last staffer exited, Reed motioned for the two agents to take a seat at the rectangular table.

The last officer exited, and the door slammed closed. "Now talk."

"In 1986, Special Agent Robert Stahl worked out of the Denver field office. He was an undercover operative implanted within an organized crime ring which set-up shop in Denver in 1984."

Detective Scott leaned in closer.

"I apologize, but I can't disclose what Agent Stahl uncovered, but once we had enough evidence, we raided the gang. There were several prominent members caught up in the bust."

"Let's get to the part where some lunatics abduct two of my citizens, shoot a teenager, and leave me to solve five homicides."

"Right. Agent Stahl testified in federal court, and everyone received a minimum of twenty-five years in prison. The bureau recommended he move as far away from Denver as possible. However, he refused."

Detective Scott squirmed in the uncomfortable chair. "I'm so lost."

"I'm getting to the part which will make sense."

The captain scoffed. "Please. Time is of the essence here."

"The gang assassinated Agent Stahl in front of his home. Broad daylight. His wife rushed to his side and held him as he died her arms. Since then, we've protected Carol and Alex Jones."

"Ah, now it's clear. They're in witness protection?"

"Yes, sir."

"Wait, a minute. Wait. A. Minute. If they're federal witnesses, why are they here? And why wasn't anyone informed?"

"It was the eighties. Someone dropped the ball."

"This is insane. Tell me how we ended up in the situation we're in?"

"No clue. We are hoping together we can figure this out."

"So, you want a joint investigation?"

Tanner nodded. "You help us, we help you."

"You first."

Agent Miller pulled out an accordion folder and tossed photos onto the table. "So far, our intelligence verifies three of the men in prison have daughters. One of those men, Yerik Smirnov, was murdered in prison."

Agent Miller set photos of three women on the table. Detective Scott gasped, turned to Reed, and tapped his finger against one of the images.

"This girl—I-I recognize her. She lives here, in this subdivision, right down the street from the Jones'."

"Who is she?" Reed asked.

"The same girl we've been searching for the last twenty-four hours."

"Heather Burgess?" Reed asked.

Tanner interrupted. "Well, that's what she goes by now. Her real name is Anja Smirnov. Her father was the leader of the Russian gang, and also the inmate murdered in prison. To complicate matters further, when she was a child she watched her mother shoot herself in the head."

"Damn, what a messed up family," Detective Scott said.

"With no other living relatives, the state placed her in foster care and a few years ago Wendy, and Frank Burgess adopted her. Last we knew they were living in Grand Junction."

Reed jumped to his feet, "They've been in Ridgewood Hills for a year. How the hell did nobody keep tabs on her?"

"It's comp—."

"It's not complicated. You're both supposed to be protecting them. Instead, you let this girl move right down the street. Detective, isn't she good friends with the Jones boy?"

He bobbed his head. "They are."

Hanging his head in shame, Agent Tanner attempted to clarify, "Captain, we weren't aware anything was off until our office received a call from Dr. Jones a few hours ago."

"You've been aware for a few hours…and you're showing up after it's too late?"

Detective Scott stood, pointed his finger in Reed's face, and in an abrasive tone lectured his superior. "Stop right now. Yelling and blaming each other won't help solve this mess. Let's focus less on how we got here and more on how we will make things right."

Captain Reed leaned forward, closed his eyes, and took a few breaths.

Scott continued. "This psychopath took these kids someplace and considering three of them are missing, she's not working alone."

"Daniel, you're right. We can blame each other after this ends on a happy note. Now let's stop sitting around and get out there and find these bastards."

Captain Reed stood and marched towards the door, slamming it closed behind him. Agent Miller leaned across the table. "Is he always so feisty?"

"He's low-key until shit gets messed up. When that happens—watch out."

17

DETECTIVE SCOTT STOOD FROM THE TABLE and walked outside to calm Reed down. He advanced as the captain paced back and forth, his beet-red face, and veins in his forehead bulged, so he cleared his throat before as to not further his anger.

Agents Tanner and Miller followed close behind the detective. Uneasy, Tanner tried to speak first. However, the captain interrupted before the words passed from his lips.

"What do you want?"

"My partner hoped he might have an opportunity to speak with the shooting victim."

Reed hung his head. "Do what you like—you federal agents always do anyhow."

"And if it's not too much to ask, I hoped Detective Scott could escort him. We aren't familiar with the town, and I'd hate for him to get lost as he often does."

Scott piped up. "I don't mind as long as it's okay with you."

"If it'll be of value, help them out."

The younger officers walked away towards the black SUV, leaving the two older men staring each other down. Agent Tanner broke the silence. "Let's head back inside where it's warmer."

Reed tried to hold his grudge, and when a gust of wind came along, it changed his mind. "Yeah, I like that idea."

They reverted to the shelter of the trailer, and Captain Reed took a seat; however, Agent Tanner lingered near the door of the claustrophobic space. He wandered about for several minutes, but the silence became too much for him.

"I didn't come here to piss you off...or steal this case. I'm coming for the person I pledged to protect. Alas, I let her and her son down."

The captain remained unaffected.

"I concede we screwed this one up. I've been an agent for thirty years, and I've lost no one."

Captain Reed squinted his eyes and clenched his jaw while he stared Agent Tanner dead in the eye. "That may be, although there's a first time for everything."

Tanner's mouth dropped, and Reed continued.

"One of my men is out there, wrapped up in this shit, so you'll excuse me if I don't have complete faith in your track record."

"No need for explanation," he contended while Captain Reed grew more relaxed, "I'd be the same way if one of my agents were in the same predicament. But can we agree to disagree and set politics aside?"

From the corner of his mouth, Captain Reed broke a smile. "Yes, let's focus on bringing everyone home safe. So, Detective Scott and your partner are en route to Memorial Hospital to speak more with John Davidson."

"Right. Hope the young man can shed more light on the case."

"Coffee?" Reed asked.

"Thanks. I take mine black."

The smile Reed abandoned a few moments earlier now graced his face. "Well, appears you and I will get along fine."

***

198

THIRTY MINUTES PASSED, AND SITTING next to the fireplace, drenched in sweat, were Alex and Amy. Moving ten feet, a simple task, drained them.

"I'm exhausted," he said.

"Me too."

Outside the door echoed two distinct muffled male voices and Alex wasn't sure what they were saying. When their voices raised and grew angry, it was evident they were upset with one another. Alex listened for anything that sounded familiar, but after a few seconds he grew irked and drowned them out. Regardless of how exhausted he was, the kidnappers could return any minute and blow their plot to escape, and Alex wasn't about to let that happen.

"On my count, I need you to lift again."

"Where are we going now?"

"On top of the hearth."

"For what?"

"I'm going to try to cut this rope off of by rubbing it against the stone."

"You've completely lost it. For once in our lives can we face the truth? That guy is going to kill us and nothing we do will change it."

"I made you a promise I'd get us out of this mess. Well, the mess is here, and unless you change your attitude and work with me, these psychos will kill us."

"Argh. Fine, one last time."

Alex counted down from five, and on zero they hoisted the chairs into the air. As quiet as possible, they moved the final five feet and set the legs of the chairs down on the stone fireplace.

Amy's body tightened with fear. "I hope you know what you're doing."

"You worry too much—I've got this."

Alex reached over towards the stone with his leg rubbed the rope tied around his ankles.

The repeated scraping of the rope against the stone frustrated Amy. "Can't you do this any quieter?"

"Now is not the time to complain."

"Shit. Might be faster if you burn the rope off."

Alex sensed her panic yet maintained calmness with his sarcasm. "Well, to do that, I need to be closer to the fire."

"Grr, I could strangle you. However, given our predicament, I'll do it later."

Again, the duo raised the chair and with one quick stroke set the chair up against the grill of the fireplace. The warm, blazing fire burned away, and Alex reached his hands as close as he could. All it took was one small ember, and the dry-rotted rope ignited. In a matter of seconds, the cord released its hold, and the blazing hemp dropped to the floor.

However excited, Alex had to keep his voice down. "I did it. I got it off."

Amy wiggled in her chair. "It worked?"

"Yeah, I got a tiny burn, but it's the price I'm willing to pay for freedom."

Alex stood and raced around to untie his best-friend. With the rope removed he tossed it on the floor and helped Amy to her feet. They exchanged a hug and pulled away.

"Hugs later, find a way out now."

They scanned the room for a possible escape route, and their choices looked impossible. That was until Alex spotted a single window tucked away in the corner of the room. He took a step and hesitated.

Is it large enough to climb out of? And if it is, who's waiting outside to catch us?

Alex pointed. "Think we can squeeze through?"

"At this point, I'm willing to try. We need to move, Alex. No telling when 'ole grumpy will return."

"Why the hell are we standing here? Let's get the hell out of here."

They tiptoed towards the window, and Alex searched for the lock. The metal latch snagged his finger, and with a quick flick, it unlatched. He slid his finger along the bottom and pulled up. It squeaked, and Amy danced in place.

"Hurry."

"Considering I'm bleeding, bruised, burned, and exhausted I'm going as fast as I can."

"I know. I know. If they catch us, we can add butchered to our list of ailments."

The window was wide open, and Alex poked his head out. He glanced towards the ground five feet below.

"It's doable."

Amy grinned.

He slid his right leg in first and followed with his left. He closed his eyes and jumped. Plop. He bowled onto the snowy ground, and the shock of the cold had him back on his feet in no time.

With her adrenaline pumping, she slid her body through the window and heaved herself towards freedom. She closed her eyes and came to a hard landing next to Alex.

"Oww."

"No time to think, we gotta go."

They scrambled to their feet, scanned the unfamiliar backdrop, and the encircling pitch-black forest greeted them. They swapped looks and sought a clue on which direction to run.

With no visible landmarks at his disposal, Alex grabbed her forearm, and they raced towards the tree-line at the edge of the property. As they hauled ass, the one thing on his mind was *anyplace is better than standing outside the cabin like sitting ducks*. His feet hit the earth with such force the powdery snow packed down. He turned his head and with a stutter in his voice yelled, "Just keep up."

"Where are we going?"

"I don't know. We'll recognize it when we find it."

***

THREE MILES FROM THE CABIN, CAROL AND Heather drove along the two-lane road which snaked through the peaks and valleys of the Rocky Mountains. The snow fell heavier, and without her snow tires, the SUV slid. In the distance, Carol saw the road blocked by a gate. She slowed, and a sign indicated 'Closed for Winter.'

Heather yelled out, "Ram it."

"But—."

Heather aimed the gun at Carol's head. "Ram it, bitch."

Carol did what Heather ordered and plowed her SUV into the metal gate. It ripped from the hinges and flew across the road. The weather grew worse the further they drove, and Carol's eyes scanned both sides of the desolate highway. One wrong move is all it would take, and they could either crash into a forest filled with spruces or into a steel guardrail.

Carol contemplated her own death yet wasn't sure if giving up was the right thing to do. All she wanted was to put an end to the chaos, and as she soul-searched for answers, it became clear that the only way for Alex to have peace boiled down to two choices. The question she had to ask herself was whether she wanted her ending to go quick and painless, or suffer while the SUV tumbled down a never-ending mountainside? Either way, she had to decide soon before they arrived wherever it was they were going.

She glanced into the passenger seat where she found Heather preoccupied with the beauty of the surroundings. Carol glanced into Heather's lap and noticed the gun pointed away, and another thing, she wasn't wearing her seatbelt.

Carol mumbled under her breath, took one final deep breath, and shouted out. "Heavenly Father, please forgive me for what I'm about to do, but I have no other choice! I have to save my son!"

Heather awoke from her daze, gripped her gun, and reached for the steering wheel. It was too late, as the uproar threw her off, Carol floored the gas pedal to the floor, swerved to the left, and screamed as the car careened off the roadway.

The crash produced an ear-piercing sound of twisting metal and shattering glass which echoed across the desolate forest. A few seconds after impact, steam rose from the vehicle.

Inside it was calm, with no movement from Carol who slumped over the steering wheel, with a large laceration across her face. The force of the crash forced the engine inward, and it came to a rest in Carol's lap.

Heather met a worse fate when she hurled through the windshield and her lifeless body wrapped around the trunk of an enormous Blue Spruce.

Smoke filled the air around the accident site, but silence remained. And a voice cut through the stillness. "This is OnStar. We have detected an airbag deployment; Dr. Jones, do you need medical assistance?"

A minute passed without a response, and the voice repeated, "Dr. Jones, are you able to respond?"

Again receiving no response, the agent sprang into action. "Dr. Jones, we have your location, and I'm sending help."

18

A MILE AHEAD, ON THE SAME two-lane road Mike drove prudently across the snow-covered roadway. Being at the forefront, he had no idea the crash occurred. The main thing on his mind was saving Alex, Amy, and Brandy from the predicament they found themselves in. Though he had no idea what he was driving into, it didn't matter; he was hell-bent on saving them.

Driving alone in silence his mind flooded with memories over the last year—the good and not so good. While things weren't always fun and perfect, there never was, nor ever would be, two people more spiritually connected than they were.

A shadowy figure walked along the road ahead, and Mike found himself catapulted back to reality. The closer he got, a familiar face came into focus; Brandy. From a distance, he could see her rosy-red cheeks were swollen from the cold, but worse, her eyes told a story of fear.

Did she escape? Where are Alex and Amy?

Mike decelerated and stopped a few feet away. She hurried to his vehicle and before Mike could unlock the doors, she yanked at the door handle.

"Hang on."

The doors unlocked, and a blast of icy air whooshed inside as she hoisted herself into the passenger seat. Once seated her teeth chattered, and her body shook nonstop while Mike reached into the backseat and grabbed a blanket to keep her warm. And as he did a premonition washed over him

He shook his head and handed her the blanket. But as any competent cop would do, he grilled her for answers. "Why the hell are you out here alone? What happened to Alex and Amy?"

"I have no idea where they are. One minute they were right behind me, but then next thing I knew they had vanished."

"People don't vanish into thin air. Are they out here?"

Overwhelmed with the onslaught of questions, Brandy stopped shaking and brandished a gun from the pocket of her hoodie. "Stop asking so many fucking questions. Keep driving."

"I should have known you were involved in this. Funny how you show up right in the middle of chaos."

Brandy stared in silence.

"You haven't seen Alex in what, a year? Why now?"

Brandy tilted her head and stared at him with a crazed smirk. "You'd have been a brilliant detective with your prying questions. Pity you won't live long enough for a promotion."

The girl he met hours earlier changed. Gone was the sweet, innocent best-friend, and whoever flipped the switch activated the psycho killer mode. He continued along the road, perplexed. Mike had new questions, and he craved answers. So, Mike matched her body language and cocked his head to the side and squinted. Their eyes locked.

"Well, since it looks like no matter what, I'm going to die, you should have no problem answering a few more questions?"

"Shoot."

"Are you working alone? Or do you have a co-conspirator? I mean, let's be frank, it's strange how Heather vanished right before you showed up."

Her villain-like laugh disturbed Mike to the core. "Heather? Oh, you're talking about my sister, Anja?"

"Who?"

"Anja. Don't act so shocked. I bet Alex already told you about the shit his father caused."

"Eh, it's a delicate subject, and we've never discussed his father in depth. He told me some guy with a Russian gang assassinated him many years ago."

"So, that gang, we're back to reclaim what's ours."

"This has nothing to do with Alex, so why implicate him in the drama?"

"To get closer to Denise."

"Who the fuck is Denise? None of this makes any sense."

She scoffed. "I don't buy it for a minute you and Alex never discussed his whole covert existence in the witness protection program."

Mike bit his bottom lip, and for once he couldn't express what he wanted to say.

She choked on a laugh. "You really didn't know?"

"It's obvious I'm not familiar with everything about his life. Since you love to cling to the past so much, please, educate me on my boyfriend."

"How much are you aware of?"

"Other than your gang killing his father, and the fact he was an FBI agent in the '80s, not much. So, it's your turn."

"Oh, where shall I start?"

Mike leaned in towards Brandy without flinching. "The beginning is best."

"Alex's father is responsible for sending mine to prison."

"That's usually where they send people who commit crimes. Did he?"

Brandy hung her head. "Yes, lots of them. Don't be fooled, Alex's father was no angel either."

Mike listened and didn't interrupt.

"During his first month in, another inmate shanked him in the shower. The ordeal sent my mother into a dark depression, and when I was eight, I watched her shoot herself in the head."

"Shit."

"That was the beginning of the end. The state separated us. I went to live with a couple of losers in Woodland Park while some wealthy people from Grand Junction adopted Anja."

"It sucks you had such an unhappy life, and so what if Alex's father was a horrible person? None of it explains why you and your sister killed five innocent people and kidnap the rest of us."

"It doesn't need a reason. I can't unleash my revenge on Alex's father since someone already took care of him for us years ago. So, instead, I'll take the next best thing: Carol and Alex."

"But why? Why them?"

She waved the gun around. "Agent Stahl took money from my family, and I want back what's mine."

"And you believe you'll get away with this?"

"Why wouldn't we?"

"For one, I'm sure my department is out looking for us, and—."

She interrupted. "And? They'll never find you. No cell service up here."

She flaunted her phone, and the screen displayed 'No Service.'

Mike clenched his jaw. "Next, Kelli Burgess. Did you have a hand in her death?"

Again, her fiendish chuckle resonated. "She eavesdropped on us making our plans—I had to stop her before she ran to tattle to the cops. I did what I had to do."

"You should have gone to Hollywood instead. Damn. I can't believe I let you sucker us into feeling sympathy for you when your whole reason for showing your face was to spy."

She didn't answer.

"And how did it feel executing Kelli? Did you enjoy it?"

"I mean, I didn't want to kill her, but once I knew a problem was brewing, I had to neutralize it."

"You're one vile, warped bitch."

The SUV approached a dimly lit cabin in the middle of nowhere. "Yup. Guilty. And we're here, back to destroying Alex's perfect world."

Brandy pointed towards a clearing next to a stack of firewood and Mike inched the vehicle to where she indicated. The SUV stopped, and Mike exhaled with both hands on the steering wheel. From the corner of his eye, two large men stood in the door frame, blocking every ray of light which gleamed from within. Mike tilted his head, and with one quick glance, his jaw dropped. When he believed it was only Brandy, he considered he might have a fighting chance. However, those odds plummeted with the latest development.

Outsmarting people was his most remarkable trait. It's what the academy trained him to do. Yet sitting in the driver's seat, he struggled to compose an exit strategy on the spot. His best option was to surrender to whatever their plans were and keep optimistic that an opportunity to break away would occur.

Mike kept still, his hands gripped the steering wheel, and he held his breath in anticipation. Brandy jabbed the gun at his chest and glared at him with pure hatred in her eyes. Her door swung open, and she grunted as she stepped onto the asphalt.

"Get out and do nothing stupid."

With one hand, Mike reached down and opened his door. The two men stepped off the stairs and approached as Mike planted his left foot onto the powder-packed driveway.

They shoved him against the side of the Escalade. "No plans to do anything irrational."

"Shocking—perhaps you're not as stupid as you appear."

"I reckon I'm not."

The goons frisked him from top to bottom while Brandy rushed around the front of the SUV, her weapon drawn and aimed. "Standard weapons check. You understand."

"I have nothing on me. When you first called, I chucked it into the field."

The older man verified, "He's clean."

Mike assumed these were the two shady persons involved in the 7-Eleven robbery and murders. The accent, the faint stench of tobacco lingered on their breath, their boldness—very distinctive traits.

Mike snapped back from his recollection with the sensation of metal against his back. Heather jabbed harder. "Move."

"Look, bitch, I'm not leaving without Alex. You need to calm your ass down."

"Shut up and speak when I tell you to. And when you do address me, you will keep your answers short and direct, without any whining involved."

They advanced towards the cabin, and the soft golden glow illuminated the timber deck. With sweaty palms and shortness of breath, Mike dreaded what awaited him on the other side of the door. He deliberated if Alex and Amy were still alive. His unease blended with relief for a reunion with Alex was on the horizon.

Over the previous month, Mike brawled with a barrage of conflicting moods during the temporary breather he and Alex endured. The volatility of their relationship, not to mention the void, lit a determination to rekindle things to the way they were before everything changed. First, they'd need to survive this ordeal.

God if you can spare us, just this once, I promise I'll be a better boyfriend. I'll be more courteous to those I meet each day. I'll devote more time to those who matter most. I need you to hear me right now.

Once inside the cabin, the first order of business was to steer Mike to a padlocked door at the furthest end of the run-down cottage. The frigid air circulated about, and Mike shuddered. The aggressive goon stepped in front and disengaged the latch. He threw the door open, and it collided with the wall inside the room. He ordered the passive one in first, and after a second, he raced out.

His arms flailed about, and he spoke with panic in his voice. "They're gone."

"What the hell do you mean they're gone?"

The man stepped aside and extended his arm. "Have a peek."

They rushed in, expecting to find Alex and Amy tied to the chair where he left them. Instead, they discovered the flame in the fireplace had dwindled and two empty chairs which once held their prisoner's captive.

Brandy glanced beyond the fireplace and stared at the blue and white plaid curtains which flap in the wind. Speechless, everyone exchanged glances until Brandy grew enraged.

"You idiots. How did you let this happen? I gave you one task—one—and you let them escape."

"I stood here the entire time. Don't you think I'd have heard them escaping?"

"Well, clearly they did. Unless you moved them somewhere else?"

The man shrugged his shoulders.

"Whatever. When did you see them last?"

"Twenty minutes ago, give or take—I'm not quite sure."

"I can't trust either of you to do anything right."

"Screw you."

Her fool-proof plot unraveled before Mike's eyes, and he did a happy dance on the inside. *He answered my prayer.*

"You two split up and find them."

"Where?"

"I have no idea. They couldn't have gotten far in this storm."

The aggressive goon pointed to Mike. "And him?"

"I'll take care of him."

Everyone shifted into the snowstorm which grew worse by the minute. The two cronies dashed off in one direction, leaving Mike and Brandy alone. She walked behind Mike as they trampled through the snow to the backside of the cabin. Underneath the window was the faint outline of footprints, which the snow-covered at a steady clip.

Brandy pointed to the south. "This way."

Mike held his hands up and walked ahead of her.

"Now, when we find them, if you do anything to tip them off, you're dead."

"So why do you need me?"

"I need you to lure them out from wherever they're hiding."

Mike couldn't keep his mouth shut. "I doubt we'll find them."

"And why's that?"

"I mean, first, they have at least a thirty-minute advantage. Second, Alex spent many years in the Boy Scouts as a kid. He can survive this."

She laughed. "In a button-down and jeans? Nah, they'll be dead in a few hours. Either the weather will take them or one of the many wild animals."

"So why go on this suicide mission? I mean, as you said yourself, they're going to die out there. Isn't that what you want?"

She didn't respond.

"There's a blizzard closing in, and you're sending us out in this? Do you have any clue where you're going?"

She struck him again on the back with the muzzle of her gun. "I'm an expert of the area, and there isn't anyone or anything around for miles. They'll die before they reach help."

"Aren't you charming?"

"Move, or I swear I'll shoot you right here and your reunion with Alex will be a distant wish."

Reluctant, Mike did as she commanded.

Situated ahead was the vast forest shrouded in deep snow and dense fog. The atmosphere complemented the mystery of what lay ahead. And the unknown terrified Mike. Was someone waiting to ambush them? Even if they did find Alex, would he realize he was a victim as well or perhaps believe Mike was involved?

The panic dug its heels in and wasn't letting up any time soon.

211

19

CAPTAIN REED SAT AT THE TABLE INSIDE THE TRAILER with both hands clasped over his face. The bleakness of the whole thing weighed on him, and the only way to relieve the tension was to massage his temples. His cheap, Casio watch beeped, and it hit him that too much time had passed since the last update.

One of the captains bragging rights was in the ten years he worked on the force, Ridgewood Hills had never lost an officer. And today was not the day he wanted the streak to end. The immense sensation of doom felt heavy on his mind, and when he couldn't take it any longer, he jumped to his feet.

Agent Tanner, engrossed in paperwork, glanced up. "Everything okay?"

"Fine. Everything's fine."

"Not to overstep my bounds, except I don't get the impression you are fine."

Captain Reed brushed off his remark.

"Sitting here idle isn't healthy for you."

Captain Reed bowed his head. "It isn't."

"I've experienced it first-hand. You allow the morbid thoughts to overtake your mind and getting rid of them takes more time. It's overwhelming and exhausting."

He dipped his head. "What's worse, I haven't had an update in over forty minutes."

"Tell you what. Let me go see if I can gather some information. You need a coffee?"

"Coffee would be great."

"Take a deep breath, and I'll be right back."

Captain Reed interjected before Agent Tanner walked to the coffeemaker. "I want some news to set my mind at ease."

Agent Tanner smirked, grabbed the empty mugs from the table, and stepped away. With two steamy cups in hand, he slid one across the table to the captain.

Agent Tanner took a sip and crouched down. "You good?"

"Yeah."

"Great. Be right back."

Agent Tanner twisted the door handle and stepped outside. He took in a deep breath and exhaled forming a cloud of mist around his head. With Tanner gone, the room fell quiet, leaving Reed and his overactive mind to simmer. Deep in thought, the captain all but missed the phone ringing. He snapped to and looked down. *Shit.*

"Reed. Give me some good news."

"Mr. Reed, my name is Jennifer Green, and I'm an employee with OnStar."

"Oh, okay? How can I help you?"

"I'm calling about an accident which happened around twenty minutes ago."

"Accident? Don't tell me it's Mike Temple."

"No, sir. The Denver Police made me aware you're searching for a Dr. Carol Jones. Is this correct?"

"I am. Is she—."

The OnStar employee interrupted. "I don't know if she's dead. All I can say with certainty is her vehicle was involved in a head-on collision."

"Doesn't sound good."

"Both airbags deployed, yet I've received no response. I've dispatched the Grand County Sheriff's Office, but with the weather, they're backlogged and revealed it may take a while to reach the accident site."

"You got a location?"

"I do. Pine Mountain Road, close to three miles north of Lake Granby."

Reed stood and snatched his heavy parka from the backside of the chair. "Thank you—this is the break I was looking for."

"I hope for a happy conclusion."

"Me too."

Reed ended the call, flung the jacket around his back, and rushed out the door on the hunt for Agent Tanner. "Tanner. Got a huge break. We need to go."

Tanner flashed a thumbs up, chugged the final drops of his coffee, and pulled his wool trench coat tighter. "What are we waiting for?"

Neither of them could reach the black SUV fast enough. Both doors flung open in unison, and Captain Reed reversed, swung a U-turn, and flipped the lights and sirens as the vehicle faded into the shadows of the countryside.

Reed grabbed his cell phone and reached out to Stevens to give him the update Reed never received. The phone rang twice, and Stevens answered with disdain in his voice. "No update, Reed. I told you I'd—."

"We found them. Agent Tanner and I are on our way to Grand County as we speak."

"What? How?"

"Long story. Do me a favor and contact the Sheriff up there. Make them aware we're on our way, and we'll require back-up."

"What's your ETA?"

"Looks like an hour, maybe longer. The weather has grown nasty out here."

"Okay, you got it. Don't get your hopes too high. They're a small department and say you do make it; they may not have the manpower. Be careful."

Reed twisted his head towards Tanner buckled into the passenger seat. "We'll take our chances. Just make sure they know we're coming."

"Got it. Again, be safe and give us updates as you can."

Reed ended the call, tossed the phone into the center console, and with a nervous tightening in his throat he declared, "Better hold on tight—shit's about to get real."

20

"**WE HAVE TO STOP**—I can't go much further," Amy whined.

Alex ran to her side. "No way in hell. Those guys could be right behind us, and I refuse to die out here in the middle of nowhere."

"Please—let me catch my breath."

He groaned. "Fine. One minute."

They hurried towards a fallen pine tree which blocked the snow-covered trail and Alex wiped his bare-hand across to brush off the pristine accumulated snow. They collapsed while the snow fell to the ground. Amy bent forward in pure exhaustion, and Alex wrapped his arm around her back. Alex took in a few deep breaths. Once calmed, Amy glanced over at Alex who bobbed his leg up and down as he waited next to her.

"How far have we run?" she asked.

"Two miles at least. My adrenaline hasn't stopped since we escaped."

"Mine either. We need shelter soon. Otherwise, neither of us will survive if we keep on. We're not trained for this crap."

Alex agreed. "One more minute. I need to gather my thoughts."

Alex skimmed the dark, dense forest for any hint of refuge while his body trembled. The size of the snowflakes increased, making it harder to make out what lie ahead. His eyelids grew weightier, and his body devoted every ounce of energy to keep warm, influencing his ability to process information.

We need to keep on.

The extra minute expired, and the wind howled across the treetops above. Alex covered his face with his hands, hopeful the unexpected onslaught of snow and ice crystals would pass. As he twisted his head away, Amy let out a groan of agony.

As fast as it commenced, it stopped, and Alex uncovered his face. Off in the distance, a flicker of optimism. A small, derelict cabin shrouded by the trees came into view. They shared an ecstatic, yet hesitant glance.

"Did we run in a circle?" Alex asked.

"Impossible. We've kept in a straight line, so there's no way it's the same place."

"I don't know about this."

"One way to find out."

The lack of feeling in his hands made the decision easier for Alex. "Any place is better than in the cold."

He grabbed Amy by her hand, and they traipsed amongst the snow towards the cabin. He wished they could move quicker, but again the wind picked up, and he lost his point of reference for a split second.

"I don't see it anymore."

Amy yelled over the wind. "Keep moving. We'll find it."

And they did. The building came into sight once more, and moments later their drive to survive paid off. They stood at the front door, prudent about their next move.

"Look inside," Amy said.

"I-I don't know about this."

She pushed him aside and peeked through one of the tiny squares of glass embedded in the door. At first glance, she saw a one-room building with a card table, two chairs, and a stack of camping supplies in the corner of the large room.

Alex shivered behind. "So? Is it safe?"

217

She banged against the door. No sense in committing a felony if someone was home. And given the fact they were in the mountains, where people believed in 'shoot first, ask questions later,' it was the right thing to do.

They waited for a response, but after thirty seconds, she jiggled the door handle—bolted.

"Stand back," she said.

Alex retreated as she forced her elbow against the glass, sending shards flying inside. She slid her thin hand inside and twisted the deadbolt. The door swung within, and she stepped through the doorsill.

"Are you crazy? They will arrest us."

Amy cocked her head. "Arrest us? We're victims, fleeing two abductors in the middle of nowhere during a blizzard. No judge with any wits would lock us up for saving ourselves."

"Good point. Let's see if there's anything handy to make it back to civilization."

Stacked in the corner near the fireplace were two large backpacks. One black and the other a hunter green. Amy rushed to the edge, kneeled, and grabbed the black bag and unzipped it. Inside she found a small blanket, various first aid supplies, and some out-of-date nibbles. Alex kneeled beside her and grabbed the second pack—the contents were identical. While to a reasonable person, it didn't seem like much, but to them, it was as if they won the lottery.

"Jackpot," Alex said.

"Right? We should check for a phone."

They zipped the bags closed, and each slung one onto their backs. In the opposite corner of the large room was a small kitchenette with a sink, stove, small refrigerator, and three cabinets. He made a beeline towards the cupboards when out of the corner of his eye he spotted an old rotary dial landline mounted to the wall.

"Found it," Alex announced.

"Oh, thank God. Fingers crossed someone paid the bill."

He lifted the receiver to his ear—no dial tone. Alex clicked the hook switch again and again; it was futile. Frustrated, he placed the receiver back on the hook.

"Shit."

"Was worth a shot, Alex. What do we do now?"

Alex paced around the room. "If we could just locate something useful to give us a clue where we are."

"Like a map?" Amy asked.

"A map, the white pages, an address. Anything."

They split up and searched through drawers. Not knowing how close their abductors were behind them, seconds grew more valuable. However, if they were to have a chance at escaping the icy, desolate woodland breathing, winter gear was a requirement.

Alex slammed the last drawer closed. "No luck. No maps, no address. We can't stay here much longer."

Amy nodded. "I'm quite aware."

"My intuition tells me they're getting closer. If we stay, they'll catch up."

"And we're dead."

"Exactly."

She reached into her pocket. "Wait—my lighter and cigarettes. That'll help, right?"

"I never imagined I'd say this but thank God you're a smoker."

"One last place to check."

"If we're lucky, whoever owns this place left behind some snow boots, or at least a heavy jacket."

"Let's hope. Given that we'll die in a short amount of time with what we're wearing."

They walked across the room to the sole closet beside the wood-burning fireplace. Alex twisted the doorknob, and it creaked as he pulled it open. Inside, on a hanger, hung a black snow parka. Alex picked it from the wooden bar and showed Amy.

"That's it?"

"Unfortunately. Here, take it."

He tossed it her direction, and she caught it one-handed. "No way—you're the brains of this mission. You need it to stay sharp enough to get us home."

"Don't be stupid. I can wrap myself in those two blankets."

She stomped her foot. "I'm a big girl, I got plenty of insulation. I'll take the blankets, and you take the damn jacket."

The jacket flew across the room again, except Alex missed, and it fell to the floor.

Alex leaned over and held the jacket in his hand. "Now you listen here, stubborn ass—you're taking the jacket. That's final."

"Me? A stubborn ass. You need some Windex to clean that dirty mirror you stare into every day."

Alex tossed it back across the room for what he hoped was the final time of their petty argument. "Whatever."

Amy conceded and slid her arms into the jacket. "I'll never win an argument with you, will I?"

"You've known me long enough to answer your own question. Never. You'll never win with your well-being."

Alex flung the black backpack onto the floor and dug out the blanket from inside. "You ready to venture back out into blizzard hell?"

"I suppose we don't have a choice."

When they emerged from the cabin, the storm intensified which made travel more perilous than when they entered. The duo resumed along the same path, uncertain of what they might encounter the deeper into the forest the ventured.

Twenty minutes passed since they exited the cabin, and the snow grew deeper the further away they trekked. With the powder up past Amy's knees, each step took more time and strength; strength neither of them had. Strenuous activities and Amy never mixed, and one of her biggest downfalls was her constant need for a break.

Alex shouted, "Come on—we are *not* stopping again. We can't risk it."

She grumbled. "I can't do it. We must have a large enough lead."

Alex stopped. "Wait. They picked this area for one reason. They know these woods. We don't. It'll be our luck, and they'll be waiting over the next hill."

She threw her hands up and plopped forward into the snowpack. Unimpressed, Alex stomped his foot against the ground. "Get up."

She laid there, waving her arm. "Go on without me."

"Jesus Christ. I'm not leaving you behind. I promise we'll find shelter and out of view."

She looked up. "You promise?"

Alex didn't answer, instead scanned the area, and noticed a small alcove in the side of a rock formation. *A cave?*

"Might happen sooner than not. Now stand up so we can move."

She struggled to her feet and dusted off the snow. "Better find it soon. If not, I'll lie down and let God have her way."

"So damn dramatic. I need you to reach down, deep inside, and find the motivation to live."

She scoffed. "What motivation? So, I can go back to an unhappy home, graduate, and leave everything behind?"

"This isn't the time for a meltdown, sweetie."

He could see it through the blinding snow; a cave. "Can you make it twenty more feet?"

"Twenty feet and that's as far as these feet take me."

They hopped over downed trees and trudged through the snow towards the enclave. There was no telling when the storm would end, but at the very least, they could set up camp for a while to warm up.

They arrived at the cave which wasn't much. Alex mumbled aloud to himself, "This is a perfect place for an extended break."

She overheard him talking to himself and could not help but crack a half smile. They squeezed through the snug opening and once out of the wind Amy grunted and dropped the backpack to the ground. She foraged through the bag, yanked out the blanket resting towards the top, and spread it out across the ground. As soon as the blanket shielded the muck, she situated herself on top, but not before she dug into her front pocket.

"Whatcha looking for?"

"A cigarette. I need a damn cigarette."

"Stressed much?"

"This isn't funny. Do you have any idea how stressed I am?"

He shook his head. "I'll suppose you are. I blame the smoking on why you can't keep up."

"How dare you pass judgment on me? This is my way of dealing with my anxiety."

"I'd never judge you; you're my best friend in the entire world. Sometimes our friends do things we may or may not like—it's part of life. It's not the life I'd choose for me."

With the pack in her hand, she plucked out a cigarette and lit it. Alex continued on his rant. "However, given our situation, I realize the stress is making you cranky, and if having a cigarette will calm you down, go for it."

She inhaled the destructive smoke, and the warm, red cherry burned in the darkened cave. "I'm scared, Alex, like scared to the point I'm convinced we aren't leaving these woods alive."

Alex squatted down next to her on the plaid blanket and reached for her free hand. "I'm won't sit here and tell you how this will end. I'm not Miss Cleo. You guys assume I have the answers to the meaning of life, well, if we're honest, I don't always know the right thing to do."

Amy sucked again at her cigarette yet remained quiet.

"It's difficult being the strong, in control Alex you've grown to love."

She grinned. "Aww, shit, your forehead's bleeding yet again."

She tunneled into the backpack and dragged out the first aid kit. Tossing out items, she found a large gauze pad and tore it open with her teeth. She

222

pressed against the wound with as much pressure as she could. The pain stung, and Alex closed his eyes while she tended to his injury. When the sting subsided, he opened his eyes, and the single thing before his eyes was her forced smile, and a cigarette drooped from her lips like an old lady.

"You have no idea how ridiculous you look right now."

"I could say the same about you…but I won't."

"We need to decide if we are going to wait out the storm here or move on. What should we do?"

"I need to rest a bit, but I also know that if we do, we're as good as sitting ducks waiting for slaughter."

"Let me be honest—we have to be close to civilization by now. We've been out here for hours, and I can't feel my hands anymore."

"Isn't numbness the first indication of frostbite?"

Alex shrugged his shoulders. "You took first aid, not me."

"Let's wait a few more minutes, warm up, and move on."

Twenty more minutes passed, and Alex's anxiety jolted into overdrive. He peeked outside the cave and, out of nowhere, the wind raged, and it dashed his hopes of it had subsided.

As he was about to postpone their departure, everything went calm. He knew it was now or never if they wanted to leave. With the unpredictable storm, there was no idea how long the latest lull would last.

Alex stepped outside first. He twirled around, doing a full three-sixty, and searched for their footprints. With the heavy snow, it covered up any trace they were ever there. While it was what Alex wanted, to throw the kidnappers off their trail, there was a con: he couldn't remember which direction they came from.

"Which way?" Alex asked.

Amy looked around and remembered the fallen trees they climbed over. "That way."

Alex followed her finger. "You sure?"

"Positive. Trust me."

They continued towards the main trail, and the visibility improved allowing Alex to see further ahead. They trudged a few hundred feet, and the trees thinned.

"Hey, isn't it a good sign?"

Amy stopped and looked up. "A sign of what?"

"The trees. They're spaced apart further. Could there be a road ahead?"

Amy shrugged her shoulders. "Let's go find out."

Fifty feet under normal conditions would have taken seconds, instead, took four minutes. Once they arrived, a breathtaking view of a vast, ice-covered lake at the base of a steep hill greeted them.

"We need to make it down this hill, and we're home free."

Amy glanced over the edge. "You've lost your damn mind."

"What, it's just a hill."

"A hill? We're in the damn mountains. Nope, there has to be another way."

Amy shook her head and walked away.

"Wait up. Where are you going?"

"You didn't see the winding road along the lake?"

"Uh, no."

"We're bound to run into the same road. That is if we won't fall off the side of a mountain first."

They followed the tree line as their guide and Alex hung behind Amy. A shout in the distance gave him pause. He stopped to concentrate for a few seconds and after silence continued. Alex shrugged it off, blaming his over-paranoid mind of playing tricks on him.

Just keep moving.

Amy, in some way, unearthed her motivation to live and when Alex looked up, she was thirty-feet away. He rushed down the trail and caught up to her, yet, every few seconds he turned his head. Somehow, the sensation of a presence behind them lingered.

As they set in motion down the steep descent, the snow thinned beneath their feet. It was a welcome relief from the knee-deep snow they were tackling before. Amy refocused and let out a sigh.

"Unbelievable. I can move faster than before."

"We may make it out of here alive after all."

"We're not out of the woods yet—pardon the pun. Let's keep on."

"I have a hunch that over the hill is a road."

"Hope you're right. I'm over these woods."

As they reached the summit, Amy's intuition proved correct. There, in its glory, was a desolate, two-lane, coiled road. "The lake was to the left, so we should take the road down."

"Wait a second."

Amy stopped. "What?"

"What if those guys are out searching for us in vehicles?"

"You have a point. I didn't consider that."

"Best we stay off the road."

"We won't be sitting ducks that way."

They walked between the trees, away from the roadway, but through the trees, Alex overheard his name echo again. He stopped and swung around for another peek. "Amy, hold up."

Amy reverted to his side. "What's wrong?"

"This is gonna sound crazy."

"What?"

"I swear that was Mike calling my name."

Amy tugged the parka closer to her body and faced into the wind. "You sure? I don't see a soul."

"Let's hang tight for a minute."

"Alex—."

"Appease me, will ya?"

The crouched behind an enormous Blue Spruce, and after a minute passed without a sound, Amy placed her hand on his shoulder. "You must be hearing things."

"No. It was clear as day."

"How? The only thing I make out is a whoosh-ish sound in my ear. Trust me, you're hungry, tired, and your emotions are out-of-whack."

"I'm telling you, I recognize his voice. He must be out here looking for us."

"And how would he have knowledge of where to find us? Hmm? It's not like we're *Hansel and Gretel*, dropping breadcrumbs across Colorado."

Alex peered through the trees towards the road, and a familiar silhouette crested the hill. Alex squinted, rubbed his eyes twice, and there stood Mike. However, he wasn't solo. As Alex went to sprint, another silhouette surfaced at his side. With so much distance and poor lighting, Alex wasn't confident who the other person was. Instead of running, he crept forward. His heart thumped in his ears—Mike found them.

Amy grabbed the blanket wrapped around his back and interrupted. "Stay still. Let them come closer."

From atop the hill, Mike shouted out. "Alex…Amy…you can come out. Everything's good."

Alex paused. "He says everything's fine—he came to rescue us. Let's move."

Amy nibbled her lower lip, narrowed her eyes, and saw it. She pulled Alex back down to the ground. "He might be here to save us, but I don't think she is."

"She? Which she?"

"Brandy."

"Of course, they're both here to save us."

"Think again; she's got a gun aimed at Mike's back."

Alex took a second glance, this time closer than before. His mouth dropped, and he shook his head. "It was Brandy this entire time. Well, there goes our happy rescue."

21

MIKE MARCHED DOWN THE STEEP HILL, with Brandy close behind. She pressed the gun hard against his back as a constant reminder she was there. Alex peeked again hoping it was a dream. However, after he rubbed his eyes, there they stood.

"What do we do?" he asked.

Amy's face froze, and she remained speechless.

Alex shook her. "I got a plan."

"Okay."

"We keep low and leave as much distance between them and us. There must be help down near the lake. There has to be."

"I mean, you've gotten us this far."

They shuffled through the trees, crouched as low as possible, and worked their way down the steep downslope. Every so often, Alex looked behind him to gauge their adversary's location.

"They're closer," he whispered.

The voice of the women he trusted most of his life shouted. "Alex, I know you're there. Come out and let's talk."

"Talk? What would you ever say?"

"She's crazy if she thinks that'll happen."

By now they were neck-and-neck moving down the slope, and Alex knew at their current pace sooner or later Brandy would corner them. He stopped, crouched, and gestured for Amy to retreat.

"Come," he said.

"Alex. No. We gotta keep moving."

"I give up. It's clear they know where we are heading, coupled with the fact there is nowhere out here to hide."

"Do I hear defeat?"

Alex scrunched his face. "This isn't surrendering. I'm realistic. If we show ourselves, we may be able to—."

Amy scoffed. "To what? Overpower her? She's clutching a gun, and has our rescuer held hostage."

"Here's the plan. We hustle down this hill, get ahead of them as far as possible, and leap out. I might be able to reason with her," Alex said.

"Or she'll kill us."

Alex grabbed her cold hand. "Sweetie, any way you cut it, we're going to die from either the cold or a gunshot. We should try to go out with a fight."

Amy closed her eyes, mumbled to herself for a minute, and with a single word threw the plan into motion. They retreated into the thicker part of the forest and somehow managed to sneak ahead of Brandy, who slowed her pace while searching along the roadside for them. Alex gauged their lead by a few hundred feet and knew it was time.

"Now, Amy."

Without hesitation, the duo raced to the roadway and as Alex predicted, they had a substantial lead over their adversary. At the crest of the hill stood Brandy and Mike.

What is he thinking at this exact moment? I hope he knows I'd give up everything that ever meant anything to me if I could make this right somehow.

However, Alex was quite aware there wasn't a damn thing he could have done to change the situation.

Amy tugged at Alex's sleeve. "What now, genius?"

"Back away, one step at a time."

"You know at some point, she'll realize we're here."

Amy mumbled under her breath.

"What?"

"Nothing. Let's try it your way and pray it works."

As Alex wanted, they moved in sync away, and without warning, a single shot pierced the still air. The two escapees stopped—paralyzed to continue their withdrawal. They stood and faced the situation atop the hill. Except for this time, they would face it head-on.

Brandy trudged downward with Mike out in front with the gun still pressed against his back.

Amy whispered as Alex locked eyes with Mike. "You realize this won't end well, don't you?"

Alex shrugged his shoulders and in a nonchalant voice replied. "We'll see."

After a minute, Brandy came within earshot and yelled. "Don't even think about doing anything stupid, Alex."

"Wasn't in the plans. Mike, you okay?"

She moved the gun from this back and pressed the muzzle against the side of Mike's head. "Don't answer him…unless you want to suffer the consequences-"

Alex interrupted. "Consequences?"

"Mess with me, and the last memories of your beloved Mike will be his brains sprayed across the road."

Her crazed tone spooked Alex, and he toned down his attitude. "Okay…okay. You win. Just don't hurt him."

A moment of tense silence ensued until Alex spoke up again. "What do you want?"

She laughed with a hint of lunacy, "I'm surprised a bright guy as you never figured it out."

Alex continued to mirror her questions with more questions. "Figured out what?"

"How this transpired. You must admit I had each of you duped."

"I don't get why, though."

"I used you to get closer to your mother."

"I'm not an idiot, Brandy. My question was why. Why her?"

"It's funny how you never saw any of this coming."

"No. Not funny. I'm gonna ask one more time; what do you want from my mother or me?"

"What your father took."

"You were there when we read the letters and they didn't explain, well, anything. What did my father allegedly take from you?"

Brandy cocked her head. "You genuinely don't know anything about him…do you?"

Alex lowered his head. "I don't. But I suppose you'll tell me you do."

"I know much more than you it seems. And let me say, I hope he continues to burn in hell each day."

Alex clenched his fist and let loose. "So, let me get this straight. You pretend to be my friend all these years, murdered five innocent people, and kidnapped us over stuff my father did over a decade ago?"

Brandy grinned. "Yup, but I didn't kill anyone. That was left to my sister Anja."

"Who the hell is Anja?"

"We're getting to her."

"Fine. So, what makes you believe me, or my mother, will help you?"

Brandy swung her head to the right and to the left. "Doesn't seem either of you has a choice."

"Is it money you want?"

"Among other things. There's so much more to the story of your father, who he was, and the role your mother played."

"I'm so confused."

"Alex let me give you a quick family history. Your father was a thief, your mother was a greedy whore who fled to the U.S. from Russia years ago. Why d'you suppose we sent those letters in Russian?"

Alex let the information overload sink in for a few moments. Amy stood behind Alex the entire time.

"She's lying, Alex," Amy whispered.

"What if she's telling the truth?"

"It'll come out in the end."

Alex held Amy's hand before he refocused on Brandy. "You'll excuse me if I don't take your word."

"I'd expect nothing less. I have proof back at the cabin."

Alex shook his head. "Nope. I won't let you lure us back there."

"Either move or Mike becomes the latest collateral damage. Neither of us wants that to happen, now do we?"

Alex clenched his jaw and fidgeted with the blanket draped around his body. "Before I do anything, you never answered who the hell your sister Anja is."

"You know who she is."

Alex forced a laugh. "I have a suspicion, but I need to hear it come from your mouth."

"Heather."

Alex looked at Amy in disbelief. "Can you believe this?"

Amy grew hysterical and blurted out. "You're both crazy and trust me, you'll never get away with any of this."

"Oh, I will. Your mother should be joining the party any minute."

And as the last syllable fell from her mouth, downslope the headlights from an approaching vehicle illuminated the pitch-blackness.

Brandy walked towards Alex and Amy. "Right on time."

"She would rather go to her grave before telling you anything."

22

DOWNHILL, CAPTAIN REED AND AGENT TANNER sped for the crash site along the same curvy road where Alex and Amy faced one of their kidnappers. The car grew nearer, and when Agent Tanner pulled out of the bend, he slammed on the brakes, which sent the car into a skid across the snow. Alex grabbed Amy, and the two cowered as the vehicle slid to a stop.

When Tanner took a quick glance around, four bodies stood before him. Brandy, Mike, Amy, and Alex. Before he could react, Reed had already thrown open the passenger side door without hesitation, drew his weapon, and crouched, using the door as a shield.

"Ridgewood Hills Police. No one move."

Still dazed by the near-death experience, Agent Tanner froze in his seat. The entire confrontation moved in slow motion, however, when he saw Reed draw his weapon, life returned to regular speed, and he too followed suit.

Alex and Amy found themselves smack-dab in their crosshairs, and Alex looked back towards the officers while Amy focused her attention on Brandy.

"How do we talk our way out of this one?" Amy asked.

Not wanting to jeopardize Mike's life, Alex whispered. "Whatever you don't make any abrupt moves."

"That's all you got?"

"Let me finish. Every few seconds take a teeny-tiny step backward towards the officers."

"You sure they won't shoot us?"

Alex swung his head around, annoyed. "We're not the one with a gun. Besides, that's Mike's boss."

"I have a bad feeling about this."

"You shouldn't. If we don't make a run for it, things ought to end nonviolently."

With neither side ready to back down, moments ticked by, each one longer than the previous. On the other hand, the impasse allowed Alex and Amy to back away five feet closer to the officers and out of the line of fire.

Fed up with the slow progress and lack of reinforcement from the local sheriff, Captain Reed broke the hushed standoff. "Miss, we can do this the entire night. Give up while we can still help."

"No way in hell you'll take me alive."

"It doesn't need to come to that. Lower your weapon, let Officer Temple go, and we'll talk about it."

She shook her head in defiance. "I have a mission to carry out, and there isn't a damn thing you can do to stop it."

Concern radiated from Mike's eyes, and Captain Reed took a bold move and stepped out from behind the cover of the SUV. With slow, smooth steps he passed Alex and Amy and waved back with his hand. "Get to the car."

Without wavering, Alex snatched Amy by the forearm, and they fled for safety. The captain held his gun in his right hand and suspended his arms above his head as he approached. "Miss, I only want to talk."

His brashness threw her off-guard, and Mike sensed a perfect moment coming up. The corner of his lip quivered; it was now, or never. He glided his hand inside his jacket and extracted a folding knife concealed in the lining. With a swift wrist flick, the blade extended, and Mike thrust the knife deep into her thigh and twisted. Brandy fell to the ground, and blood squirted out onto the alpine-white snow.

She screeched. "Son of a…"

Mike bolted towards Reed, and amongst the commotion, Agent Tanner went rogue and unshielded himself.

Mike ran away and hollered out. "What the hell are you waiting for? An invitation?"

Crouched behind the driver's side door of the SUV, not aware of what was about to transpire, Alex tugged the bulky jacket wrapped around Amy's body and pulled her down next to him. No shots had exchanged, and he glanced up towards the sky. *This may end better than I thought.*

He wrapped his arms around her and pulled her against him tight. Terror exuded from her body, and Alex tried his best to quell her shaking.

"It'll be okay. It's almost over."

Amid the shouts and her dazed state, Alex wasn't sure she even caught his comforts. He tapped her shoulder, and she jerked. "Is it over yet?"

"I don't know."

"Tell me when it's safe."

Amy squeezed her eyes in the exact moment everything grew hushed. No more yelling. No more pleas. Just stillness. Alex clenched his fist and peeked through the window in the precise moment a single shot pierced the air. He couched again and pulled Amy's head into his cold chest.

Another pause. *Is it clear?* He lifted his head again and found Agent Tanner darting towards a body sprawled out across the road. His heart sank, but there was one question he needed an answer to; where was Mike?

23

ALEX HOLLERED TO THEIR RESCUERS YET kept his eyes sealed. "Everything under control?"

A familiar voice shouted back, "Yes, we neutralized the situation."

Alex exhaled and opened his eyes. When he got the guts to get to his feet, three men encircled the lifeless body of Brandy was the first thing to catch his eye first, however, next was the bright red stained snow.

"Is she—dead?"

Reed avoided a direct answer. "It's safe to come out now."

Alex sank down and shook Amy, who still sat on the pavement with her eyes closed. He rocked harder as she opened one eye.

"Hey, it's over."

"You sure?"

"Positive."

She reached out her hands, and he hoisted her up from the wet ground. Alex brushed the snow from her backside and curved his head. Out of the corner of his eye, Alex saw him. The love of his life walking their way.

Time moved in slow motion, and when Mike reached them, Alex threw out his arms and broke down in tears. "I thought you were dead."

Mike tightened his grip and buried his face against Alex's shoulder. "It'll take more than a psycho teenager to kill me."

"I can't believe it was her this entire time. How could I be so blind?"

Mike lifted his face. "She had us all fooled. But you're safe now, and I'm never going to let you go again."

Amy stood by and watched their emotional reunion and leaned against the vehicle. "Where's John? And Heather?"

Mike pulled back from Alex and glanced at Amy. "John's safe. He took a bullet, and they took him away in an ambulance."

"Oh my God. Is he alive?"

Mike nodded.

"I can't even tell you how happy I am you found us. I worried we'd all die out here."

"I'd never let that happen."

Alex stood and shivered, rubbing his hands against his biceps. "You think we can sit in the car where there's heat?"

Mike smiled. "Sure."

From the valley below, Mike caught sight of blue and red flashing lights speeding up the mountainside. He uttered under his breath as he assisted Alex into the backseat, "Perfect timing."

Soon the ambulance skidded to a halt, and two medics jumped down. They rushed towards Mike who wrapped a blanket around Alex.

"What's going on here?" the one medic asked.

Mike yanked out his wallet and flashed his badge. "A shit-show. Got one deceased and these two have been out in this storm for the last two hours. Wait. We didn't call, so how d'you know we were here?"

"We didn't. Dispatch reported a crash ahead about a mile. You know anything about it?"

Alex trembled and attempted to get his boyfriends attention, except the words which crossed his lips came out slurred. Worried, Mike pulled the lead paramedic aside. In a whispered tone Mike spoke, "Something's not right. He needs a hospital."

"But—."

"But nothing. The crash victim will have to wait, and as far as the dead body, I'm confident she isn't going anywhere."

"Sir, with all due respect, we have a protocol to follow."

Mike wrinkled his face. "Screw protocol. He's slurring. Why?"

"You mentioned he's been out in this weather for two hours?"

Mike nodded.

The medic peeked over Mike's shoulder and studied Alex. "Two hours…in those clothes?"

Mike swung around and looked Alex up and down. "Yeah."

"Damn. I'm shocked he's not worse off."

Mike threw his hands up. "Is he going to die?"

"If he hypothermic, it's possible."

"So, shouldn't you get him out of here? Let us handle the crash site, but let dispatch know to send a couple more ambulances."

The man nodded, and they raced back to the rig and offloaded the stretcher from the rear. Forcing the wheels through the deep snow, they stopped when they reached a semi-conscious Alex in the backseat. As they hoisted him onto the firm vinyl mattress, he looked up with a lifeless gaze at Mike who stood stoically by his side.

The medics covered him in a blanket and strapped him in. The medic took his vital signs, and Mike saw Alex wince in pain. Not sure how to comfort his boyfriend, Mike did the one thing he could think of and reached out his hand to provide Alex with reassurance. However, the tight-lipped medic swatted it away. "I know you want to, but we need to get him better."

Mike bent forward and whispered into Alex's ear. "I have to go now and check on this accident ahead. You relax, and I'll be at the hospital as soon as possible."

Mike watched as they loaded Alex into the back of the ambulance. Amy stood alongside him and leaned her head on Mike's arm. "He's a fighter."

"He is. You better go and get checked too," Mike said.

She nodded and stepped into the back and sat. More or less ready to leave, the medic Mike spent the most time speaking with hopped down and slammed the rear doors closed.

Mike pressed his hand against the man's chest. "Promise me he's in good hands. He's all I have."

Nodding, the paramedic gave his word, "We'll take care of them both."

Mike banged his hand on the back to ensure it was secure. "Wait. Which hospital?"

"Medical center in Granby."

Mike stepped away and returned to Reed and Tanner who attempted to reach the sheriff's office multiple times. The radiance of red and blue lights reflected off the sides of the mountains, and it disappeared into the abyss of darkness.

"Any luck reaching the authorities out here?" Mike asked.

"Nope. Guess we're on our own."

Not even a minute after he spoke those frustrating words, two county sheriff cars sped up the road. Captain Reed glanced at Agent Tanner and uttered, "Well it's about time they showed up."

The cruisers skidded to a stop a hundred feet away, and the three waited unwearied. Exiting from the lead vehicle was a tall, heavyset man with a mustache. The man slammed the door closed, placed his hat on the top of his head, and stepped towards the trio.

With his hand extended he approached the captain. "You must be Reed? Sheriff Malone."

He returned the gesture. "Sorry to meet under this unfortunate circumstances. Got one hell of a mess on our hands here."

The sheriff shifted his weight to one side and placed both hands on his hips. "I'll say. Spoke with one of your guys earlier. I don't reckon I've ever experienced anything this twisted in my thirty-year career. You guys got the situation under control?"

"Not quite. We're about to head up the road to investigate the crash OnStar reported. As you can see, our plans were disrupted."

"I see. She one of them kidnappers or a hostage?"

"Kidnapper. Both hostages are on their way to the medical center."

"Well, glad to see at least this poor unfortunate won't cause anymore trouble. You three head on up to the crash site and let my deputies handle *this* here."

Reed motioned for Mike and Tanner to return to the SUV while the two leaders sauntered towards the SU. Reed reached for the door handle, but before he opened the door, he turned towards the sheriff. "Thanks for all your help."

The sheriff smiled and tossed over a handheld walkie-talkie. "No problem. If you need anything, use it."

"I got a feeling you'll hear from me soon."

Reed opened the door and the three officers buckled in. The vehicle passed by the deputies as they covered Brandy's body with a white sheet and Reed sat in the passenger seat and stared as they resumed along the desolate road towards the crash site.

Meanwhile, in the backseat, Mike found himself also gazing out the window. Through the thick forest, and beyond the swollen snowflakes, the twinkle of a few isolated homes in the valley below caught his attention. He exhaled. A million thoughts rattled around in his head. Gratitude, confusion, and anger topped the list.

With the distress of a psychopath shooting him in the back now a distant memory and Alex on his way someplace safe, Mike relaxed. However, the contentment was short-lived when Alex's sorrowful face flashed before his eyes. Mike mulled over how Alex looked when the paramedics whisked him away, and he felt guiltier than ever.

Reed glanced in the rearview mirror. "How are you holding up, Temple?"

"Could be worse."

Accustomed to covering up his feelings, Mike wanted to be candid. "Captain, can I be honest with you?"

Captain Reed nodded.

"I've lost sight of what's most important in my life."

"We've all been there, kid. Comes with the job."

"Therein lies the problem, sir. I've dedicated the last two years to 'the job,' and in doing so, it about cost me everything."

Tanner interrupted. "Sounds like you need an extended, relaxing vacation."

Three minutes later the black smoke from the crash site came into focus. Agent Tanner eased the car to a stop, and Mike's heart sank when he viewed the mangled mess of what remained of Carol's Land Rover. *This isn't a rescue, it's a body recovery.*

Tanner threw the car into park, and he was the first to exit. Captain Reed followed a few seconds later. From being engaged in law enforcement over fifteen years and responding to hundreds of accidents in that time, it seemed urgency was not a priority on this case.

Mike opened the rear passenger side door and planted his feet onto the unpacked snow. The cold upon his feet was an unwelcome sensation. Still, he sucked it up and with caution advanced towards the mangled wreckage.

"Be right back," Mike said.

And like that, he descended into the culvert, and as he grew closer to the rear of the Range Rover, a bloodied arm with a silver bracelet dangled motionless from the driver's side window, and he fell back onto the ground.

"What d'you see?"

Mike regained his composure and took a closer look. "It's Dr. Jones."

"You sure?"

"Yeah. I recognize the band Alex gifted her on Mother's Day."

"Anyone else with her?"

"Eh, not that I see, sir…I don't want to go any further without back-up."

Reed turned to Tanner and asked, "You don't mind lending a hand, do you?"

"Sure, no problem."

"Temple, come up and get warm in the car."

Tanner navigated down the steep and slippery embankment, gasping in several breaths of crisp mountain air along the way. He exhaled and a few seconds later found himself standing side-by-side with Mike.

"I got it from here, officer."

Mike patted him on the back and walked away. In the meantime, Agent Tanner squatted beside the driver's side door and stared at the women he vowed to protect years earlier.

"I'm sorry I let you down."

The air remained still, and he worked up the courage to reach his hand inside. With his middle and index fingers, he pressed against her neck to check for any sign of life. Thirty seconds later and without a pulse, he bowed his head and sighed. All his hopes of a happy-ending disappeared faster than a crime boss on the run.

In the end, the guilt wore off, and he stepped away. A warm mist expelled from his mouth, and he yelled up to Reed. "She's dead."

"Is anyone else with her?"

Tanner walked around the front of the vehicle. "There's a massive hole in the passenger side of the windshield. The crash probably ejected her abductor."

"You need some help?" Reed asked.

"I'm good."

The bright white light of the SUV's headlights stretched far into the darkened wilderness. Reed and Mike watched Tanner disappear into the dense forest. Unsettled, Captain Reed reached behind his back and retrieved his service weapon from his waist. Unsure of who these people were, he had to be prepared for anything underhanded they had up their sleeves.

A few minutes had passed since Agent Tanner walked into the woods, and Reed was now pacing back and forth—the suspense was driving him mad. So much time had passed that there were now two ambulances and a police cruiser on the scene.

His nervousness reached its peak and Reed raced down the embankment. "Tanner, what the hell is going on?"

Agent Tanner emerged from behind a tree and rushed from the woods at a high rate of speed. He yelled, "It's her. It's Anja Petro."

Mike cocked his head to the side and shouted down. "Who?"

"You know her better as Heather Burgess."

Mike hesitated and rushed back to the crash. "She's involved too?"

Tanner nodded.

Captain Reed tossed his hands up. "Well, don't keep me in suspense, man; is she dead or alive?"

"Considering her body is wrapped around a tree, yeah, she's dead."

"Well, at least the two masterminds are out of the way," Reed affirmed as they proceeded back to the vehicle.

"Temple, where's your vehicle?"

"Up the road about another mile."

"What's there?"

"The road dead-ends at a cabin where they held Alex and Amy hostage."

"They? You're telling me there's more than the two girls?"

"Indeed. Two Russian thugs frisked me once I arrived."

"Why are we waiting around here? Let's take down these assholes."

24

REED GRABBED THE WALKIE FROM THE SUV nestled in the cup holder and briefed the locals on what they uncovered at the wreckage.

"Sheriff Malone, come in."

"Go ahead."

"Found the crash, along with two decedents. Still, two more guys to find."

"10-4, sending back-up your way."

"Copy. Heading to the cabin now."

Tanner floored the pedal and sped onward. The ascent grew steeper and more treacherous the further they drove. The mile seemed like an eternity— Mike's heart raced the entire four-minute trek. In time, the road ended and before their eyes sat the isolated cabin. With no idea what to expect, Mike swallowed hard.

His hand trembled as he tugged at the door handle, yet aware taking the remainder of thugs down was his primary objective. *The sooner you take them out, the sooner you can get back to Alex.*

With a quick yank, he flung the door open as two additional cruisers arrived on the scene. He stepped out, raised his arms above his head, and cracked his knuckles. The atmosphere was calm, and the windows inside the cabin sat dark. Letting down his guard, Mike strolled to his Escalade, left in the exact spot he parked it hours earlier. Without notice, an onslaught of rapid gunfire greeted him, and he dove into the snow for cover along the side of his SUV.

Mike mumbled, "Are there others I'm not aware of?"

Now defenseless, his main concern was how he could fight back without a weapon and some sort of body armor. After a few seconds, he remembered his service weapon was a mere three feet away, locked away in the glove box. He reached for the passenger door handle at the exact moment more gun blasts pierced the air. He lowered his hand and rethought recovering it.

Abandoning the suicide mission, the next thought to cross his mind was if his fellow officers had adequate firepower. Time ticked by in slow motion, and the chaotic gunfire grew more intense as each second passed. The raging snowstorm, which had calmed, intensified yet again. Except for this time around the biting wind gusted more vigorous and the unconfined snow dominated the air.

Mike pinched his eyes closed tight while bullets zoomed past. His priority changed, and now all he wanted was to make it back down the mountain alive.

I have to see Alex at least one more time.

A distressing shriek amid the gunfire interrupted his internal pep-talk. His eyelids straight away opened, and the first visible thing was Captain Reed fortified behind the passenger door of one of the deputy's cruiser. His superior dodged bullets as they zoomed by even though every few seconds he managed to pop off a few rounds himself.

Where's Agent Tanner?

The wind subsided for a moment, and the tiny ice-crystals fell back to the earth. Mike scooted to the rear of his vehicle and peeked around the rear. Soon his eyes answered his question. Sprawled across the hardened earth lay the motionless body of Agent Tanner in a pool of his own blood. Mike examined the body from a distance, and it became evident what happened: a bullet to the chest.

Mike watched for any signs of life, except after a minute he gave up hope and pressed his back against the frigid vehicle.

What now? I have no weapon and no way of escape.

The gunfire ceased, and Mike scanned the area for an escape route and found one. Tanner's weapon lay inches from his body. Without hesitation, Mike stumbled to his feet and raced across the gravel lot to retrieve the unsecured gun and make it someplace where he could help make an impact.

He grabbed the weapon from the ground and sprinted to the cover of the cruiser. Neither side fired in the course of the bold action. However, the cease-fire ended when a lone gunshot rang out from the cabin. The force of the impact pitched Mike to the ground, and he cried out.

"Temple. You okay?"

Through the pain, he hollered, "My shoulder."

"Damn. Hang tight I'm coming."

As more reinforcement arrived, Captain Reed took advantage of yet another lull in the gunfire to act. Mike lay feet away from the cruiser, blood seeped from his shoulder, and Reed slipped his arms under Mike's armpits. Without thinking about his own safety, he pulled him to cover and avoided becoming a casualty himself.

He vexed to watch as six heavily armored officers stormed towards the front entrance of the cabin. The final thing before he passed out from the loss of blood was the sight of the SWAT team tossing canisters of tear gas through both front windows. Within seconds smoke billowed from the windows and Mike regained consciousness. Tension mounted as everyone waited for the attackers to flee the building.

After a minute with no movement, the team tossed two more canisters through the broken windows and soon after two large, bearded men materialized at the front door, couching nonstop and surrendered. SWAT descended upon them, tossed them to the ground while three officers stood overhead with their

M-4's pointed at their heads. With the situation controlled, Captain Reed propped a half-conscious Mike up.

"How bad is it?"

Mike groaned. "I don't know."

Mike pulled his hand away from the oozing wound, and Reed reached for the radio attached to his hip. "Sheriff Malone. Captain Reed here."

His country voice crackled through the radio. "Go ahead."

"Got two officers down at the cabin. I need medical right away."

"Copy that—hang tight."

Captain Reed propped Mike's head against his shoulder and squeezed his hand. "Son, I need you to hold on; help is on the way."

Mike opened his eyes, the usual golden color in his face faded into a milky white, yet he managed to acknowledge him with a simple nod.

The very thought of Reed losing Mike kicked his anxiety into overload. His sole wish was to forget this nightmarish evening, go back a few days before all hell broke loose, and do things differently. He gazed up to the sky for a moment and said a prayer in his mind. When he opened his eyes and down, Mike had lost consciousness once again. With a vigorous shake, Reed leaned in closer as the wetness of the puffy snowflakes melted on his face.

Before utter panic set in, two ambulances rolled up on the scene. The medics wasted no time and raced over to attend to Mike. They surrounded him as he lay on the ground, and the younger paramedic dropped his bag onto the ground and grabbed for his wrist to check for a pulse.

"Got a pulse—but it's weak."

Reed scooted away and let the medics do their job. "That's a good sign, right?"

The taller medic held out his hand in front of him. "Sir, I need you to step back."

"Oh right, sorry. He's gonna make it, yeah?"

"We'll do our best. He needs a hospital as soon as possible though."

"So, why the hell are you still here? Get him out of here."

The medics exchanged glances yet remained silent.

"Uh, like now."

The middle-aged medic pulled aside the younger one to have a private conversation. Captain Reed hovered nearby. "Is he stable enough for transport?"

"The conditions are too treacherous to work on him here. Let's get him into the back, and we can examine him closer."

The two medics loaded Mike onto a stretcher and carried him towards the ambulance. Reed followed and stood guard at the rear doors in disbelief. As they tore open Mike's uniform, Reed tilted his head away for a moment to gather his emotions. Across the way, rapid movement caught his eye, and another team of medics tended to Agent Tanner. He stepped away and stopped ten feet shy. While he wasn't sure what they said, whatever it was didn't seem comforting.

Convinced the Marshal wouldn't pull through, Reed refocused his attention to Mike. He returned, pulled open the door and hollered into the back, "Can you guys go already? He's one of the best officers I got and if he dies because you're wasting time…"

The tension reached a tipping point, and Captain Reed was edging on losing his professionalism. With a deer in the headlights expression, the younger one hollered at his partner. "Smith, let's get down the mountain."

Jumping from the back, the medic raced to close the doors. Reed snatched his forearm and pulled him close. "Where are you taking him?"

The medic stuttered, "To the medical center in Granby, about fifteen miles south of here. It's the closest hospital."

"And they have the capabilities to handle a gunshot wound?"

"Eh. From the looks of it, he'll be medevaced to either Denver or Colorado Springs."

"Go. And make sure the ER docs know I'll be there soon."

Reed slammed the door shut and pounded the palm of his hand upon the window. The rig rolled forward through the thick snow, and a few seconds later the sirens wailed, and Reed watched until it disappeared around the bend.

With one situation under control, he refocused his attention back to Agent Tanner, whose lifeless body remained sprawled across the driveway. His relaxed gait shifted into a jog and eventually he approached a new team of medics.

Reed spoke in a hushed tone, "What's his condition?"

A red-headed EMT lifted his head. "He's dead, sir. Single gunshot wound to the chest."

Reed ran his hands against his face and choked back tears. "Did he suffer?"

"I couldn't tell you, sir. Given the caliber and proximity to his heart, I'm somewhat confident he didn't feel a thing."

A rugged tough from behind and Reed twisted around. Towering over him stood Sheriff Malone. "Captain, you've been through an awful lot this evening. Let's say we get you someplace warmer."

With a double-tap, Reed stepped away, and the medics continued taking notes on their clipboard. As he slunk away, Reed bowed his head, and a flood of emotions overwhelmed him. *With all my training, how could I not see any of this coming?*

The two men reached the back of the cruiser, and Sheriff Malone helped the weary captain into the backseat. He couched, planted his strong hands against his shoulders, and spoke. "Eric, I promise you we got this under control. Can I have someone escort you to the hospital?"

Captain Reed's eyes met with his. "I'm good. How…how do I get to the hospital from here?"

"You remember where you turned off of Highway thirty-four?"

Reed nodded.

"Take a left at the intersection, continue twenty minutes until you reach Granby. From that point follow the signs for the hospital."

"Thank you for everything. If you need me, I suppose you know where I'll be."

The sheriff extended his hand and Reed. "I know where to find you. Go and take care of your officer."

Heeding the sheriff's advice, he wiped away the tears from his face and raced to the black SUV. Although he wasn't too keen on commandeering a U.S. government vehicle, time was of the essence, and he'd take the heat for it later. Right now, his top priority was getting to Granby.

As he drove away down the mountain, he pulled his dying cell phone from his jacket pocket. The first person he dialed was Detective Scott.

The detective answered without even a hello. "Thank God, I was getting worried."

"Everything's under control, well, for the most part."

"Did you find Temple? The kids?"

"They are all alive. Barely."

"Huh?"

"Temple took a bullet to the shoulder, and he's on his way to the hospital as we speak."

"Shit—how bad?"

"Critical."

"What about the others?"

"Agent Tanner is dead; they rushed Alex Jones and Amy Williams to the hospital as well. All four suspects are either dead or in custody."

"Sounds like an action-packed night. You get to the hospital in one piece, and I'll spread the word to everyone."

"Thanks for doing that. If you need me, I'll be at the medical center in a town called Granby."

"Should I drive out there?"

"No need. It's doubtful he'll be there too long."

"Okay, but you'll keep me updated…won't you?"

"I'll try. My damn cell is almost dead."

"Well save your battery or find a charger. I'll just call the hospital if I need you."

"10-4."

He ended the call and sped down the snow-packed, winding road one last time. *How did I allow a straightforward investigation to end up so twisted?*

25

REED WAITED IN THE TINY emergency department waiting room and his watched beeped, breaking him from the dazed state he found himself. It was four o'clock in the morning. It had been five hours since he arrived at the hospital. He was growing more impatient as the hours elapsed. His leg bounced up and down as the suspense of not knowing anything drove him insane.

The automatic doors from the emergency department bolted open as a gray-haired, middle-aged doctor emerged to approached. "Eric Reed?"

The captain stood to his feet. "That's me. Do you have any updates on the three patients?"

"Which news do you want first? The good or...?"

"Since I've had my day turned upside down, get the bad over with."

"Officer Temple's condition hasn't changed. But he is alert, stable, and has asked about Alex more than once."

Reed's lip trembled as he tried to smile. "That's encouraging, right? I mean he hasn't gotten worse."

"True. However, he lost a great deal of blood, and therefore I have not changed his condition from critical."

"Understood. When will he go into surgery?"

The doctor scanned the floor. "Well, there lies our problem. Our little hospital lacks the necessary resources. On the bright side, I have spoken with St. Luke's in Denver, and they have deployed a medevac."

"Is that safe with the weather?"

"It cleared up enough for them to land. Should be in about thirty minutes."

"At least he's stable. What about the kids? How are they?"

"Amy Williams suffered mild hypothermia; however she is resting. We've contacted her parents, and once they arrive, we'll probably release her."

A sense of relief washed across his face. "And Alex?"

Doctor Green flipped to the third chart in his hand. "Alex Jones. A dislocated ankle, concussion, laceration to the forehead, hypothermia, and frostbite of the right hand."

"Jeez. Doesn't sound like today was his day."

"We can treat him here. Does he have family we can contact?"

"As far as I know it's him and his mother, Carol Jones."

The doctor's eyes lit up. "Did you say, Carol Jones? As in Dr. Carol Jones?" Reed nodded.

"You are aware they brought her body in."

"I am. Does Alex know yet?"

The doctor shook his head. "He doesn't. Figure I'd let you break the news to him."

"I think we'll wait until he recovers a little more before dropping a bombshell on him. So, when can I see them?"

"Now, if you'd like. I can take you to see the two of them."

They approached the first emergency bay, and the doctor yanked back the curtain. Amy lay on the hospital bed, a beige blanket covering her, and when they entered, she curved her head away from the monitor. Without hesitation, she looked at Reed square in the eyes. "Thank you for finding us."

Reed stepped to the side of the bed and reached out his hands. "Miss Williams, how are you holding up?"

"Physically, I'm good. Now, mentally, that's a different story."

"You've been through plenty for someone your age, so it's understandable."

She struggled to prop herself up. "Have you seen Alex or Mike? How are they?"

The doctor watched her struggle from a distance and rushed to the side of the bed. "Miss Williams, why don't you rest for now. I assure you we are taking excellent care of your friends."

Amy ignored his advice and fidgeted with the blanket. "When can I see them?"

"Soon. I promise."

Doctor Green cleared his throat, and with a head, nod indicated it was time to move on. Reed released his hands from hers, flashed a smile, and followed the doctor into the corridor. The doctor stepped a few feet away, and when he was sure he was out of earshot, Reed didn't hold back. "We could have at the very least told her their conditions."

"That's not how we do things around here."

"Well, no offense, but it's a shitty policy."

"And telling her Alex is in serious condition and Mike is being flown to Denver would make her feel better? It won't."

"It's not the best news to hear, but it's the truth."

Doctor Green gritted his teeth, motioned with his hand, and they continued down the sterile corridor. The doctor kept three paces ahead of Reed, and as they approached a door, he gave a quick knock and entered.

The room was dim, and Reed stepped closer to the bed where Alex lie. He stared disengaged at the IV's which dangled across and along the bedside, and his eyes scanned upward, and an oxygen mask covered his face.

Alex's heavy eyelids fluttered open and all Reed could do was stare at the monitor which beeped sporadically. *Heart rate and blood pressure seem good. If Mike saw this, it would crush him.*

The doctor waited in the corner and jotted a few notes in Alex's chart and mumbled, "His core body temperature is still too low. We hope with time it will come up."

"Someone once told me he's a tough guy. He'll push through."

Their whispers caught Alex's attention, and he tugged away the mask from his face. "Captain Reed?"

"I'm here. How are you feeling?"

Alex ignored his question and had one of his own. "Where's Mike?"

He approached the bedside and hovered. "He's here, and he's in good hands."

"Did something happen? Why can't he come to see me?"

Reed glanced over at the doctor who sighed. "Tell you what, Alex. I'll try to get him down here to see you soon. Okay?"

Alex placed the mask against his face and Reed nodded politely as Alex closed his eyes. The captain inhaled and exhaled before he turned to the door, and like that he was back in the corridor.

The doctor exited the room and closed the door behind him. Three rooms down and they arrived at Mike's room. Reed rounded the corner and followed the doctor inside where a cheerful nurse greeted them.

"How's he doing?" the doctor asked.

"No change. He's stable though."

There rested his six-foot-three officer on the gurney. His face was lifeless and seeing him in this condition was enough to heighten his anxiety. Reed wiped his hand across his face and turned towards the doctor.

"I'll be outside if you need me."

And like that, the doctor disappeared, leaving him alone in the room. Reed moved towards the chair in the corner and trembling hands he pulled it closer. The legs of the chair scraped against the floor, and Mike opened his eyes and cocked his head.

"Captain...," his words trailed off.

Never had he seen any of his officers in this state before. Reed, never being good at reassuring people, smiled as he sat in the chair next to the bed. They sat in silence and stared for a few minutes. Reed considered what he'd say to make the situation better? However, after all his thinking he couldn't formulate a coherent sentence.

Mike saw the struggle in his eyes and pulled the mask away from his face and whispered, "Where's Alex?"

"I've seen him and Amy, they are both safe. The better question is, how are you feeling?"

"You're looking at it. I overheard them mention I'm being transferred to a trauma center in Denver soon."

"That's right."

"I need a favor before that happens."

Reed leaned closer. "Name it."

"I have to talk to Alex one more time. It could be my last."

Reed fell back in the chair. "Don't say that. You're strong."

"Please make it happen."

"I'll check with the doctor, although between you and me, he's an asshole."

Mike's lower lip curled downward, and he closed his eyes.

"Hang tight, and I'll speak to him."

Reed got to his feet and walked through the door into the hallway. The captain glanced both ways and squinted his eyes in search of Doctor Green. A few seconds later he reemerged into the hallway from Alex's room. He rushed and walked up behind the doctor.

"Excuse me, Doctor Green."

He flipped the chart closed and turned. "Yes, sir."

"He's asking to see Alex. Is there any feasible way you can make that happen? Even if for only a few minutes."

The doctor twirled the pen in between his fingers. "I feel uncomfortable moving either one of them. You are aware they both are in desperate need of recuperation, right?"

"I am. However, Officer Temple needs to see the love of his life once more before you transfer him. I'm sure you can empathize with his request, right?"

Dr. Green had qualms, and his eyes scanned the floor instead of the eye-contact he had made all evening. "Officer Temple will not die. Does he need surgery; yes. However, his injury is not life-threatening."

"Still—."

Doctor Green raised his hand and cut him off. "I'll talk with Nurse Adams and see what we can do. I'm not making any guarantees."

Doctor Green marched towards the nurse's station at the end of the corridor and leaned against the counter to speak with the nurse. Every so often the doctor's head would turn towards Reed, and his arrogance made him uneasy. Captain Reed moved to the other side of the hallway for a better view of both of them and observed her smiling and nodding. *Could this be good news for Mike? Is he going to see Alex before he leaves?*

Nurse Adams stepped around from the nurse's station, and the two advanced towards him as he waited in the shadows of the hallway. Adrenaline coursed through his veins as he awaited their decision. She stopped at Alex's room, but the doctor continued forward.

"Thanks for your patience."

"Yeah, no problem. What's the verdict?"

"Nurse Adams believes Alex is stable enough to transport. However, before you get too thrilled, I'm restricting their visit to five minutes, nothing more."

"Five minutes is ample time. I'll be sure to thank Nurse Adams when she arrives."

"I'm certain she realizes your appreciation. Besides, she says the helicopter should arrive about the same time anyhow."

Reed extended his hand to the doctor. "I know I've been very demanding; however, I am grateful for everything you've done."

"It's a tough situation. Besides, I'm used to dealing with far worse than you."

Five minutes had passed, and Reed wandered the room. The wait was agonizing. At every sixty-second mark, he'd poke his head into the hallway to survey for any hint of progress. And on his fifth or sixth peek he saw the foot of the hospital bed emerge into the hall. Standing behind was Nurse Adams with a smile painted across her face. Once the entire bed was moving, Reed grinned and advanced to Mike's bedside where he lay with his eyes closed.

In a low, gruff voice he spoke, "He's coming. I'll give you two a few minutes of private time."

"Thanks."

Reed stepped to the door and held it open for the young nurse as she pushed the bed inside Mike's room. With the painkillers wearing off, turning his head was hellish. However, Mike mustered up the strength. He whimpered as he turned his head.

"Alex? Are you there?"

"I'm here."

"You look like shit."

Alex rolled his head, and the lovers stared into each other's eyes. "You don't look any better."

The nurse reminded them of the time limit before she and Reed stepped out into the hallway.

"What happened to you?" Alex asked.

"I took a bullet, but never mind that right now. The doctors are transferring me to Denver soon–"

Alex became upset and increased his tone. "No. They can't move you. I need you here with me."

"Alex, calm down. I need surgery, and they can't do it here. Let me finish."

"Finish what?"

"I have to tell you something, the problem is I don't know how."

The tension ate away at Alex "Well, don't keep me in suspense. Spit it out."

Mike closed his eyes, let his breath out, and shifted his lips. "I never dreamed in a million years I'd tell someone so close what I'm about to say."

Alex rolled his head away, closed his eyes, and a lone tear rolled down his cheek. "I know it's bad, so get it over with…"

Mike swallowed hard. "It's about your mother. Something happened, and it's not the kind of news I ever wanted to break to you."

TWO MONTHS LATER

THE SUN STREAMED THROUGH THE HALF-OPENED shades in the study as Alex ripped off a large piece of packing tape from the roll. He smacked it hard against the gaping seam of the last moving box. Alex stood to his feet, setting the half-empty roll of tape on top of the table. Alex brushed his hands together, wiped the dust against his jeans, and cocked his hip outward. After a quick inspection of the room, he blurted out, "Finished."

In the distance, a familiar voice resounded against the empty walls of the hallway. "Anyone home?"

He raced out of the study, and hollered out, "Coming."

Once he rounded the corner into the living room, he found Mike standing in the foyer. Alex glanced at him: a body-hugging pair of jeans, a colorful button-down complemented by a white sling his right arm rested in. Alex saw a large plastic sack and raised his eyebrow.

"Whatcha got there?"

Mike approached him. "Well, I know you've been busy, and I figured dinner might cheer you up. It's your favorite."

Alex smiled and gave him a peck on the cheek. "You didn't have to go to all this trouble."

"I wanted to. And besides, and with your support these past few months of recovery—I mean it's the least I can do."

Alex wrapped his arm around his neck as gentle as he could. "Whoa, slow down. I'm not healed yet."

"Oh, shit—I keep forgetting about your shoulder."

"It's okay; I'll let it slide *this* time."

Alex stood there, not ready to let go. Mike's touch was the exact thing he sought after the traumatizing previous few months. From mourning the death of his mother to almost losing the love of his life, when the reality of everything crumbled down, so did his drive for growth. That was until one day, as he and Amy sat around talking about life, it hit him; *I survived two psychopaths, I'm stronger than I think.* And this revelation incited a renewed outlook on his life.

After a minute, he relaxed his hold on Mike and eyed the bag. "What d'you order?"

"Well, I got the General Tso chicken. And for you, because I love you, the vegetarian Lo Mein."

"Well, I've always made it known you care about others more than you do yourself." Alex pointed out as Mike grinned.

"Only when it comes to you. And there's nothing wrong with caring more about you than myself," he blurted out, looking around the empty house. "Is the table still here?"

"Yeah, of course. The movers don't come until tomorrow. Besides, that'd be the last thing to go since I need somewhere to eat."

The two wandered through the foyer towards the dining room. The battle scars from the night of his kidnapping had long healed, and the place looked like nothing sinister had ever happened there. Alex took the bag from Mike, pulling out a chair for him to sit.

"Sit down while I unpack everything."

"You're the boss," Mike joked as he could hear a vibration coming from Alex's pocket.

"Sorry, let me grab this fast." Alex walked back towards the foyer and answered the call, "This is Alex."

A familiar voice greeted him, "Hey, it's me. I'm stopping by with John in a few minutes. We both have fantastic news to share with you."

"Did it come?"

"I'm not spoiling the surprise; you'll have to wait until we arrive."

"Fine; you know I hate anticipation."

"Yes, we know, it's one of your flaws. I'll see you in a few."

Alex flipped his phone closed and headed back for the dining room. Mike sat in the chair, grinning from ear to ear. The past two months had reaffirmed their commitment to one another and brought more strength to their relationship.

Alex wasn't sure would happen now between him and Mike. Graduation came and passed, and it was a bittersweet time for him. While it thrilled him to wrap up his high school days, he couldn't help but reflect on his mother's death, and the unfinished business it brought. Her funeral happened a week before graduation and not looking out into the bleachers and seeing her smiling face shattered his heart into a million pieces.

Before the whole ordeal, Alex had his entire future mapped out; study at The University of Colorado and remain in Ridgewood Hills where he and Mike would live happily ever after. Those plans all went to hell when a quartette of vindictive assholes crushed his ambitions in the blink of an eye. Now, the reality was he was leaving Ridgewood Hills behind for greener pastures. Although he recognized Mike needed more time to recover from his near-death experience, Alex was hell-bent on moving forward with his life.

He glanced at the clock and expected Amy and John to knock on the door any minute to share their good news.

He returned to the table as Mike looked at him. "So, now that you've settled everything did you ever find what they were looking for?"

"Nope. I went through the safe, my mom's financial information, hell even closed out her safe deposit box; nothing seems out of place."

"What was in the box at the bank?"

263

"Jewelry, important paperwork, and a few of my father's keepsakes. Doubtful any of it belonged to those thugs."

"So strange they insisted your mother had something of theirs. Sucks we suffered through this, when, none of it should have ever happened."

"Yeah, I guess if you look at it that way, we could have avoided all this. You know my philosophy though: everything happens for a reason."

"True. Can I change the subject for a moment?"

"Sure."

"I hate that you're leaving me for New York."

Alex grabbed hold of Mike's hands. "As much as I love you, I can't stay. While I have so many incredible memories here, but I also have some that are not so great."

Mike dropped his head.

"If I stay here, I'll never move on with my life."

"I recognize that. I wish you didn't have to move clear across the country. New York is going to eat you alive."

"Hey, if I can survive two crazy bitches with a grudge, I can survive 7.4 million people and the subway every day."

"Well, if this is what you want, I have something to ask you." Mike pulled out a small black box from his pocket and kneeled on one knee. "I refuse to let you leave me here in this town to wallow in pity. I love you, with every fiber of my being, and I want to know—."

Alex covered his mouth. "What?"

Mike picked right back up where he left off. "Will you spend the rest of our lives together? No matter where we end up, I want to always be together."

Alex released his hands and leaned forward. "Are you asking me what I think you're asking?"

"I'm—I'm asking you if you'll marry me?"

After the initial shock wore off and reality set in, he tapped his finger against the side of his face. "Hold up. How would we make a marriage work if I'm living on the east coast and you're here?"

"Well, more good news. Amy stopped in to visit me in the hospital and broke the news you two were leaving for New York at the end of the summer."

"She did?"

He nodded. "And cooped up in the hospital gave me plenty of time to reflect on my life."

"Reflect on what?"

Mike tried hard to fend off a grin. "I applied to the NYPD."

"And?"

His grin transitioned into a full-blown smile. "And... I took the job."

"You're kidding?"

"I would never joke about something like this. I'll be off of medical leave soon; Captain Reed has given me his full support. So, what d'you say?"

A loud knock at the door broke Alex from the shock, yet he remained motionless. Mike looked at him and joked, "Oh, fine, I'll grab the door; you take a load off. Is this what it'll be like when we're married?"

Alex watched Mike approach the front door. As the door swung open, Alex mumbled under his breath, "It's only Amy and John."

Alex closed his eyes and waited to hear his friends enter before opening them. His two best friends rushed past Mike, shrieking, and flapping around papers in their hands.

"I got into NYIT," she exclaimed.

"And I got into my first pick—Notre Dame."

"NYIT? Notre Dame? I had no idea those were the schools' you guys were waiting to hear about."

Amy set her hand on her hip. "We sort of figured you'd be more excited than this—wait a second, did we interrupt something?"

Mike smiled as Amy danced around. "Possibly."

"Did you ask him?"

"I did, and now I'm awaiting his answer," he replied as everyone hovered over Alex.

He contemplated before shouting out with happiness, "Yes, of course, I'll marry you. Since the moment I first met you I knew you were the one. You're who I want to spend the rest of my life with."

"Well, screw this Chinese food—we're going out to celebrate fantastic news for a change," John said.

Everyone exchanged glances. "I'm in."

"Me too," Mike replied.

Mike wrapped his arms around Alex, leaned in and gave him a peck on the cheek. "And afterward you can stay at my place. No reason for you to come back here except to let the movers in tomorrow."

"Deal."

Mike and John filed out the door while Alex and Amy hung back. With one foot across the threshold, he rested the palm of his hands on the door handle and gave the bare living room, the place he spent so many nights with Mike, his mom, and his friends, one final look over.

Amy reached into her pants and pulled out a white envelope in her hand. Her hand shook as she leaned in to whisper into his ear. "I didn't want to bring this up in front of the guys, but I found this tucked into the door handle of your car."

"Oh."

Alex frowned and snatched it from her hand. He slid his index finger underneath the flap, and he pulled out a single page from inside. As he unfolded the letter, three scribbled words written in crude handwriting jumped from the page. *Watch your back.*

Alex folded it shut, stuffed it back inside and turned his head to Amy. "Well? What is it?"

His jaw trembled, and as the words fell from his mouth, a husky voice shouted from the driveway. "You guys coming?"

Alex raised his eyebrow and crumpled the envelope into the back pocket of his jeans. He sniggered under his breath. "Yeah, yeah. In a second."

Not wanting to rush him, Amy rubbed her hand against his back and stepped out into the sunshine. "I'll give you a second to say goodbye."

He smiled, and she strolled away along the cobblestone path. With his arm still propped against the door frame, he hung his head. Would this last-ditch intimidation ever allow him to move forward with his life.?

What other choice do I have? I can't live in fear every day of an invisible force conspiring against me.

With the flick of a finger, he switched the lights off for the final time. He sighed, and whispered under his breath, "Well, Ridgewood Hills, it's been real. I'll miss the place I called home for so long, but I need a fresh start someplace far, far away."

Alex raised his head, yanked the door, and faced his friends waiting in the driveway motioning for him to hustle. As the creaky front door latched, deep down in his soul he appreciated the first favorable decision he made since this whole traumatic nightmare surfaced—he allowed himself to leave the past where it belonged—behind him.

ACKNOWLEDGMENT

MANY THANKS TO THE FOLLOWING PEOPLE for without their contributions and support this book would never have become a reality.

First, to my husband, Jesse, for the love and support you gave me throughout this process. You were there for me when I wanted to throw in the towel, and instead of letting me, you pushed me to uncover my talents, to help me believe in myself the way you believe in me.

To my grandmother, Jeanetta, you've always believed in me since I spent weekends at your house poking away at your typewriter. Thank you for everything.

Lastly, the following people contributed time and energy, emotional support, and sometimes took me out for a drink and let me vent about the writing process. So, thank you from the bottom of my heart to everyone mentioned below:

Vickie & Vincent Sneed
Kate Kafonek
Will Greenley
Dr. Heather Pfeifer
Michelle Phillips
Kelly Milliken
Jenn Cobleigh

Curious as to what happens next in Alex's life? Check out the second installment in the series, *Dark Ending*, today.

Amazon | Kindle Unlimited | Paperback

www.ingramcontent.com/pod-product-compliance
Lightning Source LLC
Chambersburg PA
CBHW060404180626
46817CB00007B/2504